A TWISTED INFINITY CHRISTMAS

By Rhea Morrigan

Published by CleverQuill Publishing, Fiction Division

A Twisted Infinity Christmas ©2025 by Rhea Morrigan

Printed in the United States of America.

EBOOK ISBN: 978-1-969012-02-0

PAPERBACK ISBN: 978-1-969012-03-7

Adults Only Content Warning

This book contains explicit language, sexual content and adult situations that may be unsuitable for some readers.

Editor: EpochWriter

Cover Art: Rhea Morrigan

DEDICATION

For my beloved husband,
Whose love endures beyond time and season.
Your memory is the brightest star in my winter sky,
Guiding me through every twist of this story and
every day of my life.

Forever missed, forever loved.

EPIGRAPH

Bless the Broken Road

I set out on a narrow way many years ago
Hoping I would find true love along the broken road
But I got lost a time or two
Wiped my brow and kept pushing through
I couldn't see how every sign pointed straight to you

Every long-lost dream led me to where you are
Others who broke my heart, they were like Northern stars
Pointing me on my way into your loving arms
This much I know is true
That God blessed the broken road
That led me straight to you
(Yes, he did)

I think about the years I spent just passing through
I'd like to have the time I lost and give it back to you
But you just smile and take my hand
You've been there, you understand
It's all part of a grander plan that is coming true

And every long-lost dream led me to where you are
Others who broke my heart, they were like Northern stars
Pointing me on my way into your loving arms
This much I know is true
That God blessed the broken road
That led me straight to you

God blessed this broken road, yeah

And now I'm just rolling home
Into my lover's arms
This much I know is true
That God blessed the broken road
That led me straight to you

That God blessed the broken road
That led me straight to you

Co-Written by Marcus Hummon, Jeff Hanna, 1994

First recorded by the Nitty Gritty Dirt Band, 1994

TABLE OF CONTENTS

PROLOGUE 1

CHAPTER 1 9

CHAPTER 2 21

CHAPTER 3 33

CHAPTER 4 45

CHAPTER 5 53

CHAPTER 6 65

CHAPTER 7 75

CHAPTER 8 85

CHAPTER 9 95

CHAPTER 10 107

CHAPTER 11 117

CHAPTER 12 127

CHAPTER 13 137

CHAPTER 14 147

CHAPTER 15 157

CHAPTER 16 165

CHAPTER 17 175

CHAPTER 18 187

CHAPTER 19 199

CHAPTER 20 209

CHAPTER 21 221

CHAPTER 22 233

CHAPTER 23 245

CHAPTER 24 253

CHAPTER 25 261

CHAPTER 26 271

CHAPTER 27 279

CHAPTER 28 289

CHAPTER 29 299

CHAPTER 30 311

CHAPTER 31 325

CHAPTER 32 339

CHAPTER 33 349

CHAPTER 34 357

CHAPTER 35 367

EPILOGUE 379

A NOTE FROM THE AUTHOR 383

ABOUT THE AUTHOR 385

OTHER BOOKS BY RHEA MORRIGAN 387

COMING SOON BY RHEA MORRIGAN 389

ACKNOWLEDGEMENTS

With the warmth of Christmas in my heart and gratitude as endearing as holiday lights, I wish to thank those who were the spirit behind "A Twisted Infinity Christmas." Writing this book has truly been a journey shaped by the unwavering support and expertise of others.

Heartfelt thanks to **EpochWriter** for the careful editing that brought polish and clarity to every page—like snow glistening beneath festive stars.

To **Michelle Romano**, whose thoughtful editing during and after the writing process and invaluable feedback as a beta reader added joy and depth to this story, your generosity shines brighter than any ornament. Her kindness as both editor and beta reader made all the difference in shaping this book's final form—like a gift wrapped with care and hope.

Sincere gratitude to **Thuly Tyler, Gina (3 Boys and a Book), and E.N. Chanting** for the time, insight, and encouragement provided in beta reading; their observations helped refine this story's heart, just as loved ones warm the winter season.

To everyone who lent their skills and encouragement along the way: thank you for helping this story shine.

May the season's light and the memory of your support echo through every page.

PROLOGUE

Aris's eyes narrowed, and his fingers pressed against the weathered fence as Selene's truck rattled out of the driveway on its way to LaFollette, a small town about forty-five minutes north of Knoxville, and twenty-five miles from Evermist, to visit her so-called new friends. The faded deep blue pickup jolted over a rut, and Selene tossed a wave over her shoulder toward him, her hand barely making it past the window.

1

His jaw throbbed as he worked it in tight circles, as though it would dislodge the heavy weight in his chest. He knew those two girls were nothing but trouble and that they'd eventually drag her into their mess.

A movie of her laughing with those girls played through his mind, and his eyes narrowed every time it invaded his thoughts—Lisa with the chipped black nails and Maralyn always sneaking cigarettes and who knows what else behind the school. The last time he'd seen them, they'd had their arms around Selene, like the Three Musketeers, as they ducked into the convenience store.

She'd called him jealous after the fight this past week. He'd said he wasn't, but it echoed hollow inside.

I'm not jealous. I just know they're going to get her in trouble. You keep telling yourself that, Aris.

As she drove down the road, he became smaller and smaller in her mirror. Selene cranked up the classic country station, singing along to songs her mother used to listen to while working in the bakery. The music she loved growing up talked about tight-fittin' jeans, single-shot rifles and one-eyed dogs, lovin' her while holdin' you and swingin' on a porch swing, and she couldn't help but smirk, thinking about the current so-called country music and how it missed the soul the old-timers had.

Her thoughts turned to her new friends and Aris. "I don't see what's wrong with hanging out with Lisa and Maralyn, anyway. He says he's not jealous, but it sure looks as though he is. Maybe they're a little rough around the edges, but they're really nice," she muttered, fingers drumming the steering wheel. She sped up when the curves opened and took in the thick smell of sweet maple.

Just how much trouble can two high school seniors get into?

What she didn't realize was that not everyone was as invested in family or getting good grades in school as she was. It was very naïve thinking, and it could lead to issues, even later in life.

At the bakery, Aris swung open the door, the bell above it ringing twice. Warm air, heavy with cinnamon sugar, enveloped him as he walked in. Jed wiped his hands on a dish towel. "Afternoon, Son. What's with the stony look on your face?"

He grunted and shrugged, examining the crumbs strewn over the counter. Jed smirked, one eyebrow twitching. "She took off again, hunh?" His big hand squeezed Aris's shoulder. "Selene knows how to take care of herself. If those new friends of hers, Lisa and Maralyn, go too far, she'll be back here before you can blink. My girl's got more sense than you think."

Aris breathed in, nodding. After Jed finished cleaning the counter, he followed him into the bakery kitchen. Levi greeted him with a crooked smile, gesturing to the clean aprons hanging on the hooks near the hall to the employee bathroom and the office. "Grab one. I'm working on a new apple fritter recipe."

The scent of apples and frying dough always dragged up memories he'd buried deep.

Selene's older brother, Levi, was teaching him how to bake. Since his mother had died years ago, he and his father took turns cooking. Aris remembered the first meal he'd cooked by himself. He was twelve, and his mother had been gone for several months. His father had been late coming home from work.

Aris had made boxed macaroni and cheese and hot dogs. It wasn't something his father had really enjoyed, but Aris loved it. It was the start of his interest in cooking. His father was good at it, so he began showing Aris how to cook. By the time he was fourteen, he could make anything if he had a recipe. By sixteen, he was making stews from scratch on icy nights and testing all sorts of spices. At seventeen, he spent weekends baking with Levi and learning the fine art of baking—and loving it.

Six Months Later

Selene pulled into the bakery's back parking lot, the tires crunching under the wheels. Time had flown by. She had finally graduated from high school and was on her way to college in Knoxville, and her duffel bag and boxes of personal items crowded the front passenger and rear seats. She'd promised to stop by and say goodbye to her mother, father and brother.

When she walked in, her mother hugged her. "My little girl's not so little and is on her way to college," Jeanna whispered, squeezing her tightly.

Her father and older brother, Levi, hugged her, but remained silent. Jed gruffly patted her shoulder.

"Guys, it's not like I'm going to the ends of the Earth. I'm only going to Knoxville." Selene rolled her eyes.

"We know, sugar, but it's not going to be the same without you here," her mother said.

Levi handed her a large bag. "Some snacks for the trip and to hold you over for a while. I wrapped them for the freezer, so you can throw whatever you don't eat in there."

"I will," Selene said. "That *is* one thing I'm going to miss." She lifted the bag to her nose, breathing in the yeast and cinnamon. "There's nothing like fresh-baked pastries in the morning. Or for lunch. Hell, any time of the day."

"Language," Jed growled. "Well, you should get started so you're not late to orientation. We'll see you in a few weeks. And you know you're more than welcome to come home every weekend."

"Yeah, Dad, I know. I'll probably have too much homework, though. But I promise, if I don't, I'll come home. It's the only way I'll get my bakery fix."

Selene put the bag of pastries and bread onto the front passenger seat and slid inside the truck. As she shut the door, she glanced around, but didn't see Aris. She shrugged and started the truck, waving at her family as she took off down the mountain.

Aris peeked through the blinds at his friend's house, watching Selene as she got into her truck. He couldn't bring himself to be there to see her off. They'd just get into an argument again.

About her so-called friends.

Aris rolled his eyes and let the blinds fall into place long after she drove off.

When he turned away from the window, his friend Luke lifted his shoulder and hand. "What?"

"Nothing, man."

"Dude. It's not like you were banging her. So, you had a fight. You'll both get over it."

Aris shrugged. "I guess. I'm going to head home. I'll see you tomorrow."

"Yeah, man. See you tomorrow."

Aris let himself out and drove home, the empty streets pressing in on the heaviness in his chest.

CHAPTER 1

Just as she reached the grocery store in LaFollette, tiny flakes fell from the sky. She had planned on stopping, but she knew that this light snow could turn into a blizzard at any time, and she might not make it to her hometown of Evermist in the rugged mountains of East Tennessee. *I hope Dad has food in the fridge.*

Selene navigated the turn that led out of town, and the flakes got larger and fell faster. Half an hour later, as the narrow, twisting road took her farther up the

9

mountain, tears welled in her eyes when she passed the turnoff for her mother's favorite hiking trail.

She gripped the steering wheel until her knuckles whitened, and her eyes traced the outline of the trail through the swirling snow. She'd give anything to have her mother back so they could smell the fresh scent of pine as they hiked the narrow trail that wound its way up the mountain to the lake nestled at the top. It was something she hadn't taken the time to do this past summer when she visited.

Tomorrow, mourners would crowd the small church, voices muffled under layers of polite sorrow, and she would have to stand beside her father and brother as they lowered her mother into the frozen ground. Her heart ached with things she hadn't said, the grief trapped beneath a numbness she couldn't shake.

By the time Selene had driven another few miles, the snow started sticking to the ground. The county would eventually plow the road, but it wasn't at the top of its list, as very few people lived out there. As it steepened, the houses became more sporadic, as it was too difficult to build on the side of a mountain.

When she reached the sharpest hairpin curve, there were nearly two inches of snow piled up on the road. A flash of color right in the turn caught her eye. Selene shook her head as she pulled into the pull-off on the wide part of the curve.

The snow covered her brunette, waist-length hair within seconds of stepping out of the car. She walked back to the memorial that had caught her eye as she navigated the steep slope of the sharp turn. Someone had carved her mother's name into a whitewashed cross, and surrounded it by several bouquets of plastic flowers.

Selene rubbed a finger over the name. Jeanna Weaver. She sank to her knees, the snow soaking through her jeans, as she fingered the plastic flowers.

Shivering broke her out of reminiscing about her mother and the things they used to do together. Hanging Christmas lights with the family. Hot chocolate on Christmas morning. Helping make a big roast and all the fixings for dinner. As she stood, snow fell off her coat. *Shit. I know better. I need to get warm. It's easy to get frostbite up here.* As she lifted her shaking hands to wipe the tears off her face, she noticed her fingers had a blue tinge to them.

Selene's footsteps were far apart as she made her way to the car as quickly as possible without sliding on the slippery road. She pressed the key fob to unlock the car, and once she got inside, she swore as her numb hands fumbled to insert the key into the ignition.

She finally got the car started and waited as it warmed up again. As the air from the vents heated the cab, she held her hands up to it. When she finally stopped shivering, she flicked the wipers on to clear the snow.

11

As she turned the wheel to pull out onto the road, headlights cut through the near white-out the snow was causing. Selene waited as a bright red pickup made its way around the curve. She couldn't make out the stenciled name on it, but she didn't have to.

It was Aris Beckett. Selene's hand hovered over the steering wheel as the red truck idled through the curve. Once, she would have rolled down the window and called him over, or traded stories about haunted campgrounds they'd visited.

Now, their greetings had stilled to… *What? Nothing. He hadn't called her since she left for college. Hadn't texted her. Nothing.*

The memory of their last argument flickered in her mind. The sharp edge in his voice when he groused about her new friends crawled up her spine and fueled her own stubborn refusal to back down. She caught his quick, unreadable glance before he turned away.

While she had feelings for him, she had never acted on them. She wasn't sure if he'd felt the same, and she didn't want to ruin their friendship. Not that she needed to worry, since he refused to speak to her after she decided to go to Gatlinburg with her friends one weekend in their senior year, instead of spending time horseback riding on his parents' farm. The fight was so petty, but at the time, it didn't seem that way. A wide gap had formed between them, and they never fixed it before she left for college.

Selene had thrown herself into school so she couldn't feel the despair in the pit of her gut—most of the time. Before she even tossed her graduation cap into the sky, a large marketing firm had snatched her up. Back-to-back presentations and flights booked by assistants she'd never met filled her calendar. Each visit home required at least a couple of months' notice.

She knew her mother counted down the days like a rare birthday, and she wasn't taking the time to look up the likes of Aris Beckett. She drove past Aris's old farm more times than she could count, but her knuckles gripped the wheel as she forced herself to continue past.

Aris slowly made his way around the hairpin that had taken Jeanna Weaver's life not three days ago. That day, the weather had been nice, though the temperature was below freezing. While the tourist who had hit Jeanna hadn't been speeding, he'd slid on the black ice formed by the water spraying off the cliff as it made its way to a weather creek beside the road. The snow became heavier as he traveled up the mountain.

He slowed as he saw brake lights in the pull-off. He wanted to be sure the driver saw him coming before pulling out. The small car waited as he passed.

"Whoever that is shouldn't be up here in this blizzard in a compact car. I hope he has all-wheel drive, at least."

Aris shook his head. "I wonder who it is. Tourists don't like coming up here in the summer, never mind at the end of November when we could get one of these surprise blizzards."

No one in Evermist drove cars. They all drove four-wheel drive pickup trucks. They had no use for small vehicles. Not only could they not haul enough supplies, but they'd also get stuck in the snow and on some of the dirt roads after heavy rain.

Aris kept his speed down so the stranger could follow him, and he could watch to make sure he—or she—didn't slide off the side of the road. "We've already had one death…Shit." His heart fluttered, and a knot formed in his stomach. "That must be Selene. Her mother's funeral is tomorrow," he said to the otherwise empty cab of his truck.

His heart tripped again at the memory of the last time they spoke. They'd argued over some girls she'd met in LaFollette. The girls wouldn't come up the mountain, so Selene always drove down to visit them. He'd seen them a couple of times when he went into town. They always wore black goth clothing and were smokers.

Maybe he should have called her. He wondered what life could have been like had they'd stayed friends. Or, even started dating. He liked her a lot, but didn't want to screw up the friendship. The one that got screwed anyway. Every time he'd asked her brother about her, Levi said she didn't even want to hear his name. *Good*

14

Lord, but that woman can hold a grudge. He knew that it didn't matter that he was right. Not then. Not now.

The dashboard clock blinked in the half-dark as Aris gripped the warm leather of the steering wheel. He swallowed hard and tightened his jaw as a scrap of memory flickered—Selene's voice turning to ice as she slammed the door of her truck after their last argument.

At the stoplight, he drew her initials in the condensation on the glass and angrily rubbed it out before anyone could see it. *What the fuck? I'm not a teenager anymore. She moved on. I should have, too.*

The ache in his chest was familiar, sharp and soft, and it swelled every time he imagined what they might have had.

He'd argued with Selene that her new friends probably did drugs, and she shouldn't be hanging around them. She'd thought he was jealous because she hung around him less. He quit trying to talk to her about them during their senior year, even though all he could think about was kissing her lips—lips that just had to be soft— while he wrapped his arms around her curves.

Aris made the turn that led to his small farm and blacksmith shop at the edge of town. He hadn't stopped thinking about Selene. His thoughts rambled from their fight to his hidden feelings for her to seeing her again.

When she came to visit in the past, her father or brother would let him know. He'd watch her when she

15

was out and about, but never approached her. From what her family had said, she never talked about him, and she'd refused even to entertain meeting up with him, so he kept his distance.

As he followed her up the mountain, he wondered what her lips would feel like. If her breasts would fit in his hands just the way he liked. What it would feel like just holding her. What it would feel like sliding inside of her as she wrapped her legs around him and ran her fingers through his hair.

Damn. Aris adjusted the front of his jeans as he pulled up to the house. *I'm going to have to take a cold shower if I don't stop thinking about her.*

The red truck turned off the main road, and Selene could see red and green halos of dim light as they fought to shine through the blinding snow. *Typical of Evermist. Already started on Christmas.*

The small town clung to the mountain's crest, houses cupped in a shallow bowl carved by wind and time, a geography that echoed the distant lake on the next ridge. The welcome sign, which showed the population to be 2,549, hadn't needed painting in years, as visitors rarely came, and those who did didn't want to be here in the winter.

Raised beds that held black soil hauled from the bounty lay covered under the ever-thickening layer of snow, their frames lashed tight against the wind. Just past the town square, the farmer's market stall stood empty, except for storage boxes that contained items to set up each booth.

As she approached the small convenience store at the other end of town, she glanced at her gas gauge. "Not that they're going to be open in this fucking blizzard," she muttered. The trip up the mountain had taken longer than she thought, thanks to the snow. She had less than a quarter of a tank left. It'd get her to her father's and back to the convenience store when it stopped snowing. "Not that I'll be driving it up here."

Selene had a truck that her brother kept running. She'd driven it to college, but it was too hard to find parking in the crowded lots, so she'd leased a small "city car," as she called it. It was a subcompact SUV with all-wheel drive. That weekend, she drove the truck home, and then her brother gave her a ride back to school.

The SUV wasn't as good as her truck in the snow, but she didn't have a choice. It had to be small enough to navigate the crowded campus, yet practical. She tried to avoid coming home if the weather was going to be bad.

She slowly made her way down the main street of town, passing the Baptist Church opposite the convenience store, a small school that held all the grades in one building, a small co-op that carried the necessities

17

for taking care of farm animals, some seed, tools and a conservative selection of home repair materials, and on the other side of the co-op, her parents' bakery.

Turning down the dirt road on the other side of the bakery, Selene crept the mile to her parents' house. While the all-wheel drive kept her on the road, it was narrow, and one slide could send her down a five-hundred-foot drop off one side or into the steep mountain cliffs on the other side.

Aris growled as his jeans pressed against his raging, hard cock when he slid out of his truck. This wasn't the first time thoughts of Selene gave him an uncontrollable hard-on. It sure wouldn't be the last. Oh, he'd had girlfriends over the years, but none could ever match his expectations of Selene.

Once he was inside, he shut the door and leaned against it. He closed his eyes and grabbed the front of his jeans to try to stop from coming in his pants.

It was always like this with Selene. One thought of her laugh, the way she chewed her lip when she was concentrating, and his control snapped. She had no idea what she did to him, no clue that he measured every woman he'd tried to date against a version of her he'd never see.

"Fuck," he groaned as he gave in, unfastened his button-fly and reached in to stroke himself. As his hips pumped into his hand the third time, Aris tilted his head back and let out a strangled moan as he shot ribbons of cum across the entryway.

His legs gave out, and he slid down the front door to the floor.

When he finally caught his breath, he went into the master bath and stripped. He turned the shower on, and while he waited for the water to heat up, he threw his clothes in the washer.

CHAPTER 2

Selene pulled into her brother's spot in the carport. *Wonder what he's doing out in this blizzard.* They'd move her car under the cover for the tractors when the snow let up. It was getting too dark to see whether she'd be driving off the narrow dirt track and into a deep snowdrift in the fields.

As she stepped into the still blowing snow, her brother pulled in. He parked in front of her car, nosing his truck just under the edge of the carport to keep some of the snow off the front of it and hers from getting buried under the three-walled structure.

The snow that had piled on his truck slid to the ground as he slammed the door. Selene waited for him to come around.

"Jewell Selene Weaver, why are you in my spot?" he said, the twinkle in his deep blue eyes taking the harshness out of his words.

Selene grinned. "Clyde Levi Weaver. I don't want my pretty car to get buried in the snow." She caught herself dropping a syllable as she responded to Levi with a long, easy mountain drawl she hadn't used at last week's board meeting. The sharp vowels she practiced in city elevators faded with every mile the car climbed past the Knoxville highway sign.

By the time she stepped under the carport, her words settled comfortably into the old, familiar rhythm, and her tongue loosened as she greeted her brother with the Appalachian lilt she couldn't disguise once she was away from the city.

"Big city girl ain't lost that accent yet?" Levi said, trashing her like they always did, despite the reason that she was home in the middle of a snowstorm.

"I'd hardly call Knoxville a big city, Levi. And you know as well as I do, they have a deep accent there, too."

"Just not as deep as ours. Let's get inside before we freeze. We'll move your car over to the tractor barn later, unless you plan on leaving soon."

Selene lifted her hand in front of her, palm up. "You really think I'll be going anywhere in the next couple of days?"

Levi grinned. "I guess not, unless you drive your truck back to the city."

"Yeah, I don't know about that, but if I have to, I guess I have to," Selene said, shrugging. "I've already warned my boss that if it snows up here, it could be a week or better before I get out of here. I can do most of what I need to do from home.

He grabbed both of her suitcases while she shifted the straps for her laptop and overnight bag on her shoulders.

Levi led Selene down the hall to her old bedroom and put her suitcases against the wall. She put her overnight bag and laptop on the bed.

"Where's dad?" she asked.

"Probably in his room." Levi glanced down the hallway toward their father's closed door. His shoulders sagged as Selene turned toward him. "Every day, I knock, call him for supper, but he won't come out. He stays holed up in that room," he murmured, the tension evident in his tone.

Levi continued softly, "Dinner goes cold most nights, and his plates end up in the sink, untouched. He'll listen for your voice, though. Maybe you can get him to come out... I'm running out of ideas." Relief and worry flickered in his eyes as they pleaded with his sister to help.

"Let's make dinner, and I'll see if I can't rouse him out." Selene slid past Levi and made her way down the hall, her footsteps muffled by the carpeting. At the opposite end of the living room's open sprawl, a single closed door beckoned her eyes. She paused before she went into the kitchen.

Opening the fridge to a patchwork of foil-wrapped casseroles and plastic containers scribbled with familiar names in black marker. Levi nudged aside a pan of cornbread, fishing out a large tub with Mrs. Miller's steady handwriting across the lid.

He pried off the top, letting the rich peppery scent of beef stew curl into the kitchen. Selene smiled, holding the container up to her nose and breathing deeply. "No one makes it like she does," she said, her tone warming despite the chill in her bones that she'd had since Levi had called about their mother.

"I'll heat this, and you try to get Dad to come out."

Selene nodded and headed down the hall to her father's bedroom. She knocked on the door. "Dad, are you awake?"

When he didn't answer, she said, "I'm coming in, Dad." She peeked around the door as she opened it to make sure he was decent. She didn't see him in the bed, so she pushed the door all the way open and stepped into the room. "Dad?"

Her eyes adjusted to the darkness as she looked around. The bathroom door was open, and it was dark, so he wasn't in there. "What the hell," she muttered under her breath.

"Language, girl."

Selene turned toward the sound. She finally made out the form of her father in the dark reading alcove and turned on a lamp.

A half frown twisted Jed's lips, and he sat curled into an upright fetal position. He crossed his arms and grumbled, "Turn that damned light off, Selene."

"No, Dad. You need to come out and eat."

He turned to look out the window at the darkness. "Not hungry, now get out of here and leave me alone."

Selene narrowed her eyes at him. "You can't stay in here sulking. I know you miss Mom. I miss her, too, but you still have to eat." She stepped over to him and took one of his hands, pulling him. He pulled his hand back.

"Come on, Dad. Mrs. Miller sent some of her beef stew. You need to eat just a few bites. You know you love her stew."

"You're not going to leave me alone, are you. You're worse than your brother."

"Dad, don't do this. We're all trying to deal with this."

Selene knelt beside her father's chair, searching his face for the steady assurance she remembered from childhood. His eyes flickered, distant as he avoided hers when she reached for his hand.

He let it slip from her grasp as he retreated deeper into the worn cushions. She drew a careful breath, but when she tried to coax him out to supper, the words tangled and caught, trembling behind her clenched teeth. The ache in her chest tightened even more, and she tried swallowing it down as she refused to let the crack in her voice escape.

"You know Mom would be in here shooing you out with that broomstick of hers. Don't make me get it, Dad," she said softly.

He finally unfolded himself and moved toward the door. "Fine."

Jed shuffled down the church steps between Selene and Levi, his hands locked around their arms, but his gaze fixed on the churned, pale earth as they turned toward the cemetery. Each step seemed to drag, as if the snow weighed more than the coffin they followed.

Pastor Miller had hooked up a team of horses to a sled to carry the coffin to the site. The carpeted floor of the sled sat waist high, which made it easier to move the casket onto the rollers to position it. The Pastor and Levi engaged the locks to keep the casket from rolling off as the procession made its way to the tented grave site.

The pallbearers each put a hand on the casket as Pastor Miller clucked at the horses. They moved slowly through the snow-covered ground to the grave site. When they arrived, Jed wasn't in any condition to help lift his wife's coffin onto the vault-lowering device, so Selene guided him into the front row while Levi and five others—she hadn't paid attention to who—from the church lifted the casket from the sled and carried it into the tent.

When the wind turned, rustling the tent above the grave, Jed flinched and blinked hard at the wreath set beside the casket. His lips pressed thin, his shoulders a stubborn wall against the comfort of his children. He sat motionless as the pastor spoke, his eyes looking at the casket but not seeing it, as if he was waiting for his Jeanna to speak again.

Selene's heart raced as she saw Aris at the back corner of the casket, his coat dusted with snow and eyes trained on the ground. Her cheeks flushed hot, the cold unable to cool the rush crawling up her spine.

She ducked her gaze quickly, hoping he hadn't noticed the way her fingers twisted in her coat's lining.

No one had warned her that Aris would be a pallbearer, and the unexpected jolt of seeing him—close, solid hands curled around the wooden handles of her mother's casket, sent an old spark darting through her nerves.

That fucking tingle still hadn't gone away, despite not seeing him for nearly ten years. Damn.

She wanted to shake Jed and scream at him for allowing Aris to carry her mother, but kept quiet. She'd ask Levi about it later and hoped she would be able to continue avoiding him. It wasn't as if he had feelings for her—they'd only ever been friends. *Best friends, until he decided to get controlling and jealous.*

Selene kept her gaze locked on the rows of chairs, pointedly ignoring the way Aris's voice drifted through the crowd behind her. She smoothed her skirt over her knees, biting back the urge to glance his way. The space between them pulsed with everything unsaid and every call they never made.

He could have called me over the years. Phone works both ways, woman. Besides, you probably wouldn't have answered it. That's beside the point.

She continued arguing with herself, and Levi had to elbow her to get her to pay attention. Everyone filed out, speaking in low voices. Close friends stopped to offer condolences, forcing thoughts of Aris to the back of her mind.

Levi steadied Jed as he slid into the cab of the truck, his grip firm but gentle against their father's sleeve. Selene climbed into the back seat, her shoulders sagging against the window as headlights flickered through the melting snow.

At the house, Mrs. Miller bustled in the kitchen, clattering pans and stirring stew, her soft murmurs seeping into the entryway where guests shrugged off their coats.

Levi lingered by the door, rubbing his eyes and watching shadows stretch across Selene's face. She stared past him, her gaze distant. Her lips pressed into a thin line every time someone mentioned Aris's name.

The living room echoed with slow, polite conversation. Levi's eyes drifted to the bakery keys on the counter. Glancing in the direction of the bakery as dread settled in his gut, he hoped the visitors would leave early. He barely had the words to fill the silences, and he certainly couldn't unpack the ache in Selene's eyes. There would be time to sort through it all later, once the house quieted and their father went to bed.

He suspected it had to do with Aris, but he didn't have time to deal with that mess—not while he was trying to take care of his father. They'd closed his father's bakery early on the day they found out Jeanna wrecked and hadn't opened it since. He knew he had to go in and clean up the mess they'd left when they rushed to get to the hospital. He shook his head at the thought.

29

"Dad, it's been a week. We need to get down to the bakery and get it ready to reopen."

Jed sat in the same chair in the reading nook in his room. He'd gone back in there shortly after they'd arrived home from the funeral and had barely come out, even when Selene and Levi tried to coax him out.

Every time they got him to leave his room to eat, he only took a few bites and pushed his food around on his plate. Selene pulled him out of the chair, surprised at how light he felt. "You have to start eating, Dad. You've lost too much weight. You won't be able to work in the bakery if you can't lift those bags of flour. You're wasting away to nothing."

"Leave me alone, child."

Selene sighed. She pushed him toward the master bathroom. "Get in the shower, Dad, and get dressed." She closed the door behind him and went into the kitchen.

"Levi, go in there and make sure Dad gets in the shower and gets dressed. We need to do something with that bakery."

He nodded. "Yeah, we do," he said, biting his lip.

Before Selene could say anything else, he scooted down the hall to attend to Jed.

Now, what's that all about? Levi looked as though he was anxious about going to the bakery. What's going on?

She walked down the hall and heard the shower running. "Good. At least he got Dad to clean up." She cracked the bedroom door. "Levi! I'm heading down to the bakery to get started. You and Dad come down as soon as he gets out."

Levi walked over to the door and opened it. "We will. He's in there mumbling to himself, which is more than he's said since the accident. He's pissed, though. He doesn't want to mess with the bakery today."

"Well, he'll keep putting it off, so he doesn't have a choice today. And speaking of which, what was that look you gave before you took off down the hall?"

Levi turned toward the bathroom door when they heard the water shut off. "Nothing."

Selene ground her teeth. "Levi…"

He pushed her into the hall and shut the door between them, saying, "We'll see you there."

CHAPTER 3

Selene stomped down the hall and grabbed her truck keys and those to the bakery from the hook by the back door. Most of the snow had melted the day before, so she and Levi had moved her car over to the tractor barn.

She jumped into her truck and started it, letting it warm up before she headed down to the bakery. The gravel road was full of ruts from tires running over melting snow and partially frozen ground, so she drove slowly.

33

When she finally arrived at the bakery, Selene let herself in the back door, expecting to see a mess. She paused in the doorway as her gaze swept over the spotless counter. The mixer sparkled, and there wasn't a speck of flour dust in sight. Someone had even stacked the trays.

"Whoever was working here must have stayed and cleaned up. That was nice of them. Now, to see what we need to get started," Selene thought as she stepped down the hall to the office, where she dropped her keys and purse on the desk. She grabbed the inventory list from its spot on the wall.

Her eyes narrowed as she read it. "What the fuck?" She carried it into the store room, finding that they weren't stocking nearly as many ingredients as they should be for a fully functioning bakery and coffee shop. She carried the inventory list to the walk-in cooler and freezer and found the same. Low stock.

Selene flipped through the past month's inventory logs, her fingers trailing down the columns. Each week's order was shorter than the last. She counted four bags of coffee beans. Pressing her lips in a tight line, she estimated that they were only doing about a third of the business they had been—at least, based on the amount of product they'd been ordering every week.

Just as she was walking back to the office, her father and brother came in. Selene put her weight on one leg and the opposite hand on her hip as she raised her eyebrows at them. "Somebody going to explain why business is down

34

by two-thirds? Why didn't one of you tell me about this long ago?"

"Just what would you have done about it?" Jed snapped at her.

"Dad, I could have helped figure out what's wrong. Done some marketing for you. And don't tell me you couldn't afford it. How many times have I told you that your marketing doesn't cost you a dime if I work on it after hours?"

"Told you, Dad," Levi muttered under his breath.

"Fuck you, Levi. You're adult enough to tell me if they won't," Selene snapped.

"Now, don't you go getting on Levi, Little Girl. And watch that mouth of yours."

Selene sighed. "You know, Dad, I'm about at the end of my rope. I keep telling you it's easier to fix something when it first happens. On another note, someone cleaned up. I'm going into the office to see if I can't fix this. You two can sit with me so we can get you back on track."

She stomped off to the office.

Jed turned toward the walk-in.

"What are you doing, Dad?"

Jed shrugged. "You go sit with her. I'm going to prep for tomorrow."

"You know she's going to be pissed," Levi said. "And don't tell me about my language. Just because she's here doesn't mean we have to watch it. She obviously learned those words somewhere."

Jed snickered. "Yeah, I guess she did. She let loose on you, too."

Jed stepped into the office. "Let's go home, Selene. It's getting late."

She glanced up from the spreadsheets and accounting she was working on after checking the clock at the bottom of the computer screen. She opened her mouth to get on his case about not sitting in with her and Levi to straighten out what finances they could.

Instead, realizing it was futile, she sighed to herself and said, "Okay. Give me a minute to save this and make a couple of notes."

After a few minutes, she grabbed her coat. "Are you going to open tomorrow?"

"Yes. I have the dough proofing. Levi goes in at three in the morning to start baking. I'll come in around six and help him finish up," her father said curtly as he followed her out of the back door.

For the first time in a week, Selene took a good look at her father. It seemed as though he had aged twenty

36

years in the past week. She shook her head as she locked up behind them. Jed rode with Levi, and Selene followed in her truck.

As she turned out of the side lot to head home, Aris's truck passed in front of the bakery. She waited while he turned around, and then followed Levi home. *What the hell is he doing? Checking on the bakery? Looking for me? Looking for something to eat? I sure hope he's not looking for me after the way he treated me all those years ago.*

Selene walked in, and Levi was already pulling out ingredients to make steaks, mashed potatoes and gravy.

He turned and said, "Dad said he was hungry. I'm taking advantage of it. He's in the shower. He went in on his own."

Selene dropped her purse on the counter and leaned against it. "Want to tell me what the fuck is going on, Levi?"

He set several potatoes on the table and tossed the peeler to her before he turned back to the fridge to get the steaks so he could season them and let them sit while the potatoes cooked.

Selene reached up and caught the peeler. She grabbed a paper plate, the strainer and a paring knife. Picking up the first potato, she said, "You're not going to get out of telling me, and I'll figure it out sooner, so you might as well save us some fuckin' grief, Levi, and tell me what's going on with the bakery."

"Oh, there's going to be a whole lot of grief when you hear what's been going on," Levi muttered.

"What?"

When he didn't answer, Selene sighed. She rested her hands on the edge of the counter, tapping her fingers as Levi busied himself with the steaks. Her jaw tightened with every sidelong glance she shot at her brother, and her eyes narrowed each time he dodged her questions. When silence stretched between them, she blew her breath out.

"Later. When Dad goes to bed," Levi said under his breath so Jed wouldn't hear.

"You have had over a week to tell me about this, Levi. Stop putting it off."

"Later. I want to make sure Dad eats." Levi was firm with her.

Selene opened her mouth to protest, then closed it and shook her head. She snatched up the next potato, dragging the peeler over its surface with deliberate strokes. Her eyes flicked up to Levi's determined expression, and she rolled them, grumbling under her breath while she finished the potatoes.

Levi took the strainer from her and rinsed them, and then grabbed the paring knife from the table and cut them into chunks into a pot of water.

After dinner, Selene glanced at her watch. "It's early enough. Let's walk through town, and you can tell me what's new," she said to Levi. She turned to Jed. "You don't mind, do you, Dad?"

"No, I don't mind. I think I'll watch a little TV and then hit the sack."

"We won't be long. Do you want anything from the store?" Levi asked.

Jed shook his head. "No, thanks, I'm good."

Selene smiled at her father. "You're looking better already, Dad. You have more color in your face. We won't be long. It's not like the town is huge or anything."

She changed out of her sneakers and pulled on her insulated boots. Grabbing her purse and jacket, she stepped into the hall, just as Levi did.

"It's only a few blocks to the rest of the stores once we get down the mile-long driveway. Do you want to ride or walk?" he asked.

"Let's walk. It's right at freezing, and it's not far. It'll be nice to see the lights the town put up. Do you think they decorated the storefronts yet?"

Levi laughed. "You haven't been paying attention, have you, little sister?"

Selene punched his shoulder and blew out a breath as she shoved her hands into her pockets. "I haven't even had time to unpack my suitcase, let alone find my winter boots, until tonight," she muttered, glancing sideways at Levi. "Feels like every day has been a race, just to keep up."

"That's an understatement," Levi muttered.

They stepped outside, and Selene sniffed the air. "I smell snow."

"I've been smelling it since yesterday," Levi said, agreeing.

They walked in silence for a few minutes. Just as Selene was going to say something, Levi spoke up.

"Mom was having an affair. Had been for several months, as much as we could tell. She didn't know we figured it out."

Selene stopped where she was. "What?!"

Levi shook his head. "Yeah. That's what we said. Dad was going to confront her about it the night she had the accident. She never made it home. The thing is, if she

40

had been where she was supposed to be, which is right here helping out at the bakery, she would still be here."

"Was he planning on divorcing her?"

"I don't know. He never would say. I don't think he knew what he was going to do."

"Jesus, Levi. They're pushing sixty. Why now?"

"I don't know. And I know Dad is wondering if this was the first time. He won't talk about it, but I suspect he thinks there were more."

"Well, hell," Selene cursed. "They always seemed to get along just fine."

"They did. There's no telling how long she'd been putting on a front. He didn't say this, but I started thinking about the times she'd disappear. I don't know if it's the same guy or if she's had a few affairs over the past six or seven years. I'm almost afraid to ask him if he didn't realize something was up before."

They walked in silence for several minutes. Levi pointed at the small hardware store. "Old Man Cutter turned the hardware store over to his son. Other than that, everything else is the same."

They walked a few more minutes before Selene said, "The Christmas lights don't seem to have the same appeal now."

Levi nodded, agreeing. "No, they don't. The holidays are sure going to be different without Mom here." He sighed. "Want to go back? I'm getting a bit cold."

"Same. When are they doing the tree lighting?"

Levi shrugged as they turned around. "I'm not sure. This whole thing with Mom and Dad and the bakery has had me running like a chicken with its head cut off. In case you haven't figured it out yet, that's why the bakery is going downhill. He didn't want to say anything, and he's been trying to do the finances and the prepping by himself. He's not good at finances. And his product is suffering. We've had to throw some stuff away, so when we were out, people stopped coming in."

Selene stopped and dragged a hand through her hair. Her shoulders sagged. "This is a certified cluster fuck. Everything seems to be falling apart all at once."

"That language. Is that what they taught you in your job?"

Selene huffed a laugh. "You learn it pretty quickly when accounts have screwups working in their marketing department, then they call us to fix it when their sales tank."

"Do you—"

"Yeah. I can fix it. It'll take a bit. Dad's probably going to be pissed. But it's not the worst I've seen."

Levi grabbed her arm and pulled her to a stop just as they reached their front door. "I don't care if he gets pissed. This bakery is supposed to be our livelihood. You went off and got an education that you can use anywhere, but I didn't go to college. I planned on running the bakery when Mom and Dad got too old to do it. I want to keep it going, and Dad's been trying to do this alone for at least five or six months."

"You have a lot to learn. And from what I saw today, it's been longer than five or six months."

"Not really on the learning. I just didn't know what was going on. But you're right. I should have known something was up and investigated sooner."

"But you trusted him," Selene whispered.

"Yeah. There was no reason not to. He is our dad."

Selene sighed. "Yeah, I know. I probably would have been in your shoes had I been here."

CHAPTER 4

Selene hurriedly stepped around the endcap of an aisle in Whiting's Hardware, glancing at the time on her phone, and ran slap into a tall, muscular body that smelled of wood smoke. She stepped back, but not before the large, strong hands grabbed her shoulders to steady her.

She lifted her head and met the piercing blue eyes of Aris Beckett. "S-sorry," she stammered.

Aris grinned, and his eyes softened. "Hey, Selene. How have you been?"

She stepped away from him, and thankfully, his hands slid off her shoulders. She glanced down at her hands and twisted her mouth before lifting her eyes to him and scowling. "Fine. You?"

The smile left his face. "Doing well. You in town for long?"

"Uh, no." Selene took another step back. "I gotta run." She turned on her heels and almost ran down the aisle.

"Shit! I don't have time for this," she mumbled and then checked the next aisle before she went down it. At the end of it, Selene stopped and breathed deeply while her eyes scanned the back of the store. Not seeing Aris, her shoulders relaxed a bit, and she headed over to the wall full of screws.

She found what she was looking for and grabbed a large box before turning toward the front. *Fuck me. I hope he's gone by now.* She peeked down an aisle to make sure he wasn't there. As she neared the front of the store, Aris walked across the parking lot with a bag in his hand.

Selene sighed as the tension in her chest uncoiled. *Evidently, he didn't have time, either.* She paid for her purchases and headed out to her truck. After turning the key, she cranked the heat up. Selene reached for the gearshift but pulled her hand back and leaned against the seat, rubbing it across her chin.

Something happened. Something bad. Can't be. That feeling doesn't work all the time. I didn't get this feeling when Mom wrecked. Levi and Dad were working and were fine when I left. They were getting all—.

"No. That can't be. I was over him ten years ago when he decided to play all high-and-mighty," she said to the empty cab. Shaking her head, she sighed and backed out of the parking space.

Levi glanced up when Selene walked into the bakery, raising his eyebrows at her. Stomping down to the office, she grabbed an impact drill from the toolbox and headed into the storage area to finish the shelving that Levi had started building. She'd gotten one put together and affixed to the wall when her brother walked in.

"I can do that later if you have other things to do, Sis."

She jumped at the sound of his voice. "Damn, Levi. Don't sneak up on people like that."

Levi laughed. "I wasn't sneaking. Your mind must be in another world if you didn't hear me coming in."

The laughter fell from his face as Selene turned around. "What's that scowl for? Don't tell me. You ran into Aris."

Selene lifted her eyebrow as she leaned away from him. "Why would you think that?"

"That's the same look you had when you had that falling out with him. You never did reconnect, did you?"

"Now I know you know I didn't just fall off the fucking turnip truck, Levi. I know you're friends with him, which means you know that he never reconnected with me." *Or vice versa.*

"Uh, he doesn't really talk about you."

Selene rolled her eyes. "And that hesitation tells me that you're full of shit."

"Language!" Jed bellowed from the hallway.

Levi laughed, and Selene rolled her eyes again.

"For real, Sis. He really doesn't." Levi shrugged.

"Yeah, right. Are you done baking?"

"For now. Want some help?"

Levi didn't wait for her to answer and started on the next set of shelves.

They had one more left to put together and tether to the wall when the extension in the storeroom buzzed. Selene reached over and absentmindedly picked it up.

"Yeah, Dad," she said as she held the shelf in place so Levi could screw in the safety bracket.

"Can you give me a hand for a minute?"

"Sure. I'll be right there."

Once Levi got one screw in so the shelf would stay in place, she stopped in the bathroom to wash her hands and headed out front. She was wiping her hands with a paper towel and not paying attention to who was in line.

Chucking the paper towel in the trash, she asked, "Good afternoon, what can I get you today?"

When she finally lifted her head, she had all she could do to keep from rolling her eyes. Aris was standing there, the only person in line, and her father was nowhere to be found. Selene tilted her head and tightened her lips. "What, Aris?"

He leaned on the counter, and the corner of his mouth lifted in a partial smirk. "Why'd you take off so fast?"

"What are you talking about?" Selene asked, narrowing her eyes.

"In the hardware store. You took off like your ass was on fire."

"I have things to do, Aris. I was right in the middle of helping Levi with a project. Now, did you come in here just to bust my ass, or did you want something?"

The corner of Aris's mouth lifted in a slight smirk. "A little of both. I came in here to bust your ass, but now, I'm hungry. It smells so good in here. I'll take a strawberry Danish and a black coffee to go, please."

Selene's lips tightened as she made his order and handed it to him. After he swiped his card, she pleasantly said, "Have a good day," though she didn't feel pleasant.

Aris nodded. "Sure will."

He took his pastry and coffee over to a table by the front window, hoping Levi and Jed didn't come back out, twisting in his chair so he could watch Selene out of the corner of his eye.

Damn it. He said, 'To go.' Leave already. Selene wiped the counter and rearranged the baked products so that they were at the front of the case. As she worked, her eyes kept shifting to Aris.

When she realized what she was doing, she rolled her eyes at herself. *Quit looking at him. It's not like you had a romantic relationship before. But he's so...muscular. Yeah. That. And the way those jeans hug his ass. I wonder if his lips are as soft as they look.*

Her face pinked, and she hurriedly walked into the back to see if there were more pastries to put out, even though she knew there weren't. Opening the walk-in cooler door, she stepped inside and took a deep breath.

When she had composed herself, she stepped back out front.

Aris was throwing his trash away. He lifted a hand in a wave and said, "See ya 'round."

Selene nodded. "See ya."

Hopefully not.

Levi and Jed took that opportunity to walk out front. Selene narrowed her eyes at them. "Don't do that to me again," she snapped.

"What? You didn't talk to him?" Levi asked.

Selene shrugged. "We obviously don't have anything to talk about. He was an ass and never apologized. He still hasn't."

"Maybe he doesn't think he has anything to apologize for. Besides, who holds a grudge for over ten years?" Jed asked.

"It's time to close up and go home," Selene said, avoiding Jed's question. She walked to the front door and locked it, and then turned off the lights.

It wasn't until she had started her truck that her father and brother finally came out and locked the back door. They climbed into Jed's truck and followed her home.

CHAPTER 5

Aris flipped on the lights in his workshop, casting long shadows over his tools. He moved over to the forge, checked everything he needed to and flipped it on. He had an order for a large mezzaluna, a curved blade with two handles, and it would be the perfect metal to use. The blade "rocked," making it easier to chop vegetables.

His thumb ran along the blackened edge of the old high-carbon sawmill blade propped against the wall. "This will be perfect for the mezzaluna," he thought as he

53

pictured the blade's arc making a smooth roll for chopping.

As he cut a piece that was large enough for the mezzaluna, sparks popped, spraying in the air. His hand slowed as his thoughts turned to Selene.

What is with her? Selene never treated me like that. She still can't be pissed about those girls. I wonder if she even knows that both of them ended up in jail out in Nashville. Whoring for drugs and copped an attempted murder charge. I knew they were bad news.

His hand tightened on the plasma cutter when Selene's scowl flashed in his mind. He shook his head, pressing his lips tight. *Maybe she didn't know where those girls ended up after all.* The memory of their heavy-lidded eyes and reckless laughter crawled under his skin.

"Damn it!" Aris cussed. "That's what I get for not paying attention." His experienced eyes followed the too-shallow cut in the metal. "Fuck. It's not going to be big enough," he said, measuring the gap with his calloused thumb. It was a mere eighth of an inch off. It would make the knife blade too thin.

Sighing, Aris put the template on another part of the saw blade. "Head out of your ass, Beckett. Focus," he muttered, chastising himself and lining the pattern up for another try.

This time, he made the right cuts. He worked on heating and pounding the steel until it was in the shape he wanted. Checking his cell phone for the time, he switched off the roaring forge. His stomach rumbled. With the most challenging part over, he could hunt up a couple of antler tips for the handles after he grabbed a bite to eat.

He walked across the yard and into the back door of his house. Opening the fridge, he scoured the shelves for something to eat. Sandwiches. Leftover meatloaf and potatoes. Fried chicken. He settled on the fried chicken and would go to the bakery for a Danish and coffee.

You just want to see Selene. No, I don't. Yeah, you do. You know you can't keep asking Jed and Levi to send her out front. They already suspect something's going on. Ah, hell. He shoved the thought away, knowing if he showed up again, Jed and Levi would give him even more curious looks. "I already burned too many excuses to see her," he thought, tearing into a drumstick and scowling at himself.

Aris cleaned up from lunch and grabbed a chocolate bar out of the fridge. He paused at the door, his hand hovering over his keys. He'd already made his bakery rounds for the week, having picked up pastries twice. If he showed up again, no one would believe that it was just for the pastries. *They would know. Or at least suspect.*

Selene folded the last shirt into the suitcase, her fingers hesitating on the pile of clothes she'd so neatly

55

arranged. While she could work from home, she'd stayed longer than expected and had to show her face at the office—at the very least.

She'd done all she could to straighten out the books and had started on a marketing plan for the bakery. Since she would be the one implementing it, she could finish that chore from home. "First thing after breakfast, I'm out of here," she whispered as she packed the notebooks and documents she'd need for her marketing efforts.

She padded down the hallway toward the kitchen to fix dinner just as Jed and Levi walked in the back door.

"All packed and ready to go?" Jed asked.

"Yep. I'll leave after breakfast in the morning."

"Have you talked to Aris?" Levi asked as he leaned against the counter.

Selene raised her eyebrow at him. "Why? And get out of my way if you want me to make dinner." She gave him a light shove.

"Just wondering."

"Really, Levi, I thought I told you. We don't have anything to say to each other. We were only friends in high school, nothing more. And there won't be anything more."

"You need to hear what he has to say, Selene," Jed interjected.

"Why? He has my number. It's never changed. If he wanted to talk that badly, he could have called at least once over the past ten years."

Jed held his hands up in surrender. "Okay. Just saying, though."

He sat at the table next to Levi. "What are you making? Do you need help?"

Selene wiped the surprised look off her face before she turned around. "No, thanks, Dad. The pork chops are on, and all I have to do is heat up some leftover potatoes and creamed peas."

"Is there any more of that broccoli and cheese left?" Levi asked.

"Not much," Selene said. "I can heat that up, too, if you want."

"Yes, please," Levi said, rubbing his hands. "That cheese sauce you made the other day is really good."

Selene laughed. "It's the same recipe you use when you cook."

"Yeah, but it tastes better when someone else makes it."

As she walked past Levi to grab the broccoli out of the fridge, she flicked his shoulder with her hand. "You're just being lazy."

Jed snickered at both of his children and then got up to set the table.

Selene fixed three plates, handing the first two to Levi. He set them on the table and reached into the fridge for three bottles of water.

"Thanks, Son," Jed grunted. He scooped some of the broccoli and cheese onto his fork, stabbed a piece of pork chop, and wiped it through the cheese sauce. "Mm, good," he grunted around the food in his mouth.

"Next time, I'll make extra cheese sauce just to dip the meat in," Selene said. "Hmm…you know what would be good? Bleu cheese dressing on steak."

Jed and Levi nodded. "Yeah," Levi said after he swallowed the food in his mouth. "That is good. I've done that before."

When they finished eating, Levi said he'd clean up since Selene had cooked. Jed went into the living room to catch the news, their words drifting off as the anchor's voice sounded in the living room.

"I have a couple of emails to respond to, and then I'm going to head to bed. I want to make sure I get a good night's sleep before I drive back," Selene said.

Levi opened his mouth to say something about the drive, but Selene held her hand up.

"I know, it's not a long drive, but if I hit weather, I want to be on my game, Big Brother."

Selene headed down the hall to take a shower. She put her pajamas on and wrapped a robe around herself. Once she got into her room, she lifted the blinds to look outside, knowing it would be one of the few times she'd see the Tennessee countryside for a while.

She let the blind fall back into place and then swore under her breath. Lifting the blind again, she craned her head toward the carport. Heavy flakes tumbled down, swallowing the trees and distant barn in grey-white silence. "Shit. I guess I won't be going anywhere tomorrow."

Grabbing her phone off the nightstand, she navigated to her favorite weather app. She tied the belt to her robe and walked out into the kitchen, holding her phone in front of her as if it were a light guiding her way.

Jed glanced up when he saw movement out of the corner of his eye. A phone made its way around the corner, followed by Selene. He grinned and asked, "Girl, what are you doing? That phone isn't going to bite you."

"No, but the weather just did. Did you know it's snowing out there?" she asked in disbelief.

"For real?" Levi asked. "It wasn't supposed to snow."

"I know. Why do you think I decided to leave now? They are expecting a mess of snow next week."

Jed slid his chair back and opened the back door. "Uh, Selene."

"Yeah, Dad?"

"Does that thing say how much we're supposed to get?"

She swiped the screen a few times. "Well, fuck my life."

"Language!" Jed yelled.

Levi laughed, and Jed turned around. "Don't egg her on. She's bad enough."

"So, Little Girl, how much snow?" Jed asked snarkily.

"You'd better go turn the TV on. This thing says over a foot by morning, and they don't expect it to stop until the day after."

"Well, hell," Jed mumbled under his breath.

"Language, Dad," Selene said with a grin.

"Never you mind my language. Best mind your own."

Levi turned the TV on and switched to a local news station. "It's nine, but they'll break in for something like this."

They all knew that the news didn't start until ten, but were hoping they would break in.

"Commercial," Levi muttered. "We pay for cable, and they still put commercials on."

"That's because—"

"I know why, Sis. But they make more than I could ever hope to make in ten lifetimes. Those cable companies could at least give us a couple of channels without commercials."

"True that," Selene muttered as she pointed at the TV. "Good timing."

Levi slouched on the couch, arms crossed, muttering about commercials. His hate for them was no worse than anyone else's, but he always complained about them.

"Breaking news," the newscaster said. "We have an unexpected winter storm moving in. Let's go to Brett Anderson in our weather station for more."

The shot panned over to Brett in front of the weather map, showing blue arrows swirling across the map as he straightened his tie.

"Good evening, folks. I'm Brett Anderson on TV14 weather, and I'm breaking in with a major, unexpected weather alert for LaFollette and the surrounding communities. If you're just tuning in, here's the latest. The weather models are showing a rare and rapidly developing winter storm, headed directly for our area, and it's set to take everyone by surprise.

"Let me explain what's happening. Usually, we can spot these storms from days away, but tonight, a perfect storm of atmospheric conditions is coming together. Earlier today, a surge of unusually cold Arctic air slipped further south than normal, colliding overhead with a strong, moisture-packed warm front traveling in from the Gulf. This surprise clash of temperatures and moisture is creating intense uplift in the atmosphere. That's triggering heavy snow bands to form almost instantly, right above Campbell County.

"Now, here's what you need to know: This winter storm is expected to settle in for three days, blanketing LaFollette and Evermist with a massive two feet of snow before it moves out. The most astonishing part? The first foot is forecasted to fall overnight, starting in just a few hours. By sunrise, snowdrifts could make travel nearly impossible.

"This sudden system, called a "bombogenesis," happens when pressure drops very rapidly in a short period, causing storm conditions to explode in severity with little warning. That's exactly what's unfolding—heavy snow, reduced visibility, gusty winds, and plummeting temperatures, all ramping up tonight through the weekend."

"Well, they're even late with that," Jed said.

"Unless this snow we're getting isn't part of that mess," Selene added.

"I guess you'd better go unpack, Selene. Looks like you're going to be here for at least another week," Levi added.

Selene sighed. "I'd better shoot off an email to my boss. They were expecting me the day after tomorrow."

She went into her room and came back with her laptop. She set it up on the kitchen table and typed out an email. "I might as well work on some of the marketing for the bakery," she said to the two men sitting at the table with her. "I'm not tired now."

"I'll put some coffee on," Jed said. "I'm not tired either, and it's a cinch we're not opening the bakery tomorrow. Levi?"

He nodded. "Sure, Dad. I'll take a cup. Tomorrow is the day we bake the extra loaves for those who need a little help, though. Maybe I should take the four-wheeler down—"

"You might make it there, but you won't make it back. Not without a Ski-Doo," Jed said at the same time Selene started to ask about the free bread.

His gaze shifted to Selene. "Sorry, you were going to say?"

"Guys. We can't be giving away product right now. We can't afford it."

"But these are older people who don't have the means to get any bread. They have very little Social Security, and they often have to go without food, heat or medication because they can't afford all three."

"I know, Dad, but we're going to be in that boat if we don't watch it. You can go back to doing that when we get back on our feet."

Jed's lips tightened. "Let's work on that marketing plan." He didn't feel like arguing, and he knew it would turn into one, because he wasn't going to give up on making bread for those who needed it.

CHAPTER 6

Two days later, the snow had finally tapered off. Only thin, lazy flakes floated to the ground. It was a far cry from the blinding curtain that blanketed the house for days. Levi stood at the window, gazing longingly toward town.

"Don't even think about it, Son," Jed said, sighing.

"Our trucks have four-wheel drive, Dad."

"It's not worth your life. The bakery will still be there when this starts to melt."

Jed heaved a long sigh, watching the worry pull Levi's brows together as he stared out at the covered road. He knew Levi only cared about making bread for those who couldn't buy it. "It's not going to melt. We have another storm coming in this week, too."

Selene put her hand on Levi's shoulder. "We can try to get in tomorrow. But we're not making free bread."

"Might as well. People aren't going to be coming into the bakery in this mess, and we'll need to use up some of those ingredients or throw them away."

"What are you using that's going to expire? We used dried milk and eggs."

"For this particular bread recipe, we've been using fresh milk."

"Damn it, Levi. Dad." Selene sighed. "You were already in trouble, yet you continued with a recipe that uses fresh instead of dried? Do you know how much extra that costs? And I suppose you're not getting any extra for this bread to make up for the extra cost."

Levi lifted one shoulder and twisted his mouth into a partial smile, while Jed's curved in that quiet, apologetic way Selene had seen when he'd already made up his mind.

"It looks like I need to help you with more than the marketing."

Selene shut down her marketing program and logged into the server for the bakery. "I was going to leave this part up to you guys, since you are the ones working this every day. Dad, this is our future. We want to be able to hand this down to our kids. We won't be able to do that if the bakery goes under and we have to sell, or worse, the bank forecloses on us."

Neither man said anything. Jed hadn't told either of his children just how bad the finances had gotten. They were about to find out, and it wasn't going to be pretty.

"I need a drink," he said.

Selene's eyes lifted from the computer screen. "You don't even drink, Dad."

"Maybe on special occasions," he muttered as he walked over to the cabinet and took out a bottle of whiskey. He held the half-full bottle up and lifted his eyebrows.

Selene glanced at Levi, who shrugged. "Sure, Dad. Just one finger, though. I can't have a fucked-up head if I'm going to straighten this mess out. And you will need to help, so you don't get crazy on it, either."

Jed poured them each a finger's worth in whiskey glasses he took from the cupboard and put the bottle away.

Levi and Selene waited for him to come back to the table.

Jed lifted his glass. "A new day. No more secrets— you're about to find out the last one—and to better days," he said as he lifted his glass toward his adult children.

"Better days," they both parroted.

Selene noticed her father wringing his hands under the table. "Dad. Chill. I already know it's bad."

Selene grunted as she rolled over to turn off the alarm on her cell phone. "Shit."

It was six in the morning, and they had gone through the finances until after two in the morning. But they knew exactly where they stood. It wasn't good, but Selene supposed it could have been much worse. It would have been, if it hadn't been for her mother's death. She and Levi may have never caught it in time.

She lay in the bed for a few minutes, and her mind wandered to the crux of the problems.

"Hell, it wouldn't have gotten to this point if she'd have kept her legs closed. Selene could have been her father's twin, so she knew who her father was. But Levi? He had his mother's looks. He didn't even get an ounce of his father's genes," she mumbled.

He doesn't look exactly like Mom, either. That's questionable. I wonder if that thought went through his head. I'm certainly not going to bring it up. But, damn.

Selene shoved back the covers and wandered into the bathroom she shared with Levi to do her morning routine. She heard her father in the master bath. If Levi were still sleeping, she'd wake him up when breakfast was ready.

She walked into the kitchen to start making it, but Levi was putting bacon in the pan. "Good morning," she mumbled.

Levi grunted at her. Despite having to get up early every day, he'd never been and never would be a morning person.

Selene walked over to the coffee pot and poured herself a cup. She sat at the table with both hands wrapped around the warm mug.

Jed had just walked into the kitchen when a strange notification sounded from his phone. He pulled it from his pocket. "Well, fuck."

"Language, Dad," Selene muttered.

"That was the sheriff. There's water all over the front of the bakery. A pipe must have busted. He turned the water off at the street."

"Well, there's no rush, then. Sit and eat. Breakfast is almost ready," Levi said.

69

"I guess you're right," Jed said, shaking his head.

After breakfast, they put their plates in the sink.

"You two go ahead. I'll clean up here, and then I'll be there," Selene said.

Jed opened his mouth to object, but Selene shook her head at him. "No, go ahead. It won't take me but a few minutes to do this."

She turned the hot water on and waited for it to warm up. Once it did, she made quick work of the dishes and then pulled her coat and boots on.

She carefully made her way down to the bakery. Most of the snow had melted, but it had barely made it above freezing, so there was a considerable risk of black ice.

Levi and Jed were already cleaning up the water off the floor. They had the heat turned up in the bakery. Typically, they set it at sixty degrees when no one was there to save on utility bills. But even when they were open, it was rarely over seventy degrees, as the ovens put out a lot of heat.

"Did you guys find the leak?" Selene asked.

"No. In the kitchen somewhere," Jed said crossly.

"Okay, I'll go hunt it down."

She checked everything in the kitchen and couldn't find the source of the leak. She checked the bathrooms and finally remembered the sink in the storage room. When she opened the door, she stepped into water on the floor. It had leaked under the walls and into the kitchen and the retail area.

Opening the cabinet under the sink, she shone a flashlight inside and found the problem. The pipe coming out of the floor was broken right at the base of the cabinet. They'd have to replace the cabinet.

She walked out into the retail area. "I found the leak. The pipe in the storeroom busted. We'll need to replace the cabinet and the pipe. I know what we need. I'll just go over to the hardware store and get it."

"Okay," said Jed. "Just be careful out there."

"I will," Selene said as she went to the office to grab her coat and purse.

One of the clerks helped her load the new cabinet and sink into the back of her truck. She'd decided to get a larger sink, as the one that was in there was really too small for maintenance purposes. She set the bag with the plumbing stuff and pipe on the front seat and climbed in. Selene rolled down the window.

"Thanks, Mack!" she called as he went back into the store.

He waved at her and said, "Be careful out there!"

Selene rolled up the window and turned the heat on. A smile tugged at Selene's lips as Mack lifted a hand, waving. She couldn't remember the last time anyone had helped her load boxes, let alone send her off with a reminder to drive safely.

She waited for the one vehicle that was passing the hardware store before she pulled out into the road. She'd only gone a block when the truck spun out of control.

"Well, fuck," she muttered as she turned into the skid and eased off the brake. Selene's hands moved on instinct, nudging the wheel and feathering the brakes just like Dad had taught her when she was barely tall enough to reach the pedals in the old Chevy. However, her rear wheels still hit the edge of the sidewalk and caused the truck to slide the other way.

She corrected, but the rear of the truck hit a telephone pole when it came back around. Selene let out a long string of curse words that would make a sailor blush. She was still cussing when she stepped out of the truck to check the damage…right into Aris's strong chest.

He put his hands on her waist to steady her. "Whoa. Take it easy there, Selene. You're gonna fall and bust your ass."

Fuck. Just what I need.

Aris.

Here.

72

Now.

"Aris." She pushed his hands away and stepped around him so she could check the damage. She hurried around the back, jaw clenched, not even looking at the dented fender. Her eyes locked on the sturdy utility pole, and she crossed her fingers that she wouldn't owe the county for damage. Luckily, the pole was fine. But the bed of her truck had a massive dent right above the wheel well.

Selene bent down to check the axle and whether the dent would rub the tire.

"Fuck my life," she muttered. The body wasn't touching the wheel, but it was really close, and she wasn't going to risk driving it and getting stranded because an errant bump knocked the tire into the sharp crease in the metal body.

They didn't do much body work at the local shop, so she'd have to tow it to LaFollette.

"You know you can't drive that like that," Aris said. He was trying to be friendly.

"No shit, dipwad," Selene shot back. She rolled her eyes. "Sorry. It's a shitty day, and I'm still pissed at you—"

"You're still pissed because of those girls? From like, what? Ten years ago?" It was Aris's turn to roll his eyes. "You can't be ser..."

She wasn't paying attention to him as she pulled her phone out of her pocket to call for a tow truck. They could stop at the bakery on the way out of town to drop her and the plumbing stuff off.

CHAPTER 7

Aris leaned against Selene's bumper while she called for a tow. He shifted his weight forward as he adjusted his stance against the smashed truck.

"Selene." Aris bit his lip and wiped his hand on his pants.

She sighed. "What, Aris?"

"Are you going to answer my question?"

Selene clenched her fists and set her jaw as she glared at him. "No. It doesn't deserve an answer. Why do you insist on fucking with me? And what are you doing here, anyway?"

"Why are you holding a grudge all these years later?"

"Why? Really, Aris? You withdraw your friendship—a friendship we had for fucking years—because you were jealous of my friends, and now you wonder why I don't want a fucking thing to do with you? You're denser than I thought."

Selene pulled her phone out of her pocket. "I need to call Dad so he doesn't worry. Do you fucking mind?" She turned her back and walked away from him, almost slipping on the black ice that caused this mess in the first place.

"Damn it," she muttered. "Why does he have to be everywhere I turn?"

Aris could hear her side of the conversation.

"Hey, Dad. I'll be there shortly. I spun out on black ice. I didn't want you to worry."

Selene rolled her eyes at the phone.

"No, Dad. I'm fine." She kicked at a small pile of snow and ice while she listened to her father worrying about her and the truck.

"The truck will be fine. It's got a massive dent in the bed, right over the rear wheel. I'll have the tow truck drop me off and take it to that body shop in LaFollette."

Aris knew her father was giving her the third degree by the way her shoulders stiffened, revealing her frustration with his questions.

"Yes, I'm sure I'm not hurt. I'll be there in a bit, and then I'll tell you what happened."

Aris waited until she finished her call and then walked up to her. "It's cold. Wait in my truck with me so you can keep warm."

"I can wait in my truck. There's nothing wrong with the engine. And you still didn't answer my question." Selene pulled her truck door open and slid into the warm cab. Before she could hit the lock button, Aris had the passenger door open.

"Persistent, ain't you." Selene said as she tilted her head and pursed her lips.

Aris huffed a laugh. "You haven't changed one bit."

"If that bothers you, don't let that door hit you in the ass on the way out."

Aris rolled his eyes at her as he adjusted himself on the seat. *Fuck. Even when she's being an asshole, she makes me hard. Hopefully, she doesn't notice.*

He sighed, finally answering her question. "I didn't want you to get hurt."

Selene tilted her head back against the headrest and closed her eyes. "My patience is wearing thin, Aris. How was I going to get hurt, and How. The. Fuck. Do. You. Think. What. I. Was. Doing. Was. Any. Of. Your. Business?"

Aris waited a few minutes before he answered. "Do you know what happened to those girls? Did you keep in touch with them?"

"Out, Aris," she growled.

"Wait. There's a point to that question. That you won't answer tells me you don't know what happened. They're both in jail. They got busted for hooking for their drug habit and an attempted murder charge. Attempted murder, Selene!"

Selene gripped the steering wheel hard enough to turn her knuckles white.

"And?"

Aris sighed and shook his head. "I was fucking right, Selene. I told you they were bad news. You didn't believe me. Just be lucky you didn't get tied up in that mess."

"And why do you think I would get tied up in that mess? Do you think I'm that stupid? And why do you keep showing up wherever I am?"

"No, Selene. It's not that, but you were impressionable and might not have thought—"

"Enough! You obviously didn't think enough of me to know that I'd never get involved in anything like that."

"And if they did something while you were with them? How do you think you would have gotten out of that?"

Selene rolled her eyes. "All we ever did—you know what? It's none of your business. Now either shut up or get out of my truck."

She turned her head when she heard the rumble of the tow truck. "Good. They're here. Out."

Aris muttered under his breath, "I was on my way to see Levi at the bakery when I saw you wreck. You act like I'm stalking you or something."

Selene slid out of the truck and slammed the door. *He is stalking me.*

Aris eased out and closed his door more gently. She smiled at the tow truck driver, even though she was fuming. She explained where she wanted her truck towed, and the driver agreed to drop her off at the bakery.

Aris pulled into the bakery behind the tow truck and went inside to get Levi. The driver tipped the bed, and he

79

and Levi wrangled the counter and sink out of Selene's truck and onto the bed of the tow truck. Once they slid it off the tow bed, the driver worked the levers to lower it in place and headed down the mountain to LaFollette.

Levi and Aris carried the awkward box containing the counter into the storeroom and then went back out for the sink.

Selene handed the bag with the plumbing supplies to Levi. "I'll be in the office since Dad is working the front." She turned to Aris. "Try not to disturb me."

Levi glared at him. "Damn, Aris, did you piss in her Wheaties?"

Aris shrugged. "I'll help you set this up."

They went into the storeroom and unboxed the counter. Aris pawed through the bag. "At least she got the right stuff."

"Don't knock her, Aris. She can put this together faster than you and me together."

Aris raised his eyebrows.

"Yeah," Levi said. "She's good at doing stuff like this. Always has been." He motioned for Aris to hand him the pipe glue.

"I never knew that."

Levi sat back on his heels and looked up at Aris. "You were too concerned with shit you shouldn't have been when it came to her."

"Oh, hell. Not you, too."

"She's not wrong, Aris. Give it a break and apologize to her. You might get somewhere with that."

Aris shrugged. "I don't know. She's pretty pissed."

"She doesn't like others to control her. She butts heads with Dad all the time."

The clinking of tools filled the room as they finished installing the sink and cabinet. Aris stuck his head under it. "Turn the water on so I can see if there are any leaks." He shone the flashlight around as the water gurgled down the drain.

"No leaks." Aris washed his hands and continued, "I'm going to head out. I have a couple of small orders to do in the blacksmith shop."

"Okay. Thanks for the help. Do you want to take some pastries with you?"

"No thanks. I have several in the freezer." Aris grinned. "I must have a couple of dozen Danish in there, five or six apple fritters."

Levi nodded and followed Aris out to the front of the bakery.

He watched as Aris hopped in his truck and left, and then went back to the office.

"Hey."

Selene glanced up from her laptop and then back down, grunting a greeting.

Levi leaned back in his chair. "What are you working on?"

"A Facebook page, reels, posts and other stuff. I can schedule them for a couple of weeks at a time."

He stood and grabbed one of the folding chairs leaning against the wall and set it next to Selene's so he could watch what she was doing. After several minutes, he said, "I can do that. Once you get it set up, do you want me to continue with it?"

Selene leaned back in her chair and raised an eyebrow as Levi scrolled through his phone, a string of notifications lighting up. She knew he was really good with social media because of all the followers he had.

"Let's see what you come up with over the next few days. If you are on point with your content, then I might turn it over to you."

She worked for another hour, with Levi watching and learning. They both startled when Jed poked his head into the office.

"Time to go home, kids."

Selene glanced at her watch. "Well, hell. I guess we got involved in that. Why didn't you come get us to help clean up?"

"It was slow, so I cleaned up between customers. When the last one left, I only had a couple of things to wash and put away. Now, I'm hungry. Let's go."

Selene saved her work and closed the laptop. "Okay. I have a good marketing plan started for social media. Levi said he wanted to help, so if he comes up with acceptable content, we'll both work on it."

Jed nodded. "Do you really think you can pull us out of this mess?"

Selene glanced at Levi and then at her father. "Yeah, Dad. This time. I've seen worse, but not much worse. You won't be able to recover if it happens again."

Jed nodded as he turned and locked the back door behind them. They climbed in their trucks and made their way to the house, but not before the snow started falling again. The second storm—the one that everyone knew about—had started earlier than expected.

And that's not the only storm brewing. Aris was spending way too much time around her—and her family.

CHAPTER 8

Morning sunlight glimmered off the shallow snowdrifts, barely three inches deep. Jed eyed the driveway, then shot Selene and Levi a quick nod. "Looks like we're opening. The roads in town will be clear enough. The trucks will have spread ice melt on the main roads the day before the storm hit, so it won't take them long to clear, especially once everyone gets out and about."

The one good thing about this storm was that their rutted gravel drive had frozen over again, so driving it wasn't as hairy as it was once the last snow had partially melted in the forty-degree days they'd had between storms.

Selene walked into the front of the bakery while Levi helped Jed into the back. Since they weren't sure how much it would snow, Levi hadn't gone to work until six. All three of them rode in his truck. They had some product left from yesterday and would sell it at their day-old prices, and hoped it would last until today's bake came out of the ovens.

She turned on the open sign and unlocked the front door, and then started the commercial coffee pots. She had a regular and decaf brewing in two, plus vanilla bean and raspberry in the other two.

The bell on the front door jingled when the first customer of the morning walked in. Selene finished pouring the first pot of regular coffee into the large insulated carafe and had just pressed the button to start another pot when the hair stood up on the back of her neck.

She turned slowly, meeting Aris's deep blue eyes. "Good morning, Aris," she said grudgingly. He was a customer, and she had to be polite to him while he was in the store. At least, until he stepped out of line.

He smiled at her and nodded. "I'm here to help this morning. I figured you'd be starting late because of the snow."

Selene nodded and pointed toward the back with her thumb. "Dad and Levi are in there."

He walked around the counter, but before he could push through the swinging doors, she asked, "Do you want a coffee?"

Aris hesitated. "Uh, sure. I could use a cup."

"Still take it black?"

"Yeah," Aris said, leaning against the counter while she fixed it.

She handed him the cup of steaming liquid and almost dropped it when his fingers touched hers, causing them to tingle. Just then, she seized the distraction of the bell, pivoting away from Aris and greeting the next customer, leaving him lingering awkwardly by the counter.

Aris left after the breakfast rush, so Jed helped with the crowd that came in for lunch. When it slowed down, Selene decided to walk down the street to check out some of the shops, since it didn't feel as cold as it had been, even though it was still snowing.

She went into the back to let Levi know so that he could watch the front. The smell of the cinnamon buns he was baking and the mulled cider that was simmering on the stovetop made her realize that Christmas was a mere week and a half away.

She wanted to see the Christmas tree lighting that the town had postponed because of all the snow. As she stepped out the front door of the bakery, the light snow that was still falling melted as soon as it touched her warm jacket. *At least this storm doesn't have as much accumulation, and it's the powdery, dry snow instead of that heavy wet slop we got last time.*

While some of the businesses were closed because of the weather, the bookstore was still open. She was hoping that Jolene was still working there. Levi had told her that nothing had changed, except the hardware store, and she really didn't consider that a change, since it was still in the family.

She stepped into the warm, welcoming bookstore, and a display up front caught her eye. The bookstore—or the author—had set up an extensive display with the author's Christmas swag and piles of her books.

Selene ran her fingers over the smooth cover. "A Chance at Christmas." *Sweet-looking couple. I haven't read a good romance in a long time. This must be an indie author. Never heard of her before. It's great she got her books in here. I wonder how they found her?*

She read the blurb on the back of the book. "Hmm.. she lets him move in—as a friend. Oh, he had relationship issues. That should be some good drama."

She flipped through the pages and stopped to read a couple of paragraphs to see if she liked the author's style. "Might have found me a new author," she muttered, tucking the book under her arm.

Selene stepped around the display and headed toward the rear of the store, since no one was at the checkout counter. She'd only taken a few steps when Jolene came out of the back.

"Can I help you—Selene! When did you get back?" She rushed over and pulled her friend into a bear hug before letting her go. "You look great. I haven't seen you in forever."

Selene grinned, and her friend finally slowed down enough to let her get a word in edgewise. "I've been in town for a few weeks, dealing with Mom's funeral, Dad and Levi, the bakery and," she rolled her eyes, "this snow!"

Jolene laughed. "We're getting a lot more than we normally get, that's for sure. How long are you home?"

Selene turned toward the checkout counter as she talked. "I don't know. It wasn't supposed to be for more than a week, but here I am." She placed the book on the counter.

"I came to ask if you knew when they moved the Christmas tree lighting to, and I ran across this." Selene pointed to the book. "Have you read it?"

"First things first. The lighting ceremony is this Saturday. Second, no, I haven't read it, but it looks good, so I bought a copy. Plus, I've read some of Rowen's other books. She's good."

"I guess we'll both find out soon enough," Selene said, shrugging.

"That we will. Do you wanna meet me at the tree lighting?" Jolene asked.

"Yes! That would be great. Levi and Dad can do their thing for a bit."

"Awesome! We haven't spent any time together since you were here last spring."

"Yeah, that's right. When I was here in the summer, you had the flu."

"Ugh. Don't remind me." Jolene shuddered. "I wouldn't wish that on my worst enemy."

The bell over the door dinged, so Jolene rang up the book and bagged it. As she handed it to Selene, she said, "I'll meet you at the bakery at six. We can both walk from there, and we'll have decent parking."

"Sounds good. See you then!"

"Don't be a stranger," Jolene called after her as she made her way out the door.

Selene turned and waved. "I won't!"

When she got back to the bakery, Levi was working the front counter. He had a short line of people, so Selene slid the book under the front counter and washed her hands in the hand sink. She helped the next person in line.

When they finished, she asked Levi, "Where's Dad?"

"He took the mail to the office. Come to think of it, he's been in there for over fifteen minutes. He said he was coming right back to help me. I'm glad you showed up when you did."

"I'll go check on him," Selene said.

Levi nodded as she went through the double swinging doors.

Selene poked her head into the office. Her father was reading a document with a scowl on his face. "What do you have there, Dad?"

"That fucking bitch was cheating on me." He leaned back on the chair. "I know Levi told you that I suspected it. You kids never did keep anything from each other. I wasn't sure, but I was pretty suspicious."

He waved the document. "This confirms it."

Selene walked over to the desk and reached for the document. Her father handed it over. As she read the charges on the credit card statement, her eyebrows rose higher and higher on her forehead. "What the fuck, Dad? There are a couple of thousand dollars in charges on here just for the past month!"

"Yeah. And ain't a one of them mine. I've been here every day. You can ask Levi."

"I don't have to, Dad. I believe you. First, you never would have spent this kind of money on trips, and second, you don't have time to take off this often."

Selene leaned against the wall as she studied the list of charges again. Her hand clenched the coffee cup so tightly that Jed thought it would break.

"Is this a joint account, Dad?"

"Unfortunately, it is. I have to pay it."

"Yeah, you do. Damn. Obviously, she didn't care if you found out, so she was probably planning on filing for divorce. I know she's my mother, but I really hate her right now. And I mean it when I say that this whole mess with her death is probably a blessing in disguise."

Jed turned toward her and lifted one eyebrow.

"Dad, she would have taken a percentage of everything you own together, including the bakery."

"Well, fuck," Jed muttered.

"You can say that again."

Jed growled, "Not that there's much left after all this."

She handed the statement to her father. "We'll fix it, Dad, don't worry." Selene felt her anger temper a bit.

"I'll just pay the whole thing off. I normally keep a zero balance on this card—I use it for gas, groceries, and stuff like that, so I don't want to pay interest on the balance, since those are everyday things. It helps me keep track of my personal expenses. I certainly don't want to pay interest on her fling, though."

Selene nodded. "I know you dipped into your retirement to cover the shortfalls for the last several months. This is what we're going to do. I have money saved. I'll give you the money for her charges. And I know we didn't discuss it, but when the bakery gets going again, it will pay you back for those loans from your retirement savings."

Jed opened his mouth to disagree with her, but Selene held up her hand. "No, Dad. It's only right. But your taxes are going to be a certified cluster fuck this year."

"Language," Jed growled, but the twinkle in his eye gave away that he was only busting her ass.

Selene cocked her head to the side and lifted an eyebrow.

Jed grinned and said, "Well, if I can't get you to stop cussing like a sailor, then I guess I might as well embrace it."

Laughing, she said, "If you think that's going to stop me, you've got another thing coming, Dad."

CHAPTER 9

"Levi! Dad! Hurry! We're going to be late!"

Jed sauntered into the kitchen. "Levi's still in the shower. Why don't you just take your truck down? I can ride with Levi. That way, if you're having fun with your friend, you can stay if we decide to leave early."

Selene sighed, her shoulders drooping as she gave in. "Okay. I'd rather we all went as a group, though. Besides,

I just got my truck back. I'd rather Levi smash his up this time."

Jed laughed and said, "Be nice to your brother."

She shook her head. "Nope. We never were when we were kids. No sense in starting now."

Jed shooed her with his hand. "Get out of here and have fun."

Before she stepped out of the door, she turned to Jed. "You'll look for us when you get there, so we can see the tree lighting together?"

"I promise," he said as he waved at her.

She texted Jolene to tell her she was on her way and would be in the bakery parking lot in about ten minutes.

Her phone binged when she was about halfway down the long driveway. Selene knew it was Jolene, so she didn't stop to read it. She pulled into the parking lot next to her truck.

Jolene jumped up and down next to her truck, waving wildly. Selene could hear her squealing and rolled her eyes. Her friend was always over-the-top excited for stuff like this. Not that Selene wasn't—she simply didn't go over the top crazy.

Selene grabbed her purse and slammed the door shut. She pressed the key fob to lock the truck and stuck it in her pocket so she could put her gloves on.

Jolene grabbed her hand. "Let's go! We have some time to walk around and check out the lights. They won't light the tree for another hour."

Grinning, Selene said, "Let's start at the bookstore. I can do some quick shopping since Dad and Levi aren't around."

"Okay. My helper is keeping it open until fifteen minutes before the lighting. I think all of the stores that are open are doing the same, so no one misses the tree lighting."

The women headed out to the street. They stopped to browse the window displays in stores they didn't need to go into and went into some others after Selene picked out a couple of novels at the bookstore.

The market had a large nativity scene in its window. The hardware store had a sleigh filled with merchandise from its shelves. Even the gas station had snowmen painted on its windows instead of the usual advertisements for beer and soda.

The bookstore's display was the best, though. Santa and Mrs. Claus were sitting in front of a cozy fire. Santa was going through long lists of naughty and good children while Mrs. Claus was reading a copy of Rowen Burrows' Christmas romance.

Jolene pulled her phone out of her pocket. "If we head back now, we'll have time to drop our stuff off at the trucks and get back to the town square for the lighting."

Selene nodded. "Sounds good. I got more done than I thought I would, and got some ideas for others."

"I did, too," Jolene said, agreeing.

By the time they dropped their bags off at their trucks and made their way back to the square, people crowded it. Selene guided Jolene over to a food truck to get a cup of hot chocolate and some Christmas cookies.

Aris was several people ahead of them in line. Selene's lips tightened at the sight of him.

Jolene obliviously chattered away while Selene stared at Aris's back, her fists clenching in her pocket. She elbowed Selene. "That tall guy in front of the Millers. He's so hot!"

"*That* is Aris," Selene said with an exasperated sigh.

"*That* is Aris? Girl, I never pictured him being an ass. I've seen him around town, but never talked to him."

Selene harrumphed under her breath. "Yeah, I never thought he was an ass, either, until he got a little too controlling for my liking."

The two women moved forward in line as Jolene filled Selene in on other happenings in town. Her words stopped registering when Aris paid for his purchases and stepped out of line. Selene stared at him as he headed in the opposite direction without looking back.

She jumped when she felt a nudge in her side. "What the hell, Jolene?"

"You didn't hear a word I said, did you?" Jolene asked, smirking.

"Uh, yeah, I did. What's with you?"

Jolene laughed. "No, you didn't. You were too busy staring down that hunk."

Selene growled under her breath. "Bullshit."

Jolene laughed harder as they stepped up to place their order.

The food truck worker held her hand up when Selene handed over enough to cover two hot chocolates and a half-dozen sugar cookies. "That tall, gorgeous guy paid for you."

Selene raised her eyebrows, but didn't want to make a scene, so she handed the worker money and said, "I'll pay it forward for the next person in line."

Jolene grabbed both hot chocolates while Selene grabbed the box of cookies. They made their way over to one of the tables the town had set up around the huge Christmas tree. It wasn't an ordinary tree—not one the town put up every year.

This one—a huge Norway Spruce—grew right in the middle of the town square. Every year, the fire department uses its ladder trucks to decorate it. This year, they had outdone themselves with new lights and strings of garland and brightly colored balls and plastic ornaments, including sleighs, Santas, snowmen, skis and more.

There were fake presents under the tree's oversized bottom boughs, and a North Pole scene off to the side.

Selene climbed up on a bench so she could look for Jed and Levi. She finally spotted them on the other side of the square and waved. She stomped her foot on the bench and muttered, "Damn it. Look over here."

Jolene stood on the bench next to her. "Who are you looking for?"

Selene pointed. "Dad and Levi."

Jolene put two fingers in her mouth and whistled loudly. When Levi looked up, they both waved.

Levi elbowed Jed and pointed. They made their way through the crowd toward Jolene and Selene. Just as they were about to reach Selene, Aris walked up to the women.

Jed pulled Levi's arm, and they stepped back several steps.

"Uh, oh, this ought to be good," Levi muttered.

"What is with those two, anyway?" Jed asked.

"She's still pissed at him for butting in her business about those two friends from high school."

Jed stopped and grabbed Levi's arm. "What?!"

Levi laughed. "Yeah. You heard right."

Jed shook his head, and they moved back toward Selene.

"Hey, Selene. Hey, Aris. Jolene," Levi said.

Jed stuck his hand out. "Aris."

He turned to Jolene. "You're the lady from the bookstore."

"That's me. I actually met Selene in Knoxville in her first year there. We've been like this ever since." Jolene crossed her fingers, holding them up.

"I'm Jed, her dad." He motioned to Levi. "Her brother, Levi. We've both seen you around town, but I don't go to the bookstore, and I'm betting Levi doesn't either, since he's in the bakery all day."

"Levi and I have met, but only because I go into the bakery quite often in the afternoon when he's working out front. We never seem to have time for more than a 'hello.' Either he's busy, or I'm in a rush," Jolene said, smiling.

Selene grinned. "Y'all need to slow down a bit."

Jolene lightly punched her shoulder.

"Ow!" Selene said.

"You should talk about slowing down. You're like a speed demon everywhere you go. And if that punch hurt you, I'm Mike-fucking-Tyson."

"Language!" Jed thundered.

Levi and Selene laughed.

Jolene grinned. "Not gonna happen. Surely not."

"I could use some hot chocolate," Aris said. "Anyone else? I'm buying."

They all nodded, and Levi handed a twenty-dollar bill to Aris. "You fly, I'll buy," he said.

"Thanks," Aris said. "I'll get the next round."

"Selene, go with him and help carry all those hot chocolates back," Jed said.

She rolled her eyes at her father. "Dad."

Jed pointed at Aris, who was making his way through the crowd. "And, be nice, while you're at it."

"Fuck," she muttered under her breath as she turned to follow Aris.

Aris felt the hair on the back of his neck rise. It was something that happened when Selene was around or when there was danger nearby. He turned. "What are you doing here?"

"Dad made me come help you carry those."

Aris laughed.

"It's not funny," Selene said.

"Yes, it is. He's trying his best to get us back together."

"It's not working," she muttered.

"Well, at least you don't have a constant scowl on your face when you're around me. Most of the time, but not constantly like it was before."

"I don't want my face to freeze in a scowl. I have to straighten it out sometimes."

They stood until it was their turn. Aris ordered five hot chocolates and a dozen Christmas cookies and paid the lady.

He handed the box of cookies to Selene. "I guess you know I can carry it myself, but I'll humor your dad and let you carry something."

"Kiss-ass," Selene muttered.

After a few minutes of silence, Aris said, "Your brother told me I was too controlling over you all those years ago."

"You were." She didn't mean for the words to sound so sharp.

"I was just looking out for you. Nothing more."

"You cut our friendship off, Aris. I didn't care what you said. What pissed me off is that you threw me away like I was nothing when I didn't listen to you. I didn't have time for that kind of shit in my life then, and I don't now."

By then, they reached the spot where Jed, Levi and Jolene were standing, so Aris didn't respond. He handed out the hot chocolates while Selene took two cookies and passed the box around.

Was I really wrong for refusing to talk to her? I mean, I tried a few times in that last year before she left, but she always blew me off. I always figured she'd come around. Holy fuck, that woman can hold a grudge. It just didn't make sense to bother her at college.

Aris realized that he should have never walked away from her, especially since he had feelings for her. *I wonder what that could have turned into. Though I don't think she felt the same.*

He shrugged to himself. *What a fuckin' mess.*

They listened as the mayor called the crowd to order. When he finally had everyone's attention, he began speaking. Selene and her family and friends sipped the rich hot chocolate and ate the sweet cookies while they listened.

Several children stood around the podium that held the button to turn on the Christmas tree lights.

104

"Good evening, friends and neighbors of Evermist. Tonight, we gather not just to light a tree, but to shine a light on the warmth, kindness, and togetherness that make our town so special. In these winter nights, may this glow remind us of the love we share, the memories we cherish, and the hope we carry into the new year. Now, let's count down together and welcome the magic of Christmas to Evermist!"

"Ten!"

"Nine!"

Heavy, wet flakes of snow began falling. The mayor continued the countdown. When he reached "one," the children reached in, and as one, they pressed the button to light the tree.

CHAPTER 10

Selene stared at the Christmas tree lights as the snow turned heavy and fell faster. The colors reflected off the snowflakes as they fell, creating a beautiful sight. *I wonder if that will show up in pictures.*

She pulled her phone out of her pocket and climbed on a nearby bench so she could get above the crowd. Selene snapped photo after photo, and then switched to video mode. She meant to video the tree lights and the falling snow, but then panned around to catch the large crowd.

As she turned, Jed, Jolene, Levi and Aris came into the viewfinder. "Wave, guys!" she said loud enough to catch their attention. All of them, plus several in the crowd around them, waved at the camera.

Smiling, Selene turned the video off and jumped down from the bench.

Aris had turned toward Selene when she yelled at everyone to wave. Her joyous smile punched him in the gut. It was the first time he'd seen a genuine smile aimed at him. *Well, to be fair, she's smiling at everyone. But at least she doesn't have a scowl on her face when I'm in the crowd.*

She seemed to be more accepting after he tried to apologize.

The crowd broke up as people headed home. Stores that had stayed open during the lighting ceremony were closing earlier than expected, thanks to the heavy snowfall.

Jolene hugged her sides, her pink cheeks glowing with the cold. "I'm going to head home. I don't want to get caught having to walk up my road if this gets too bad."

Her road was as long as the one to Jed's house, and just as steep.

"We should head out, too," Jed said. "Hopefully, we'll make it up. The temperature dropped pretty fast, so whatever melted during the day will freeze over quickly, and that will make it hairy getting up our driveway."

He turned to Aris. "Where did you park?"

"Same place you did." Aris grinned. "My driveway isn't nearly as steep as yours, but it's long. It's better to get home now. By then, there's probably going to be a few inches. I have a new idea I want to work on anyway."

"You're not going out to the blacksmith shop this late, are you?" Levi asked.

As a group, they ambled down the street toward the bakery, where they were all parked.

"No. I have to design it first. It's a delicate design, so it's going to be a difficult one to make."

As they made their way toward the bakery, Aris stepped next to Selene, his heart thumping against his chest. He thought of pulling the gloves off his sweaty hands, but then she'd know he was nervous.

"Selene," he said quietly, reaching out to her, but not touching her.

As she slowed to match his pace, a warmth heated her core. *What the hell is he waiting for? Is he going to talk or not? And what the fuck is with this feeling in the pit of my stomach? I have never felt that for anyone. Ever.*

109

Her heart skipped a beat. *No way in hell. There's no way I feel that for him. Girl, you're wet as hell for him. No. No, no, no.* Her inner conscience laughed. *Oh, yeah.*

Finally, he asked, "Can we be friends again? I didn't mean to push you away. You were so mad at me, so I wanted to give you time. Or, so I thought. That time grew into a huge void because it seemed as though you hated me. I didn't realize not contacting you was pissing you off even more. I made a mess of things. Can you forgive me?"

Selene walked in silence for a few minutes, but Aris didn't press. She turned toward him and sighed. "I can forgive you, but I don't know if I can ever trust you with my feelings again."

Aris took a deep breath. "Okay."

"Okay?" Selene asked.

He stopped and put his hand on her shoulder. "It's not what I want, but it's a start. I understand why you feel that way."

He removed his hand and continued walking. Now that he wasn't worried about her response, the front of his jeans became uncomfortable. "The snow is getting heavier," he said, trying to keep his voice even.

"Yeah. It looks as though we'll be snowed in for a couple of days again. Do you know how long this is supposed to last?" she asked.

110

Aris shook his head, keeping his eyes on the ground. "I didn't even know it was supposed to snow. I think this is another one of those surprise storms. You're going to be stuck here again, aren't you?"

"Looks like it," she said, shrugging.

They reached the parking lot. Jolene had already left, but Jed and Levi were sitting in Levi's truck, waiting for them. When Selene pressed the button on the key fob to open her vehicle, Aris opened the door for her and took her hand to help her in. *That was a mistake, touching her.* He swallowed a moan. "Thanks for giving me another chance. I'll see you later?"

"Sure," Selene said as she reached for the door to close it.

"I got it," Aris said as he pushed her door closed. He waved at her through the window and turned toward his truck.

Selene waited until she saw his light come on and then waved as she pulled out. With Levi following her, they made their way up the treacherous driveway.

As soon as Aris slid into his truck, he turned the key with one hand and adjusted his jeans with the other. "God damn," he moaned. He didn't bother turning the heat on, hoping the cold would cool his ardor.

The quickly freezing slush made the roads dangerous, but Aris drove home as fast as he could. As soon as he pulled up to the house, he ran inside, haphazardly throwing his coat on the rack and kicking his boots off. He went into his office, grabbed a notepad and a pencil, and then put them on the kitchen table.

He set a pot of coffee to brew and put a bowl of leftover beef stew in the microwave. He needed something more than sugar cookies in his stomach. Without waiting for the whole pot to brew, Aris stuck his cup under the dripping coffee until it filled and then slid the pot back onto the burner. He grabbed his dinner and sat at the table.

While shoveling food in his mouth with one hand and drawing with the other, he began planning the piece he had pictured in his head. This one wouldn't be for sale, and he wouldn't make another one like it to sell.

When he finally thought he had the process down, he'd gone through the whole pot of coffee. Sighing, he glanced at the clock.

"Hell, I didn't think it was this late." He rubbed his face and put his supper dishes and coffee cup in the sink. He'd take care of them in the morning.

After watching a Christmas movie with Levi and Jed, Selene showered and then crawled into bed. She had barely stayed awake through the movie. Jed snored in his recliner for most of it. Once she was in bed, her eyes wouldn't close, and worries pounded through her head.

"Fuck my life," she muttered.

She tried reading, but that didn't work—she was too invested in the characters in the book. She put the book down and turned off the light. At first, thoughts of the financial trouble the bakery was in filled her head. It'd only been about a month, but they were doing better.

Aris had done a lot of free work for them, and that helped. *He is trying to be nicer to me. It sounds like he truly regrets pushing me away. But I just don't think I can trust him not to pull some shit like that again.*

He looks at me differently, even when I'm scowling at him or cussing him out. I wonder what his lips on my skin would feel like? Are they as soft as they look? They are definitely kissable. I wonder why he doesn't have a girlfriend or isn't married yet. Plenty of women constantly stare at him. Can't say I blame them. He does look scrumptious.

Stop. You can't think of him like that. He's just a friend. If that. Even back in high school, he was only ever a friend. He didn't act like he wanted anything more, but he also didn't go out with other girls.

Selene sat up in bed, and her breath hitched. "I wonder… is he gay? He certainly doesn't seem to be. I mean, he does look at other women. He just doesn't do anything about it. Maybe he's bi. Maybe that's why he never took anything further when we were teenagers."

She put a robe on and sneaked into the kitchen. She stood staring in the refrigerator, not knowing what she wanted. *Well. That's not a good sign that I'm only eating because I'm bored.* She grabbed a bottle of water and closed the door.

Halfway back to her room, she said, "Fuck it." She crept back to the kitchen and grabbed the last piece of French apple pie.

She grabbed a plastic fork from the tray that was still sitting on the counter, and, sitting with her chin propped up by her hand, she stabbed a bite of the sweet treat, eating it right out of the pie plate. The coolness of the spiced apples slid over her taste buds while thoughts about her time in Evermist raced through her mind. Selene shook her head. *My forced time, though it hasn't been that bad. At least I got to see some of the places I loved as a kid.*

She'd been to the library and hiked the old stream, which brought back memories. Of Aris. A few days ago, she visited the church. She used to go every Sunday, but when she left for college, she stopped going. Studies and her grueling schedule got in the way. And then, she got used to not going, so she didn't.

Maybe I should start going again. But I wouldn't know where to go in Knoxville. I guess I could find a church there.

Her thoughts rambled on about Evermist and the people here. They were a lot friendlier, even those who didn't know her. While the town was small, it did have enough people so that not everyone knew everyone. People came and left. Though more left than moved here. Kids took off as soon as they could—they wanted the big city lights. *Just like I did. But is it really worth it? It's so peaceful here. Not like the city, that's for sure.*

CHAPTER 11

Selene shot upright, her heart thudding as the alarm sliced through the air. She groaned, squinting at the clock. Five in the morning. She hadn't fallen asleep until after three. Sitting on the edge of the bed, she rubbed her eyes and listened for Levi or Jed.

She didn't hear anyone and didn't smell coffee, so she walked over to the window and lifted the blinds with her finger. "Oh, shit." Her shoulders slumped.

A blanket of white covered the ground, and she could see the blinding snow in the light over the barn door. "Damn. We got a lot of snow up here. This is the third storm in…"

Her eyes moved up and to the right as she counted the days. *I came up here a few days after Thanksgiving. Fourteen days left until Christmas Day.* "Holy shit. Three storms in as many weeks. Hell, not even three weeks. That's gotta be some kind of record. Thankfully, the snow mostly melts between storms." Though this last time, snow had still piled in shady areas.

Selene went into the bathroom to brush her teeth and pull her hair up into a ponytail. Levi hadn't taken a shower yet, and he hadn't taken one last night, so she doubted he was even up. She turned the light on in the darkened kitchen and then fumbled through the junk drawer for a flashlight.

Grabbing her jacket from the hook by the door, she slid into it and, without zipping it, opened the back door to see how deep the snow was. She reared back. "What the hell?!"

Another foot of snow covered the ground, and the wet, driving flakes didn't give any indication that it was going to let up anytime soon. Levi must have checked at three when he usually got up to go into the bakery, and then crawled back into his warm bed.

"Well, hell. I'm wide awake now. No sense in trying to go back to sleep." She hung her coat on the rack and put the flashlight where she found it. She rinsed the coffee pot and was putting grounds in the basket when Jed stumbled into the kitchen.

"Why didn't anyone wake me up? Did Levi go to the bakery? What time is it?"

Selene grinned. "Dad, there's over a foot of snow out there. I dare say that Levi's the only smart one and is still sleeping."

Jed sat at the kitchen table and rubbed the sleep out of his eyes. "I guess this is another snow day for the whole town."

"I don't doubt it," Selene said as she waited impatiently for the coffee to brew. She grabbed two mugs from the cabinet and poured them both a cup. "Do you want breakfast?"

"Not yet. Let's wait until Levi gets up. If he's not up in a half hour, we can make it. That'll wake him up," Jed said. "That boy won't ever turn down food, even when he's sleeping."

Selene grinned. "True that."

A few minutes later, Levi sauntered into the kitchen. "It's about time you got your lazy ass up," Jed commented.

"Language," Selene said.

"Both of you can kiss my ass, and I'm not watching my language." Levi poured himself a cup of coffee. "What's for breakfast?" he asked as he turned toward Selene.

"If you're gonna be like that, you can make *fucking* breakfast yourself." She swore to get a reaction out of Jed.

"Watch your mouth," Jed growled, but had a twinkle in his eye.

Selene pulled her bottom lip out. "Fuckity fuckity fuck. See, that doesn't help," she said and let her lip go just as Levi lifted a cup of coffee to his mouth.

Levi covered his face, trying not to laugh. He turned to the sink, a high-pitched sound coming from him as coffee spewed out of his nose. "Oh, my God, Selene," Levi said, laughing as he wiped his face.

Jed's fist pounded the table repeatedly as he bent at the waist, tears streaming from his eyes. He finally got control of himself. "I'm glad I wasn't the one who had a mouthful of coffee when you did that."

Selene's heart swelled to see her father laughing and cutting up. Even before Jeanna's death, he rarely smiled. She couldn't remember the last time he'd really looked and felt happy.

Still trying not to laugh, he said, "I was going to make breakfast, but just for that, you can make it."

"That's fine, because I'm in the mood for a quiche. Since we're obviously not going into work today, I'll make it. After breakfast, Levi can help me make a mess of social media posts."

"That works. I guess I'll veg out in front of the TV, then," Jed said.

Selene had just tested the quiche when they heard a pounding outside. She pulled it out of the oven and set it on top of the stove, and then followed her father and Levi to the front door.

Aris was outside, stomping the snow off his feet and brushing it off his clothes.

"What are you doing here? How did you get here? Are you crazy?" Jed asked, firing off one question after another.

Levi gently shoved him aside. "Let the man in so he can warm up, Dad."

Aris brushed more snow off himself. He pointed to the skis leaning against the front of the house. "I decided I wanted to go for a cross-country ski. Hmm... something smells really good."

Selene stood there with her hands on her hips. "And you think *I'm* reckless?"

He winked at her. "Well, good morning, Selene. Uh, I'm not even going to answer that except to say that this is skiing weather."

Jed snickered, pulling on Aris's arm. "Come on in the kitchen, and I'll get you a cup of coffee. Selene just took a breakfast quiche out of the oven."

While the men settled at the table, Selene grabbed four plates and forks and handed them to Levi. She cut the quiche into eight slices, set it on a trivet in the center of the table, and gave a pie server to Aris.

He took a piece and handed the pie server to Jed, who took two pieces. Levi also took two, and Selene one. As soon as everyone had their breakfast, Jed said, "Well, what are you waiting for? Dig in."

Aris took a bite, chewed, and then pointed at it with his fork, talking around a mouthful of food. "This is really good."

"Thanks," Selene said, nodding.

He picked over the food on his plate to see what she had put in it. He saw green peppers, onions, sausage, bacon and ham. "What kind of cheese did you use? It has a strong flavor that I really like."

"Cabot Seriously Sharp Cheddar. But you can't use it when you first get it. It's sharp, but not sharp enough for our taste. You need to let it sit in the fridge for several months. The longer you leave it in there, the more it ages,

122

and the sharper it gets. My grandmother taught us that trick. This particular block is two years out of date."

Aris raised his eyebrows. "It doesn't go bad?"

"Nope." Selene stood and walked to the fridge. She hadn't used the whole block in the quiche and had cut some up to snack on with crackers and summer sausage. She handed the airtight bowl to Aris.

He lifted the lid and sniffed it.

"I don't see any of that green gunk on it."

"If you leave it sealed in the original vacuum pack it comes in, it doesn't get moldy. If, for some reason, it does, you just cut it off," she explained. "Uh, don't do that with any food—it can make you really sick, but it's okay to do with cheddar. Go ahead and taste it, but be careful. That cheese is so sharp it'll cut your tongue."

Aris took a small piece and put it in his mouth. He chewed slowly, savoring the taste. "Oh, my God. This is to die for."

"The only problem with aging it that long is that it gets really crumbly. The longer it ages, the worse it gets. That's why you see a mess of tiny bits in there."

"Hell, I can work with that." He put the lid on and handed the bowl to her. "If it's going to taste like that, it's worth dealing with crumbles."

Selene put the bowl of cheese in the fridge and sat down to finish her breakfast.

Levi and Selene cleaned up after breakfast while Jed and Aris moved into the living room. Despite joking about wanting to go out skiing, he did have something to discuss, but wasn't sure how to approach it.

Luckily, Levi volunteered to help Selene clean up, leaving him alone with Jed for a few minutes.

"I need to ask you about something, Jed, but it's private," Aris said.

Jed nodded and motioned down the hall to his home office. He followed Aris in and closed the door. "What's up?" he asked, leaning against the door.

"Do you mind if I sit?" Aris asked.

"Go ahead. I'll stand right here. Since those two were knee-high to a grasshopper, they'd sneak down the hall and listen at the door. I've learned to keep an ear close to it."

Aris laughed. "That doesn't surprise me." He sat in Jed's comfortable office chair and leaned back. "You know that I'm on the town board, right?"

"Yep," Jed said, nodding.

"I know Jeanna always organized the Christmas lighting ceremony. She had gotten it started this year, but one of the other board members had to finish it. No one on the board is very good at organizing stuff."

Jed raised his eyebrow. "If you think I'm going to be any better, you've got another thing coming."

Aris laughed. "Not you. Selene."

"You're going to get me into all kinds of trouble with her. I'm already in enough trouble of my own."

"I just need to know how long she plans on staying."

"Oh, hell, Aris. I don't know." Jed shrugged. "I don't even think she knows. She's been pretty antsy about getting back, even though she can do her job from here. How's she going to do that when she goes back?"

"We'd have to pick someone else. It's not just the Christmas thing—"

"I know," Jed interrupted. "There's supposedly a lot of 'meeting people' going on." His eyebrows lifted, and the corner of his mouth formed a grimace.

Aris raised his eyebrows at Jed's sudden harsh tone. "Uh, am I missing something here?"

CHAPTER 12

Levi pulled the shade aside. The windowpane was a blur of white. A low groan escaped him. "Damn. The snow is getting heavier."

Jed and Aris clomped down the hall in their boots. "Really?" Aris asked as he moved over to the window. "I guess I'd better get back before it gets too deep for the skis."

"That's quite a way to go on skis. Why don't you stay here?" Jed asked.

Aris glanced into the kitchen, where Selene was putting the dried dishes into the cabinets. "I don't think that's a good idea."

"She's going to have to get over herself," Jed said.

He squirmed under Jed's stare. It wasn't that. He didn't know if he could spend the night in the same house as Selene without sneaking into her room, and that wouldn't end well for him. He could feel himself getting hard just thinking about it.

"It's-it's, uh, not that." Aris stuttered, glancing into the kitchen again. He'd managed to keep himself under control all morning, despite the minor discomfort at the front of his jeans. *At least it's not so damned hard that it's noticeable.* Or, so he thought.

Levi cut his eyes to Jed and pursed his lips, trying to hide the smirk. Jed rolled his eyes and sighed. He had a pretty good idea what Aris was talking about, thanks to the look Levi gave him behind Aris's back.

"Hey, do you know how to water ski?" Levi asked.

"Yeah, but I don't think we'll be doing any of that any time soon," Aris said, smirking.

"Nope. But I can tow you with the four-wheeler if the snow isn't too deep yet. That will be fun, and it will get you home before it gets too deep out there."

Aris shifted his weight to one leg while he thought about that. "That might work. It'd surely be fun!" He shivered. "Cold but fun," he said, putting his coat on.

Levi put his boots on and grabbed his coat. "Hold on, and I'll check the depth."

He stepped off the porch and kicked at the snow with his foot. Back on the porch, he stomped the snow off his boots before going back inside. "It'll work. Just. The snow is about eight inches deep. I'll make it there, but I don't know if I'll make it back because of the hill. But I can get you home if I can stay with you."

"You can do that. Pack yourself an overnight bag. You can sleep in the spare room."

Levi grinned as he went down the hall to pack a bag. When he came out, Aris was dressed and ready to go. Levi slipped back into his coat and made sure his thick knit mittens were in his pockets. He turned to Jed. "I highly doubt the town will open tomorrow. I don't know when I'll be back. It depends on when this snow stops and how much we get. I'll call and let you know if I'm going to open the bakery the day after tomorrow. I can go right from Aris's to there."

Jed nodded. "Sounds like a plan. You boys be careful."

129

"We will," Aris and Levi said at the same time.

"Little Girl, come in here and talk to me," Jed said.

Selene dried her hands and sauntered into the living room. "I guess we'll have the house to ourselves for at least today and tonight."

"Humph. By the looks of it, it's going to be a couple of days. We haven't had this much snow in I can't remember when." Jed pushed the recliner back so his feet were up.

Selene sat on the sofa and curled her feet under her. "So, what do you want to know?"

"Do you know that Aris is in love with you?"

"Oh, we're gonna go *there*?"

"I'm serious, Selene."

"Dad, he's not in love with me. He's an arrogant ass."

Jed didn't even yell at her for her language. "No, he's not. He cares too much for you. Levi is towing him home on those damned skis because he can't keep his hands off you."

"He said that?"

Jed took a sip of his coffee. "Nope. But he did say he couldn't sleep in the same house as you."

Selene sighed. "Dad, that's because we can barely stand each other."

"Oh, no, Little Girl. When a man says that, he's afraid he can't control himself. It used to be like that with—"

He knew she was waiting for him to continue, but Jed couldn't. Wrapping his arms around himself, he stared at the hot coals in the fireplace. Pieces of flame licked up, looking for something else to burn. Much like his soul burned whenever he thought of Jeanna cheating on him.

"With mom?" Selene asked after several long minutes.

"Hunh?" Jed forced his eyes away from the coals. "Uh, yeah. But that was before."

"When did you first suspect something, Dad?" she asked quietly. He'd never spoken of it with her, and she didn't know how much he'd told Levi.

"It's been a while, but I was in denial. I didn't want to believe it." He shook his head. "I was going to confront her the night of the accident. I still hadn't had concrete proof, but…"

"I'd ask why she did that, but there's never a good reason," Selene said quietly.

"We were happy, if that's what you're getting at. At least, I thought we were. She didn't give any indication that she wasn't."

"It's not your fault, Dad. If she wasn't happy, she could have—should have—said something. Do you even know who it was?"

Jed shook his head. "I have no clue. It had to be someone from down in LaFollette or even Knoxville. My friends would have said something if the guy were from here and if they knew about it. You know there's no way this town can keep a secret like that."

"That's the God's honest truth," Selene said.

"About Aris."

"He blew it, Dad. He blew our friendship, and then he tells you and Levi that he had feelings for me?"

"He didn't tell me that, Little Girl. I can tell by his actions. Like, not staying over here. Following you around town. Helping more in the bakery to be around you."

"That's bullshit, Dad. He could have called me. I never changed my number. And, even if I had changed it, he could have gotten it from you or Levi or Mom."

Jed sighed. "It is what it is, Selene. Take my word for it."

"He needs to get his head on straight." She crossed her arms and stared at the floor.

Jed shook his head. He was more than familiar with her body language.

Selene stuck a knife into the middle of the cake she was baking. "Just a few more minutes." She closed the oven door and noted the time. As she reached for the coffee pot, her phone binged. It was a text from Mrs. Miller.

MRS. MILLER: Hey, Selene. I got your number from Levi. I need to ask you about something before you leave. Can I meet you in the bakery when you open?

SELENE: I don't think we're opening tomorrow. We're hoping to open the day after, so yes. I'll be there all day.

MRS. MILLER: Great. I'll catch up with you then. Do you know how long you are staying?

"That's weird," Selene muttered.

"Dad, why would Mrs. Miller want to know how long I'm staying?"

Jed shrugged. "Got me."

Selene stared at her phone until the screen went dark. *I wasn't even supposed to be here this long. But now, I don't know about going back. I really should, though. But I really miss Evermist. And Christmas is not far off. Dad acts like I'll be here for Christmas. He's been making noises about cooking Christmas dinner.*

She sighed and shrugged to herself. *Might as well.*

SELENE: Probably until a day or two after Christmas.

MRS. MILLER: 👍

"What does she want?" Jed asked.

"She didn't say. Just that she'll come to the bakery when we open. I guess she figures the whole town will stay closed tomorrow."

Jed stood and walked over to the window. "Snow's falling even heavier. At least Levi made a good call deciding to stay at Aris's instead of trying to make it back." He turned from the window. "That smells good. What are you making for dinner?"

"Something that'll stick to our bones and keep us warm. Beef stew."

"I can't wait until it's done." Jed sat in his recliner and picked up the remote for the TV. "Wanna watch something in particular?"

"No, I'm going to work on the marketing for a client and do some for the shop," Selene said as she stood to go back into the kitchen. She lifted the lid on the slow-cooker, stirred the beef broth, and then warmed up her cup of coffee before she sat at her computer.

CHAPTER 13

Jed glanced up from cleaning the front counter when he heard the bell ring. "Hello, Mrs. Miller," he said, smiling. "Are you here to visit Selene?

"Yes. How are you doing, Jed?"

"I'm doing fine. Do you want a coffee or tea?"

"A large black coffee would be great," she said, digging in her purse.

Jed handed her two coffees and waved her money away. "On the house, and there's one for Selene, too. They're both black."

"Well, thank you, Jed."

"It's nothing. You did a lot for my family when Jeanna died."

"You know I don't mind helping any of you folks. We've known each other for years."

Jed smiled at her and said, "Do you know where to go, or do you want me to show you back?"

"I've been in the office before. I'll find my way." She briefly rested her hand on his shoulder before she stepped through the double doors.

"Hey, Mrs. Miller!" Levi called from the far side of the kitchen, where he was scraping the sides of the large commercial mixing bowl. "Selene's in the office," he added, pointing down the hall.

"Thanks, Levi!"

Mrs. Miller stuck her head in the open office door and held up the coffee.

"Hi, Mrs. Miller. Is that for me?"

"It sure is. Jed sent it back. Do you have a few minutes?"

"I sure do. Come on in and have a seat. Let me save this real quick." Selene hit the keys on the computer to save her work. "What can I do for you?"

"Well, I don't know if you can help me, but all I can do is ask."

Selene nodded. She was familiar with the way Mrs. Miller would build up to her final question.

"I know you said you don't know when you're leaving, but I'm in a bit of a pickle. Your mother used to be the one who arranged the Christmas tree lighting and got the vendors. I don't have anyone else whom I can trust to get it done as well as she could. I was wondering…"

Selene shook her head. "I'm not normally here this often. I'm only here now because I got snowed in. I'm not sure I could do that from Knoxville."

"Well, you let me know. I can help with the stuff that has to be done locally. You can do a lot from your computer. I'll send you what your mother had done, and you can look it over. If it's something you think you can help with, let me know, and we'll work the local stuff out."

"Believe it or not, I'm not that great at organizing things. I'm better when someone tells me to do something."

Selene grinned. "Now, I know better than that. You organize all the church functions and do a great job."

"That's only because I've been doing it for years and years. You should have seen the first couple of years when I started doing that. Oh, my."

"Tell you what. You go ahead and send that stuff to me, and I'll have a look. I'm not promising anything, but the least I can do is to look and see if it's something I can do."

Mrs. Miller smiled. "I would really appreciate it."

Selene rifled through the desk drawer and came up with a small notepad. She scribbled something on it, ripped the page off, and handed it to Mrs. Miller. "My email and cell phone. It's better if you text first in case I'm with a client."

"Thank you," Mrs. Miller said, looking at Selene's information. She tucked it into her pocket. "Now, we haven't had time to chat with all that's been going on and the snow keeping us all home."

Selene leaned back in her chair and smiled. "I'd be glad for the distraction. I'm working on marketing for a client, and I need a break."

She sighed as she heard the bell ding and some loud yelling. Selene narrowed her eyes. "What the hell is going on?"

She stood and walked through the bakery kitchen and out front. Several people and kids were in the front parking lot where the plow had piled snow. They were throwing snowballs at each other.

Turning to go back to the office, a bright orange hat caught her attention. She stepped out to yell at Levi to stop fooling around and get back to work. Before she could open her mouth, a snowball hit her in the chest.

Her eyes widened as she swung her head around, searching for the culprit. "Oh, hell no."

When she looked to see which person had a guilty look on his face, she saw Aris standing at the edge of the group. He was smirking. She shook her head and went back inside.

The smirk fell off Aris's face. Levi bumped shoulders with him. "I guess that didn't work. You know her pretty well. It's going to take her a while to come around."

Aris shrugged and bent down to scoop up a handful of snow for his next target. Just as he stood, someone hit him in the back of the head with a snowball. He hurriedly turned, scooped up a handful of snow and packed it into a ball. He raised his arm to throw it, but before he could, another snowball hit his shoulder from the opposite direction.

He turned and saw Selene forming another snowball.

Levi stood there laughing. "You deserved that one."

Suddenly, Levi wasn't laughing as Selene lobbed two snowballs in quick succession. One at Levi and the other at Aris. She joined the younger kids, who were throwing at the older kids and the two men.

"Everyone gets Levi and Aris at the same time!" she yelled. The kids and adults on that side of the snowball fight were only too happy to oblige. They all yelled and scooped up handfuls of snow, packing it as tight as they could to form the missiles.

Aris ducked and tried to avoid the barrage of snowballs coming his way, and while some missed, more than a few hit him. He ran behind the group Selene was with to come from the back and take her group by surprise.

Selene pedaled backward to avoid a snowball Levi threw at her and tripped over Aris's feet. She felt strong arms wrap around her, keeping her from falling in the snow. Even through her coat, she felt the charge of electricity zip through her.

What the fuck?

She turned her head to see who caught her. "Aris."

He grinned at her as she struggled to get away from him. "I don't bite, Sugar," he whisper-growled in her ear. He let her go, and she stood, staring at him. After a few long seconds, she shot him a half smile and grabbed a big handful of snow.

Aris held up his hands. "I didn't do it. I could have let you fall."

Selene smirked and lifted her arm. At the last second, she turned and lobbed the snowball at her brother, hitting him in the ear. She heard Aris laughing behind her. "Oh, you're not safe yet."

By then, many of the kids were shivering, so the snowball fight broke up as everyone went home, to their cars or inside the bakery. Selene headed toward the bakery, and Levi and Aris followed.

When they walked in, Jed had a line of cold kids and parents in front of him, so Levi went into the kitchen to make sure they had enough hot soup for their soup and sandwich special.

Aris followed him, and Selene went to help her father, but before she stepped behind the counter, she dropped the snowball she'd hidden in her pocket down the back of Aris's shirt. "Payback's a bitch," she whispered.

He had no choice but to quietly step into the kitchen to try to get the cold snow out of his shirt. Selene tilted her head and smirked. Her eyebrows lifted and lowered briefly.

"Told ya," she mouthed at him.

"I can get this if you want to warm up first," Jed said.

"I'm good. I'll grab a bowl of soup when we get this line down."

Jed nodded. "That works."

When the line was half gone, Selene pushed the swinging doors open. "More soup, Levi!"

"Coming right up!" he yelled from across the kitchen.

He set the large tureen of their homemade vegetable beef soup on a cart and waved his hand at Aris. "If you can do the honors, I'll get more base out of the fridge and get it heating."

"Gladly." Aris pushed the cart through the doors. He set the tureen on the counter and then slid past Selene to grab the nearly empty one out of the soup warmer. "Behind you," he warned her, as Jed had taught him.

Selene acknowledged that she heard him. Before she turned to place the lunch order on the counter and call out the customer's name, she stepped sideways so she wouldn't run into Aris.

He manhandled the full tureen and then slid it into the soup warmer without pinching his fingers between the large container and the countertop. As he passed behind Selene again, he touched her arm and warned, "Behind you again."

The touch was fleeting, but her hands shook as she placed the customer's drinks on his tray. "Let us know if you need anything else, and have a good day," she said with a smile, even though she could still feel the tingling where Aris had touched her. And the heat between her legs.

Holy shit. Why does his touch do that to me? I can barely stand him. She glanced through the windows in the swinging doors. Aris was helping Levi cut vegetables for a new batch of base for the next day's soup. She shivered and hoped no one noticed.

CHAPTER 14

Selene had taken a shower and gone to her room earlier than usual, claiming she was tired. At least she thought she was, but her mind wouldn't shut off. Aris, organizing the Christmas lighting ceremony, the bakery's financial position—those were at the top of her mind.

The bakery was already doing better, which was a good thing. It would most likely recover. She and Levi had worked out a marketing strategy, and he quickly picked up on creating attention-grabbing social media posts. They had even picked up a couple of wholesale accounts.

As for organizing the Christmas festival for next year, Selene wasn't sure about that. She'd reviewed Mrs. Miller's and her mother's notes, and she could do a lot of it from Knoxville, but that was her mother's pet project.

I don't know whether to hate her, feel glad she died, or continue loving her and wishing she hadn't died. I feel bad for the guy who hit her. It wasn't his fault. That black ice is hard to see, and who would expect it at that time of year? But can I feel bad for her?

Selene shook her head. "Why did she have to do that? What did she think she was missing from her marriage? I know they worked long hours, but damn. The bakery was her idea. It was her "baby." Not Dad's. And he gets to suffer through all of the stress of running it, just because she had to fuck around."

She sat up and rubbed her face. *I'm never going to get to sleep if I don't shut my mind off. Maybe if I read a little... That romance should take my mind off stuff.*

Her e-reader was in her suitcase. She hadn't unpacked it since she tried to go home the other day. Once she had her book in her hand, Selene fluffed the pillows and stacked them against the headboard so she could lean on them.

Jed and Levi were watching a movie. During a commercial, Jed paused the TV to make a pot of coffee, and Levi followed him into the kitchen. "Did Aris tell you anything about that special project he was working on?"

"Nope. Didn't even know he was working on a special project. Why?" Jed asked as he poured two cups.

"It's some big secret with him, then. He wouldn't even go out in the workshop to work on it when I was there, since he knows I want to learn more about 'smithing."

"Well, I guess that will have to be his secret. Ain't much you can do about it if he's not gonna tell you."

Levi shrugged. "True." He stood and checked the hall to make sure his sister wasn't eavesdropping. He sat in his chair and leaned forward, speaking quietly. "Do you think Selene might stay this time?"

"She hasn't given any indication of it. Why?"

"She's never stayed this long."

"It's not like she could help it, Levi. The snow trapped her up here. Same as us. I wouldn't be surprised if she hauls ass in the next day or two. You know she hates driving in this slop, even though she's a better driver than most I know." Jed leaned back in his chair.

Hmmph. I wonder what made Levi come to that conclusion. Sometimes that boy sees more than he should be seeing.

Levi shrugged. "I don't know. Maybe when she had a chance to get out of here, and she didn't. I mean, it's only a couple of hours to get to her place."

Jed shrugged noncommittally. "It would be nice, but I doubt she'll stay."

Selene read for an hour, but still couldn't fall asleep. *Not that reading had ever helped. I must have read the same paragraph ten times.*

Since she wasn't getting anywhere with that, she turned out the light. *Maybe I'll eventually fall asleep.*

Instead, thoughts of Aris infiltrated her mind. *What the hell does he mean about these 'feelings' in high school? I don't think I can believe him. Why didn't he act on them if he had so-called feelings? Why didn't he call me for all these years?*

And what the fuck was that when he touched me? Twice today. I wonder if he felt it? Why the hell would I feel that now? I've managed to avoid him all these years. He's putting himself in my path this time. Not just once or twice, so it's not a coincidence.

I wonder what it would be like to kiss him. I have always wondered that. Not that I'd ever admit that to him.

Think, Selene. He never went out with anyone in high school. You hung out together. You went to school dances together. As friends. You thought he might be gay because

150

he never paid attention to any other girl, but wouldn't go after you.

"Aw, fuck. I have no idea what to do with him. On top of it, he still pisses me off." *Not really.*

Selene mumbled as she rolled over to turn off that god-awful noise. She missed the alarm clock the first time, but finally silenced it. She sat on the edge of the bed and rubbed her face. "Hell, I have one nasty headache. I didn't even do anything to deserve it, either."

She stumbled to the bathroom to wash her face with cool water and went back to her room. When she couldn't find the bottle of aspirin in her purse, her frustration boiled over. Dumping the contents of her purse on the bed, she pawed through them until she found what she was looking for. Selene swallowed two aspirin dry and made a face at the bitter taste.

When she stumbled into the kitchen, Jed grinned and handed her a cup of coffee. "You look like shit. You got a bottle hidden in your room or something?" he said jokingly. He knew Selene didn't drink.

"Damned mind wouldn't turn off. Last time I looked at the clock, it was four in the morning. And that alarm was blasting in my ear at five-thirty."

"Want some breakfast?"

Selene shrugged. "Maybe in a bit."

"I'll make French toast."

"Did I hear something about French toast?" Levi asked as he stepped into the kitchen.

"Oh, hell," Jed muttered as he pulled the large griddle pan out of the cabinet. He lined a pound of hickory-smoked, thick-sliced bacon on it. While that was cooking, he mixed six eggs with a bit of sugar, cinnamon and nutmeg.

By then, the bacon was ready to flip. "Levi, grab me a plate and line it with paper towels."

"Thanks," Jed said as he put the plate next to the griddle. He took the bacon off and laid it on the plate. The paper towels would soak up some of the grease.

He tested the temperature of the griddle by dropping a small bit of the egg mixture on it. "Perfect." Grabbing a loaf of bread, he dipped the slices in the eggs and spices and put them right in the bacon grease on the griddle.

Selene stood to get another cup of coffee. "I'm feeling better, Dad. I think I will have some of that French toast."

"Figured you would, Little Girl. I got plenty here." Jed flipped the first eight pieces and added eight more to the griddle. "Y'all come get this. I'll get mine from the second batch."

They ate in silence and then headed to the bakery in Jed's truck. It was an easy day, since Levi had prepped all of his dough the night before. They were trying a new schedule for a week. Instead of going in at three in the morning, Levi would stay later to prep the various doughs he needed and let them go through the first proofing in the afternoon. At six in the morning, he'd pull what he needed from the walk-in and let it proof from six to seven, and then start the day's baking.

They would open at eight instead of six, because they were so slow in the early morning hours. If enough people wanted them to open earlier, they'd go back to the old schedule. Jed figured it would work, even for the wholesalers, because most people didn't get to work and stores didn't open until nine. It wasn't like when he was younger—people's work hours changed. They saw more office workers and bankers than construction workers.

Many people worked in LaFollette unless they owned a business in Evermist. The town was changing. Jed couldn't make up his mind whether it was for better or worse. Many people, like Selene, left for the so-called big city lights. Not that Knoxville was very big compared to places such as Las Vegas or New York, but it was big to them.

Once they prepped for opening, they had a few minutes, so Selene grabbed a cup of coffee and leaned against the counter. "So, you guys had been baking bread for some of the less fortunate. Do you know how much you were spending on that?"

By the time Levi went over the numbers with them, it was time to open. "I'll think about doing that again. We'll talk about it tonight," she said as she walked across the retail space to open the front door.

Selene walked behind the counter as a few regulars stepped inside. Levi had just finished stocking the display case with fresh-baked goods. He also had some day-old items to put in that section.

She finished waiting on them and was wiping down the counter when the bell over the door dinged.

"Hey, Selene."

"Aris. How are you?" she asked stiffly.

He smiled at her. "I came to see what day-old stuff you have. I'm taking it to a few people who need help with food."

Selene pointed. "We don't have much today. We were quite busy yesterday, but you're more than welcome to it."

"Oh, no. I'll pay for it. I know you guys are still trying to catch up. If I don't get stuff from you, I get it from other places, and more often than not, pay retail, so I don't mind."

She shrugged, as she wasn't going to argue with him about it. *If he wants to pay, then he can pay. It will undoubtedly help the finances.*

On his way out, he said, "I'll stop by later. I need to get some for my freezer. I'm almost out."

"Okay. See you later," she mumbled as she wiped crumbs from the counter.

Levi came out front. "Was that Aris?"

"Yeah, why?"

"No reason. I thought I heard his voice. I didn't hear you taking his head off for once."

"Bite me, Levi. Get in the back where you belong." Selene lifted her middle finger at him.

Levi laughed as he went through the doors.

CHAPTER 15

After the lunch rush, Selene went to the office to grab some much-needed downtime. The pounding in her head had stopped, but the dull ache wouldn't let up. *At least it's not so bad that it stopped me from working.*

She reached into her purse, pulled out a bottle of aspirin and swallowed two with a gulp of coffee. Knowing that staring at the computer would only make the headache worse, she booted it up anyway. Selene wanted to compare the numbers for the last two months with those from the past few weeks. It would determine whether she allowed Levi to start baking bread for the less fortunate now or made him wait.

Aris sauntered into the office and made himself comfortable. He had a cup of coffee and two blueberry muffins in his hands. "Good morning."

Without looking up, Selene mumbled, "Good morning."

"I brought you a blueberry muffin."

She finally lifted her eyes from the screen and rubbed them. "Thanks, but I ate a pretty big breakfast this morning. You can eat it."

"Uh…"

"Spit it out, Aris. I'm trying to figure this out."

"You asked for it. You look like shit. You didn't sleep last night?"

"No. My mind wouldn't turn off." Selene leaned forward to continue comparing the financials.

Aris set his coffee and muffins on the corner of her desk. *Well, here goes nothing. She'll either like it or kick me out forever.*

He walked around to stand behind her. Placing his hands on her shoulders, he used his strong fingers to massage the kinks out of her shoulders and the base of her neck.

Selene jumped when he touched her, but his hands felt so good on her. She moaned, "Jesus, Aris, that feels good."

"You need a better office chair. These short-backed chairs aren't good for your back. Does it adjust any lower?"

"Yeah, but it's not comfortable."

"This is bad for your posture. Lower it so you are sitting up straight instead of being hunched over to see the screen."

She knew he wouldn't leave her alone until she did, so, to humor him, Selene adjusted the chair.

"It'll take you a few hours to get used to typing in that position, but it will be better for your back." He continued massaging the tight muscles on her shoulders.

"This might hurt a bit." Using his thumbs, he worked his way down her neck and upper spine, pressing firmly.

Selene continued working until he reached a particularly sore spot she didn't know was there—until he pressed it with his thumbs. She sat straight up and groaned when the pain hit. A few seconds later, she felt her shoulders and back loosen.

"I think you found it. That hurt, but now it feels so good. Thanks, Aris."

"You're welcome. I gotta get going. I, uh, have some orders to work on."

Selene glanced up briefly. "Okay. Thanks again."

Before he could move, her eyes were back on her spreadsheets.

Probably a good thing, or she wouldn't be able to miss this. Aris resisted the urge to adjust the front of his jeans and sneaked out the back door.

Levi already suspects. Not that there's anything wrong with it, but if she's not interested, there's no sense in embarrassing myself with him and Jed. Being turned down is bad enough when I'm the only one who knows about it, never mind if they know about it.

When Aris got home, he went inside, stripped and took a cold shower. After he dressed, he went out to the workshop. He didn't have any orders to work on, but he hadn't totally lied to Selene. He was working on his special project.

He'd managed to get the metal thin enough and pounded it into the shape he wanted. Now, he had to make it even so that it looked nice. He ran his fingers over the piece, feeling for the areas he needed to work on. One little mistake and he'd have to start all over.

Once the piece was complete, it would be strong enough to withstand handling. Aris fired up the forge and made sure the bucket of oil for cooling was nearby. He heated the piece and worked on hammering the edges and flaws out of the piece. He'd just tempered it in the oil when his phone binged.

Carefully setting the piece on the counter, he pulled his phone from his pocket.

LEVI: Where'd you go?

ARIS: Had an order to work on. I'll be back in a bit.

LEVI: K. I'm working on a new recipe you might like.

Aries walked over to the counter and picked up the piece. *That's enough for today.*

ARIS: Be there in 20 or 30.

LEVI: 👍

"Levi, you got a minute?" Selene asked.

"Sure. This dough needs another forty-five minutes to proof." He followed her to the office and sat in the chair, putting his feet up on the corner of the desk.

Selene rolled her eyes, but didn't bother wasting her breath to tell him to put his feet on the floor where they belonged. She sat in her chair and pulled up a spreadsheet she'd been working on.

"Okay, we can afford to make ten loaves of bread per month for those who don't have much."

Levi put his feet on the floor and leaned forward.

Selene held her hand up. "Not yet. There are stipulations. You have to make the bread by the original recipe, using powdered milk and eggs. You will need to deliver this bread, and you can't use the business van."

He nodded. "I was making about thirty loaves per month."

"We're not there yet. We really shouldn't be doing this much yet, but many of those families are friends. You can rotate. Ten families this month, ten next month, and so on. Aris has been buying the day-old stuff and delivering it."

"Did I hear my name?" his deep voice came from the hallway.

"Yes. You might as well come in here," Selene said.

Aris stepped through the doorway. Selene sat in her chair, chewing on the end of a pencil.

Damn. I wish I were that pencil. His cock pressed against the front of his jeans, so he hurriedly sat in the other chair.

Selene raised one eyebrow at him as he squirmed in the chair.

God damn. That made it worse.

Aris leaned back and said, "What's going on?"

"You two need to get together and decide which of the families are getting free bread and the day-old stuff you've been buying for them." Selene continued, "Levi can make ten loaves per month. Whether he makes them all at once, a couple per week or whatever he wants to do, it's a good idea if you both don't give to the same families. Until we can afford to make more, that's just the way it will have to be."

"Okay, that sounds good." *I need to get the hell out of here.* Aris stood and turned toward the door. "Let's go figure this out and let Selene get back to what she was doing," he said as he tapped Levi's shoulder.

Levi narrowed his eyes at Aris, then at Selene, before turning back to Aris. "Uh, okay." He leaned over and grabbed a notepad and a pen from the desk. "I need to check that dough anyway."

He handed the pad and pen to Aris. "You take notes while I check this dough."

Aris followed Levi into the kitchen and leaned against the counter, hoping the cool metal would cool his ardor and that no one had noticed the lump in the front of his jeans.

163

Levi pulled the covers off the proofing dough to check it. "Needs a bit more time." He leaned against the counter where Aris was writing. They went back and forth with each other until they had a schedule that would work for all of the families, and Selene would let Levi make extra bread.

Aris agreed to deliver the baked goods and bread if Levi could have everything ready by seven-thirty.

CHAPTER 16

Selene walked into the bakery kitchen to find Levi scowling at the ovens. She watched him try to light them again.

"Fuck my life," he muttered.

"What's going on, Levi?"

He jumped. "You scared the shit out of me, Selene!"

She shrugged. "And? What's going on that's got you cussing your life?"

"The damned ovens won't light. And, before you ask, yes, I checked the gas. We have three-quarters of a tank. I also put the tester on the tank, and it's flowing."

"Are the pilots lit?" she asked.

"Yeah. It doesn't make any sense. Can you call Aris? He knows how to fix gas ovens."

"I'll go out front and get set up. You call him. Dad can help you when he gets here. He said he'd be another fifteen or twenty minutes."

No way was she calling Aris. It was bad enough that she let him massage her back. That never should have happened, either, but it felt so good. She rolled her shoulders at the memory of his strong hands.

Selene walked out front and flipped the coffee pots on, and then added the grounds. She pulled the day-old product left over from the fridge and filled that part of the case. After checking the floor to ensure they didn't miss anything from cleaning the night before, she put the chairs down.

As she walked into the kitchen, Aris emerged from the hall.

"Hey, Selene."

166

"Aris," she said, nodding. "Levi's looking for you. There's coffee out front. Might as well have some. If you can't fix the ovens, we won't be opening today. If it's not one thing, it's another. I'll be in the office."

He nodded. "It'll all work out. The ovens were fine yesterday, so it shouldn't be anything major."

"Anything is major now, since we're just getting back on our feet."

"True," Aris said as she turned away.

He stood stock still, his eyes on her ass as she made her way down the hall. *Damn. I bet her skin is soft. I'd love to take her from behind, right up against the wall. Fuck.*

"Hey, Levi!"

"Yeah?"

"I forgot something. I'll be right back." Aris rushed out to his truck. He moaned as he slid in and started it. Just after making the turn to his house, he pulled to the side of the driveway where it would be difficult for anyone to see him.

Moaning Selene's name, he unfastened his jeans. He grabbed a handful of napkins from the center console as he wrapped his hand around his cock. His hips jerked as his hand moved up and down. On the third stroke, he held the napkins against the head of his cock and tilted his head back. His hips jerked against his hand once more, and he yelled as the napkins caught the ropes of hot cum that spewed from him.

Aris stroked himself a couple more times as he moaned and twisted his head back and forth. *Fuck. I can't move. I hope no one comes down here for the next few minutes.*

After his breathing calmed, he cleaned himself up and turned the truck around.

When he walked in the back door to the bakery, Selene was in the office. He waved and said a quick 'Hey, Selene,' as he hurried past the door. It wouldn't do to have to run out of there again. He needed to keep his mind on what he was doing and stop looking at her. At least while he was helping Levi.

He set his toolbox on the counter across from the ovens. "What have you checked so far?"

Levi told him what he'd done, and then, "It can only be electrical. I pulled the panel, but I have no idea what I'm looking at. The breakers are still on."

After an hour of the two men checking electrical connections and trying to trace the problem, Selene came out to get a cup of coffee. Jed walked in with a tray of pastries. "Where'd you get those, Dad?"

"I took some dough up to the house to bake it. We're just about out of the day-old stuff. I figured we could keep some of the people happy and still make a little money. I was able to bake three batches."

"Good thinking. I'm going to check on the guys."

Jed nodded as he added the pastries to the case.

Selene walked into the back and leaned against the counter. "Any luck?" she asked.

"Not yet," Levi said. "Aris figured out the control panel isn't getting electricity to it."

"I know you probably know, but did you check the breakers? That oven also has a thermal fuse that cuts power to the control panel and the heating elements."

"Checked both. How did you know about the thermal fuse? Not many people realize some ovens have those," Aris said.

"It's blown before, but it's been a while. At least before Levi came on full-time."

Aris grunted.

After a few minutes, he pulled his head away from the mess of wires and turned his headlamp off. "I need to stretch for a minute. Standing half bent over is killing my back."

He lifted his arms in the air, interlacing his fingers, and then tilted from side to side at his waist as he stretched his muscles.

And such fine muscles, too. Shit. Selene averted her eyes, hoping he hadn't noticed that she was staring at him.

Aris grinned.

Damn. No such luck.

"So, are you planning next year's Christmas celebration?" Aris asked.

"I don't know yet. It might be too much of a pain in the ass from out of town."

"Why not come back at Christmas?"

"I'd rather come up during the warmer months, and I can only get so much time off from work." It was a little white lie, but he wouldn't know that. She could work from home whenever she wanted.

Aris knew not to push it, so he put his headlamp on and adjusted it. He leaned in to check more of the wires.

"Whatever happened with that guy we used to call Einstein? Wasn't he supposed to marry Mindy?" Selene asked.

"You mean Justin?" Aris asked.

"Yeah. Levi said he didn't keep up with them. I was wondering if you had."

"Not really, but I heard they did get married and moved to Colorado. Her parents died before they left. I didn't know him that well, so I have no idea if his parents

170

are still around. Hell, I can't even remember his last name."

For the next half-hour, they discussed some of their old classmates.

"Whatever happened to—"

"Found it!" Aris exclaimed, interrupting Levi.

Selene stepped closer and went up on her toes to see over Aris's shoulder. She stepped back quickly when Aris turned so he wouldn't run into her.

He grinned, holding up a burnt wire he'd cut out of the circuit. "I think I have some of this wire over in my toolbox, if you can grab it for me, Selene."

She reached over and lifted the top tray out of his toolbox. "Well, I guess we got lucky. It's the only wire you have in there, and it's not a very long piece."

"It'll do us. Might even have a few inches to play with." Aris grabbed a handful of butt connectors from his pocket. He picked two out of the multi-colored pieces and put the rest back in his pocket.

Holding them up, he said, "Don't want to drop this. I only have two in this size, and I'll need both of them. Lucky day today."

Just then, Jed stepped into the kitchen with them. "No worries. I have some of those in my truck."

Aris carefully spliced the new wire into the wires inside the oven where he'd cut them. "Okay, let's give it a try. I didn't see any reason why this wire burned, so it may have been rubbing against something whenever the fan came on. Just keep an eye on it for smoke."

He turned the oven on. All three of them stared into the cavity that was full of wires. After a few minutes, Aris shut his headlamp off. "Should be good to go. I didn't see any smoke. Y'all?"

"No," Selene and Levi said together.

Aris put the cover back on the control panel. "As soon as they warm up, you should be good to go. I'll hang out for a bit just to make sure you don't have any more trouble with it."

Levi nodded and set the oven temperature to 375. He slid a thermometer into the oven and closed the door. "It'll probably take a good ten-fifteen minutes for it to heat properly."

By the time Aris had grabbed a coffee for the three of them and chatted with Jed for a bit, the oven temperature was at 375. Levi slid two trays of croissants into one oven and two trays of puff pastries into the other.

Aris hung around until they came out of the ovens. "Looks like we got it fixed."

"Sure does. Thanks, Aris," Levi said.

"What do we owe you, Aris?" Selene asked.

"Not a thing. I'm always getting coffee and stuff from you guys. Consider it paid in full."

CHAPTER 17

Aris glanced at his phone when the text notification went off. *Mrs. Miller? What could she want?* He tapped on her name to bring up the text.

MRS. MILLER: Aris, I'm in a lurch. Our soloist, Kandy, has the flu and she won't be able to sing tonight. Do you know anyone who can take her place at the last minute?

Aris started typing a reply, and then backspaced over it. He did know someone. She was going to kill him if he sent Mrs. Miller her name, and he was already on poor footing with her. He shrugged as his fingers flew over the keyboard.

ARIS: Selene can sing. Remember, she was in the school choir?

MRS. MILLER: Perfect! Thank you.

Aris could picture the preacher's wife jumping up and down in excitement, clapping her hands. She was a really nice lady, but she could be flighty sometimes. Bless her heart.

Maybe I should avoid the bakery today. No, then she'll really know I'm the one who gave Mrs. Miller her name.

"Nuts. I'm hungry anyway." Aris slid his boots and jacket on and headed out to his truck. They'd gotten a light dusting of snow last night, and it covered the road where the previous snows had melted, but the sun was shining.

He glanced at the sky, hoping it wouldn't snow again. The forecast wasn't calling for it, but it's been wrong several times this year. Already. *I hate to see what January and February will bring us. I can't wait until April.*

It was thirty-five degrees, which meant the little snow they did get was already melting—and that meant more black ice in shaded areas. He drove slowly, even on the main road, until he arrived at the bakery.

"Well, here goes nothing," he said to the empty cab of his truck.

Jed was behind the counter. "Hi, Aris. How are you this morning?"

"Doing just fine, Jed. Do you have any of those apple fritters today?"

"We sure do. You want one before you head out with your deliveries?"

"I could eat one."

Jed plated the sweet breakfast treat and poured a large cup of coffee for Aris. He handed it over with a smirk. "You're in trouble," he whispered. "Selene got a call from Mrs. Miller, and she deduced that you are the only one who could have given her name."

Aris grinned. "Levi, or you could have easily done the same."

"But we didn't get a phone call asking us, and she knows it. She's been with us all morning."

"Well, shit. Maybe I should make myself scarce."

Just then, Levi walked out front. "Hey, Aris," he said a little too loudly for Aris's liking.

"Shh!" Aris said. "I don't want Selene to know I'm here."

"Ooooh. Yeah. She's not too happy with you." Levi smirked. "But she should get out and do some singing. It'd do her good."

"I thought so, too, but you know we're not exactly the best of friends right now." Aris shrugged.

"I don't think that would matter. The way she was going on, she'd tear into a best friend for that one," Jed said, snickering.

"Oh, hell. Thanks for the vote of confidence, Jed."

"Go eat your breakfast, and I'll get your delivery order ready," Levi said. He glanced down the hall as he walked into the kitchen. The office door was closed. *At least Aris might get a break this morning.*

Selene pulled into the church parking lot a few minutes before six that evening. They would be singing Christmas carols from seven until nine for today's part of the Christmas celebration on the town square. The temperature had dropped to twenty-nine degrees, but she had hand warmers for her mittens.

She stepped inside the warm church to find Mrs. Miller and several other singers gathered around a table with hot chocolate and snacks. *I love her hot chocolate. She always makes it from scratch with heavy cream.*

Selene approached the small group, who made room for her to grab a large cup of cocoa and some cookies.

"We're just waiting on a few more people, then we can get started," Mrs. Miller said as she arranged and rearranged the plates of cookies. Selene knew she didn't like to organize things, and was betting her mother usually did this.

When the other singers arrived a few minutes later, Mrs. Miller clapped her hands.

"Because of the potential for ice on the stands, Mr. Miller put carpet pieces in the risers, so be careful when stepping up, especially those on the top riser. Since Kandy has the flu, Selene has agreed to take her place.

"Luckily for us, she knows all these songs." She turned to Selene. "And even luckier, they're the same arrangement you sang all through school." She handed her a copy of the songbook.

"We'll have a break at the halfway mark so you can come to the church and get warm. Our actual singing time is about an hour and twenty minutes."

Selene turned to the table of contents to ensure she knew all the songs—and which ones they would be singing. Mrs. Miller had included two of her favorites this year: Little Drummer Boy and White Christmas.

Aris paused mid-step as two familiar figures appeared. Levi nudged his way past a group of people, laughing under his breath. Jed followed, hands tucked in his pockets. He whistled loudly and waved at his friends as he saved them a seat near the front.

"There's Aris, Dad," Levi said, pointing. The closer they got to the front, the more crowded it was.

"I'm glad Aris got here and saved us a seat," Jed said.

"Me, too. I'll go get us some hot chocolate and cookies." Levi peeled off in the opposite direction to get the snacks while Jed made his way to Aris.

When Jed finally made his way through the throngs of people, Aris asked, "Where's Levi going?"

"He's grabbing us some hot chocolate and cookies. I hope he gets here before they start singing." Jed's eyes roamed over the risers that stood in front of them.

Aris grunted his agreement and then pointed at the church across the street. "He'd better hurry." The singers were on their way over.

Just as the last singer filed onto the risers in front of the crowd, Levi made his way to where Jed and Aris were sitting. Selene had just counted off the start to the first song when he handed the drinks and snacks to the other men.

After the first set, the crowd made its way to the portable bathrooms and the food trucks. "I'm glad I decided to get the snacks when we first got here. It'd be a bear standing in those lines now," Levi said.

"That it would. Where's Selene?" Jed asked.

"They go to the church for the break so that they can warm up before the next set. I'll wait until this crowd around the food trucks dies down a bit, and then I'll grab us a coffee," Aris said.

They stood in silence for several minutes, when Aris remembered the bonfire. "Hey, are you guys going to the bonfire up at the overlook after this?"

"There's a bonfire?" Levi asked.

"You two go. I'll head home. Aris, can you give Levi a ride?"

"Sure can. We'll ask Selene, too."

"Okay. If she decides not to go, text me so I know not to look out for her."

"That'll work," Levi said.

The conversation stopped as the singers made their way back onto the risers for the second set of songs. Many people in the crowd sang along to their favorites.

The crowd had loosened up considerably, and Aris bet they had spiked their own drinks as much for the warmth whiskey provided as to enjoy a drink.

When the choir got to the last song, Selene finally glanced around the crowd. She'd seen Aris getting drinks earlier, but wasn't paying attention to where he was sitting. She finally found him with her brother and father a few rows back from the front.

Mrs. Miller expected them to go to the church before they took off for the rest of the evening. They would return the songbooks and would be able to get a hot drink. *I wonder if Levi and Jed are going to stay.*

She didn't have time to dwell as she counted the beats for the last song.

When the singers finished, the crowd headed away from the stage, which allowed Levi, Jed and Aris to reach the front before the choir took off for the church.

"Levi and I are going to the bonfire up at the outlook. Do you want to come with us?"

Selene paused for a minute and then shrugged. "Sure, why not? You're not coming, Dad?"

"No. I've had enough of this cold. I'm not young anymore like y'uns. Have fun. I won't wait up. Aris, if you want to stay, the guest bedroom is ready."

182

"Thanks, Jed. I'll probably drop these two off at Selene's truck and make my way home."

Jed nodded and then headed to his truck.

Levi walked over to the church with Selene while Aris got his truck. As he pulled into the parking lot, Selene and Levi walked out of the front doors.

Aris leaned across the front seat to open the passenger door for Selene. Levi climbed into the rear seat.

"I brought some chairs and blankets. They're in the back, and I have a thermos of spiked cocoa," he said.

"You trying to get me drunk, Aris?" Selene asked, grinning.

"Nope. Didn't say you had to drink any. Don't think there's enough for you to get drunk on, anyway."

"You must have forgotten that she's a lightweight," Levi said with a smirk.

Selene reached into the rear seat and playfully punched his shoulder.

"Ow!" Levi complained.

"Whimp," Selene and Aris said at the same time.

When she turned toward Aris, both of them laughing, she saw the love in his eyes.

Aris's heart fell as her gaze moved back to the window, and the smile slipped off her face. He didn't realize that his eyes shone with how much he loved her every time he was around her or talked about her.

They were early enough to the bonfire that Aris was able to park close. They each grabbed a chair and a blanket, and Aris handed cups to Levi while he grabbed the thermos. "We'll sit close, but not too close, so we won't get too hot."

"Or smoked out," Selene said, agreeing.

The organizers had created a large fire pit on one of the vast flat rocks that lined the overlook. Aris led them to a mostly level area and set up his chair. When Selene set hers up, Levi set his on the other side of her, so she was between the two men.

Selene narrowed her eyes at both of them, but didn't say anything. *I guess I can put up with being this close to Aris for tonight. It wouldn't be nice to make a scene.*

Just after they sat down and wrapped themselves in the blankets, someone started playing a guitar and singing. Aris and Levi moved their chairs closer to Selene, so they could talk quietly and still hear each other over the music.

Aris poured the spiked cocoa. They were so close together that his knee rested against Selene's. He felt a tingle where their bodies touched through his jeans and long-johns and swallowed a moan. He didn't want to

184

move, but the contact was making the pressure build at the front of his jeans.

CHAPTER 18

Throughout the evening, Aris, Selene and Levi remembered their high school days, and Aris and Levi shared things that happened to them during the years Selene had been gone. She regaled them with tales of her college days and some of the marketing bloopers people, including herself, had made at work.

Every so often, Aris would place his hand on her knee or shoulder when he told a story, like he had before they had their falling out. Selene tried hard not to flinch at first, but as she drank more spiked cocoa, her anger at him dissipated. She found herself remembering his touches and wondering why they never sent heat through her core as they did now.

They'd only had two cups of the spiked cocoa and had been eating cookies, so despite being a lightweight, she knew she wasn't drunk.

Unless he put a lot of whiskey in that cocoa. But I can barely taste it, so it's not that.

When the fire finally burned down, and people got up to leave, Selene checked her phone. Her eyebrows raised. "Midnight already. I didn't realize it was this late. We really need to get back since Levi and I have to get up at five."

"I didn't think it was that late, either," Aris said, standing. "It might take us a bit to get out of here, though. Everyone's leaving at the same time."

"Not much anyone can do about that," Levi said.

They gathered up the chairs, blankets, thermoses and the cooler and headed back toward the truck. Selene slipped on a slick spot, and Aris grabbed her arm to steady her.

"Thanks," she said quietly.

"No problem." He left his hand on her arm for a few long seconds before he finally removed it. He had to force it to stay by his side instead of around her waist.

The trail narrowed so that two people could barely walk side by side, so Levi moved ahead of them. Aris should have dropped back, but he couldn't. He placed his hand at the small of her back as they made their way through the narrow trail head and into the parking lot.

When she felt his hand on her back, Selene shivered.

"Cold?" Aris asked.

"Uh—no, I—maybe…" Selene jerked back slightly when Aris's fingers brushed hers, her pulse tripping over itself. She couldn't look at him—every nerve in her hand still burned where he'd touched her.

When she turned her head slightly to the left, his face was right there. Her eyes dropped to his lips. *I wonder if they're as soft as they look.* Her head slowly swiveled toward him of its own accord. *He's going to kiss me. I know he wants to. But I should not do this. No. No, no, no.*

Aris barely moved his lips closer to hers and hesitated. "Selene," he moaned in a whisper.

"Hey! You two coming?" Levi yelled from the head of the trail.

They both started walking again. "Hold your horses, boy," Aris said, trying to keep the frustration out of his voice.

Selene breathed a sigh of relief. When had her willpower and anger disappeared? *Damn. That was close.*

They caught up with Levi at the edge of the parking lot and took the last steps to Aris's truck together. After putting everything in its bed, Levi and Selene waited on the passenger side while Aris dug in his pocket for his keys. He hit the button to unlock the vehicle and adjusted the front of his jeans.

"It'll take a minute to warm the truck up," he said, climbing in the driver's seat.

"It got pretty cold once we got away from the fire," Levi said, and then added, "I bet it dropped another ten degrees from the time we left town, and that didn't help."

Selene pulled her phone out of her pocket. "It was thirty-five when we left." Her screen lit up. "Says it's twenty-two, now, so that was a big drop."

"Might be a little warmer in town," Aris said.

Selene shrugged and turned to watch others getting into their trucks as Aris waited for a break in the line in front of them. Someone finally stopped to let him in, and he gave them a 'thank you' wave.

Fifteen minutes later, they finally made it to the road. Aris glanced at Selene, only to find that she had fallen asleep. His eyes darted to the rearview mirror. "Damn. Levi's passed out, too. Oh, well. They do have to get up early. Might as well let them sleep," he mumbled to ears that couldn't hear him.

When they got back to the church where Selene had left her truck, Aris leaned over and stroked Selene's cheek with his knuckles. "Selene. Wake up, we're here."

"Can't be time yet," she mumbled in her sleep.

Aris checked the back. Levi was still asleep, too. "Selene, baby, wake up," he said quietly.

"Aris," Selene moaned in her sleep.

He squeezed her shoulder. "Wake up, Selene. We're here."

She finally woke up, but it took her a minute to realize where they were. "Damn. I guess I fell asleep."

"We both did," Levi muttered from the back seat.

"Well, we're gonna be wide awake in a minute when we get out in that cold."

"I can drive you guys home if you want to leave your truck here tonight."

"Uh, that might not be a good idea, seeing as how unpredictable this weather has been lately," Levi said, yawning.

"Yeah, it's probably not a good idea," Selene said as she opened her door. "Thanks for the invite, Aris. I had a good time."

"Me, too," Levi said.

"Anytime, you guys. I'll see you in a few hours. I'll definitely need some good coffee and some of those apple fritters to keep my ass going tomorrow," Aris said, grinning.

Aris waited until they got into Selene's truck before he pulled out and headed home.

Selene started the truck and let it warm up for a minute before she made her way out of the church parking lot and down the road to their driveway.

She was grateful that Levi didn't feel like talking for the short drive home. They were both tired, and she didn't want to hash through her almost-kiss with Aris. She knew he would eventually get around to making a crack about it to tease her.

When they finally got home, the house was dark except for the glow of the porch light and a faint shimmer from the kitchen. "At least Dad left a light on so we don't trip over ourselves and wake him up," Selene said.

"Yeah," Levi mumbled, barely awake.

When he didn't move, Selene gently shoved his shoulder. "You coming in and going to bed, or are you gonna sleep out here?"

Levi sat straight up. "Damn, I can't believe I fell asleep again. Let's get inside. I guess I'm more tired than I thought."

Selene laughed as she slid out of the truck. She didn't bother locking it—no one would mess with it in their yard—and she didn't want to take a chance on waking Jed with the horn's sharp beep when she hit the lock button. They both took their boots off in the entry and left them on the mat they used to catch mud and snow. They both managed to get to their rooms without waking Jed.

Aris glanced at the clock as he walked into the kitchen. He knew he should get some sleep, but he was wide awake. Maybe if he worked on something that always seemed to knock him out—business finances—he would be able to get a couple of hours of sleep.

He brewed a pot of coffee and then walked down to his office to boot the computer. It was warm in the house, so he turned the heat down a couple of degrees and made his way down the hall to his bedroom.

After stripping his clothes off, he found a pair of shorts and a light t-shirt and slipped them on. Padding barefoot down the hall, he entered the kitchen, poured himself a cup of coffee and then went into his home office to pull up his financial records.

Between thoughts of Selene and how he could get back into her good graces, he entered the pile of business receipts that sat on the corner of his desk, and then balanced that bank account.

She was pleasant to him all evening, but he knew that she was well-versed in acting friendly when she had to put on a front for others. *She could have moved a few inches away from me, but she didn't. Does the heat from my touch race through her like it does when she touches me?*

Once he completed that chore, he was still wide awake, so he opened the spreadsheet he was working on. It listed the date a piece sold, the customer's name, whether he or she was a repeat customer, and some other information.

Once he added other pieces he could make, he could sort the spreadsheet by any of the columns. He was primarily interested in the number of each piece he sold. Since business was picking up, he wanted to make popular pieces ahead of time. Those that did not need personalization and were common requests were perfect to keep in stock. He could work on those when he didn't have an active order.

194

That would also allow him to expand the business and sell certain pieces online. Handmade knives were common requests, whether people wanted them for the kitchen, hunting or as utility knives.

The numbers glowed faintly on the screen, pulsing in steady rhythm with the hum of the computer. He rubbed his thumb over the edge of the desk where the grain was smooth and cool. The scent of books and sandalwood drifted above the faint tang of coffee cooling beside him.

Light flickered in the corner of his vision. He blinked, but it didn't go away—it shimmered, gold pooling in the lines of the spreadsheet like sunlight spilled over water. His eyes drifted shut for just a moment, and the light warmed. The hum deepened, steady as breath, drifting now to a memory carried on longing.

It wasn't the computer anymore he was hearing, but her laugh. It was low, teasing, and close. The smell of books, sandalwood and coffee melted into the warmth of skin. His hand brushed the desk again, but now it was softer, smoother, like sliding over the curve of her thigh.

The back of her hand grazed his; heat flared, sharp and low, impossible to ignore. Even when her words bit, her touch didn't. It lingered, deliberate, soft enough to haunt. She glanced up through her lashes, and Aris forgot how to breathe.

The light grew richer, golden against the shadow. Heat bloomed around him, her breath where the air had been cold only seconds before. His chest tightened, and the want tangled with the fear that she would laugh or pull away. He thought he was still at his desk, but the chair felt wrong—the angle, the height. There was nowhere to rest his hands but her body.

Pressing her naked body against the door, his hips ground against her. Her leg found its way around his hip. Holding it, he lifted the other one. Her arms snaked around the back of his neck as she arched her back, giving him access to breasts that fit perfectly in his hand.

Pulling a nipple into his mouth, he sucked on it and then raked his teeth across it. Pressing her legs against him for leverage, she lifted enough so the head of his cock was at her entrance. It twitched when her muscles gripped it.

"Fuck, I'm gonna cum," he cried out as her hips bucked against him.

The sound cracked through the haze. The gold light fractured. For a heartbeat, he didn't know where he was. The glow broke apart into the cool blue of his monitor, the hum thinned into silence.

Aris sat up hard, hand still clutching himself, breath heavy in his throat. After a moment, the room steadied. He looked down at the damp mark spreading across his shorts, muttering, "Well, fuck. That was some dream."

Aris lifted the cup of coffee, only to find it empty. His eyes tracked to the bottom of his computer screen to check the time. So much for his theory that working with numbers would make him sleepy. It was nearly five in the morning. He wouldn't call what little sleep he got real—how could it be when that dream was so real?

CHAPTER 19

Aris rubbed his eyes, the strain of the highway still buzzing behind them, and took the Caryville exit. The dashboard clock flicked past ten. Another hour, maybe a little more, before he'd be home.

His cousin's couch hadn't offered any better sleep than his own bed, just a different ceiling to stare at. Selene had followed him there, too, bleeding through every thought, no matter how he tried to shut her out.

Even on Jack's roof, with sweat in his eyes and the hammer beating steadily against the shingles, she intruded. She was the shadow between breaths and the pull behind his ribs that never seemed to ease.

By the time he reached the switchbacks that curled toward Evermist, the night had deepened into inky black. There wasn't a star in the sky, and Aris could smell snow on the tail-end of the wind. The smell was sharp enough to sting his nose awake. He rolled the window down a crack, letting in the chill to keep him from falling asleep.

At the edge of town, the bakery's glow flickered faintly through the fog. Aris hesitated, caught between habit and longing and had to force himself to make the turn toward home.

"Well, you dumbass," he muttered, voice rough from disuse. "They always leave the lights on." He huffed out a breath that might've been a laugh. "Maybe you'll sleep this time."

Silence filled the cab again, heavy as the fog. Then softer, almost an admission: "Now I'm talking to myself."

Selene pulled into the bakery just a couple of hours after Levi and Jed. The smell of cinnamon and apples engulfed her as she opened the back door. She put her coat and purse in the office and waved at her father and brother as she made her way out front.

She paused, catching sight of the town square through the front glass. Strings of warm white lights zigzagged from lamppost to lamppost, glowing against the haze of the lightly falling snow. It was early for people to set up, but the townsfolk always got excited for the culmination of the Christmas festival and claimed their spot on the square to set up and decorate their booths.

Every year, the same spell seemed to settle over Evermist. The shop doors stayed open late, the bell above each one chiming in rhythm with carols playing from hidden speakers. Kids darted between clusters of shoppers, mittens dotted with snow, their laughter carrying above the low hum of conversation.

After she made the various flavors of coffee, she pushed through the swinging doors. "Do I have enough room on the stove to fix a big pot of cider?" she asked Levi.

"Sure do. I'm almost done with making the pie filling, so you can have the whole stove if you want. Are you making enough for customers, or is this just for us?"

Selene leaned against the counter, watching Levi's hands fold dough into neat twists for apple fritters. She traced a small circle in the flour dust near her elbow, and then brushed it away before it could form into anything.

"I have time to order more apples, and that might be a good idea, but not for the store in regular hours. It would be a draw for the Christmas bash long weekend."

Her voice was steady enough, but there was a pause before she looked up, a flicker of something distant in her expression, as if her mind had wandered somewhere she didn't mean to go.

"Exactly." Levi's eyes flicked to her and then back to the dough he was forming. "It's gonna be packed this weekend. It always is." He spooned homemade apple pie filling onto the dough, which was waiting to go into the oven.

Movement on the street caught Selene's attention. A group of volunteers hoisted a fresh wreath onto the lamppost across from the bakery. The sound of Christmas carols blasting from the speakers in the square as they tested the sound system found its way inside, blending with the droning hum of the ventilation fans.

For the first time in days, the heaviness pressed against Selene's ribs in a different way—less ache, more warmth. She rubbed her arms, smiled faintly, and said, "I'll order more apples and get the cider started."

The light slipping through the blinds was too sharp for December, all silver and cold. Aris groaned and dragged a pillow over his face, but the effort did nothing.

Sleep had been a lost cause hours ago. He'd only drifted in and out, caught between dreams and the familiar ache that followed him there.

When he finally rolled out of bed, the floorboards were cold under his bare feet, their chill biting enough to wake him fully. The house still smelled faintly of last night's burnt, stale coffee. He'd drifted off with the warmer on.

He stood at the counter for a moment, staring at the empty mug he hadn't bothered to wash, then decided fresh caffeine might do what rest hadn't. He rinsed the pot and threw out the used grounds to make another pot.

Outside, the world was gray-blue and soft. It looked as if it was going to snow. Again. After his second cup of coffee, Aris decided to head into town. He showered and dressed in a pair of tight button-fly jeans and a heavy flannel shirt.

By the time he reached Main Street, Evermist was alive. Strings of lights shimmered over the sidewalks, and laughter spilled from somewhere near the square. The sound of Christmas music drifted through the crisp air, blending with the steady rhythm of footsteps and chatter.

He parked at the corner, pulled his coat tighter, and crossed toward the bakery. The smell hit him before he reached the door—apple, cinnamon, butter melting into sugar. It wrapped around him like a memory he didn't want to admit he missed.

Inside, the heat flushed his face instantly. Levi was behind the counter, sliding a new tray of fritters onto the rack.

"Morning," Aris said, voice rough.

Levi glanced up, grinning. "If you can call it that. You look like you slept in a ditch."

"Close enough," Aris muttered, half-smiling. "Coffee and a fritter, if you've got any left."

Levi passed him a mug, the steam curling between them. "They're still warm. Help yourself before the crowd gets back from the square."

Aris nodded, taking a slow sip. The coffee was strong and dark, which was precisely what he needed. He turned toward the window while Levi went back to work, the faint hum of holiday chatter spilling in each time the door opened.

He hadn't planned on staying long, but something about the glow of the lights outside, the hum of activity, made it hard to leave. He let the warmth soak in, eyes tracing the reflection of the town's decorations in the window glass.

After he finished the fourth cup of coffee—and the second since he entered the bakery—the grogginess had lifted. Aris stretched, setting his mug down, but movement through the server's window attracted his attention. Selene stood at the stove, hair pinned in a tight

French twist, dumping spices into a huge stock pot, her movements steady and unhurried.

The scent hit him—sweet apples, sugar, cinnamon and other spices. He thought he detected cloves and maybe a hint of allspice. Aris threw his trash away and pushed through the swinging doors.

He silently leaned against the wall, the flex of her strong shoulders rippling the fabric of her shirt, drawing his eyes to her. They slowly worked their way from the bare neck beneath the French twist past her shoulders, narrow waist and curvy hips. His pulse quickened as he swallowed a grunt and the front of his jeans tightened.

Selene turned at the faint sound behind her, hand on her hip, as her gaze followed his as it made its way, slowly and deliberately, back up her body. She huffed a quiet breath as his eyes stopped on her breasts.

When they finally lifted to her face, she asked, "Enjoying the view?" Her lips twitched despite the edge to her tone.

Aris's jaw worked as a flush found its way up his neck and onto his face. "Didn't mean to stare," he muttered in a low voice that was rough around the edges.

"Sure you didn't," she said, turning back to the pot. He caught the quick rise of her breath before she spoke again. "Hand me those cinnamon sticks, would you?"

His fingers brushed hers as he did, and for one dangerous second, neither pulled away.

The subtle and hot tension between Aris and Selene was just starting to vibrate when the sharp slam of the back door cut through the kitchen. Jed strode in, boots leaving damp prints across the tile, his hair dusted with sawdust.

He blinked, brow furrowing as he caught Aris's hand brushing Selene's—a bundle of cinnamon sticks passing between them—and something in the air he hadn't expected.

"Sorry, y'all. Didn't mean to interrupt," Jed drawled, flashing his crooked grin.

He turned to Levi. "You about done in here, Son? That booth's stuck on stupid and needs a second brain."

Levi wiped his hands on his apron, shooting Aris a look that hovered between amusement and apology. "It's kind of busy in here, Dad. Let it be until this evening. You can warm up and help in the front, and we'll work on it after dinner."

Jed, undeterred, made himself at home near the counter and stacked cooling racks for Levi, his presence shifting the mood from private to bustling. He'd break off when a customer came in, and then make his way back into the kitchen.

Selene turned back to the bubbling pot of cider, stirring with deliberate focus, while Aris busied himself by checking the oven and tidying scraps of parchment paper he didn't need to touch.

As the morning wore into noon, the cider thickened and filled the bakery with a deep, sweet warmth, sinking into every corner. After the lunch rush, the four of them loaded steaming mugs for tasting, then poured the rest into wide-necked jars, fogging the glass as they sealed each one and tucked it away in the walk-in.

By closing time, the last customer was gone, and the streetlights were blinking on outside. Levi flipped stools on tables, and Selene wiped the counters clean, humming absentmindedly. Aris carried the last tray to the kitchen, feeling Jed's eyes on him in that easy, knowing way.

"You mind coming out, Aris?" Jed asked, shouldering his coat. "Could use a hand with the set-up for the market."

Aris nodded. "I'll meet you up there. My truck's across the street."

Levi grinned, zipped his jacket, and flicked off the lights. "Let's get this over with before we lose steam."

Selene gave him a thumbs-up, grabbing her own coat and purse. She followed Aris to the front door, her eyes on his taut, rounded ass, and locked it behind him.

"What the fuck?" she muttered as she felt a wave of heat flow through her core.

CHAPTER 20

The chill outside had followed them into the barn, clinging to their coats and breath. Aris shoved his hands into his pockets, scanning the half-finished booth laid out across the sawhorses. The scent of fresh-cut pine reminded him of cutting trees with his father when he was a kid.

Selene stood opposite him, sketching quick measurements in her notebook. "If we angle the display on the street just right," she said, pointing, "people coming up from the square will see it first. The lights will draw them in."

Aris gave a small huff of a laugh. "You make it sound like a trap."

She looked up at him, one corner of her mouth curving. "It's marketing. You'd be surprised how similar the two are."

He rolled one shoulder in a shrug, stepping closer to adjust the hinge she'd marked. Their arms nearly brushed. The faint sweetness of apples and clove clung to her from the hours she'd spent in the bakery. It curled under his ribs, pulling at something he'd been trying not to name.

"You hold, I'll drill," he said, his voice low from focus, or maybe from the effort of keeping it steady.

Selene gripped the edge of the wood, knuckles paling as the drill whirred to life. The vibration sent a tremor through the board and up her arms. When he cut the power, silence filled the space too quickly, the tension humming louder than the drill.

"That's solid," he said, testing the joint.

They continued working for a couple of hours and finished the framing and exterior boards. With Jed's and Levi's help, they loaded it onto the trailer.

"Now that we have the frame together, we still have to add shelving and decorate it," Levi said. "We're gonna be here a while."

Selene cleared her throat, then reached for the string of white lights in the box. She climbed on the trailer, stretching up to hook one end over the edge of the booth. Her sweater lifted slightly, revealing a sliver of skin just above her waistband.

Aris turned back to the boards with a muttered curse under his breath, tightening another screw that didn't need it.

She caught the flick of his gaze when she stepped off the trailer, but ignored it. Instead, she grabbed the end of one of the shelves he'd just finished. Levi grabbed the other, and they held it in place while Aris screwed it onto the booth. They installed two more shelves.

"The counter is next." Selene pointed to a pile of longer boards. "We'll use those on top, and since it's wider, we'll need more than braces. Use those two-by-fours to create a frame for the countertop. There should be enough to build five braces."

Her tone stayed light, but the air between them felt heavier with every breath.

For a few seconds, neither spoke. The low glow of the work lamp softened the edges of everything—tools, wood, restraint. When she finally looked up, his eyes were waiting for hers.

211

Levi broke the silence. "It'll be easier to screw the frame and braces onto the booth, and then add the wood for the countertop."

Aris nodded, and the silence grew. The moment stretched thin before Selene broke it with a quiet exhale. "We've got a lot more to finish before the market."

"Let's put this on hold for tonight. We can finish it up tomorrow and the next night, and then we can bring it down to the bakery. No one will bother the trailer. When it's time to set up, all we need to do is pull it to our spot," Jed said.

"Sounds good. I'm hungry," Levi added.

Selene nodded, heading toward the door, "We have beef stew in the fridge that I can heat up. Aris, you want to get a bite to eat?"

He forced a smile, hoping it looked casual. "Sure. Thanks, I'd like that," he said, the words catching in his throat.

He smoothed his hands over his jeans, wishing his palms weren't damp, and followed the others inside. The scent of simmering stew drifted through the hallway, warm and homey, and he tried to let it settle his nerves. Every footstep echoed on the tile, and his skin prickled with the familiar ache of not quite belonging pressing in at the edges.

He kept his expression easy, nodding and trading light words, hiding the twist of unease in his stomach. As Jed and Levi bantered about the next phase of the project, Aris joined in, careful to keep his voice steady.

After dinner, Selene and Levi cleaned up, while Aris and Jed went into the living room. The tight coil inside Aris slowly released. The living room settled into a softer, less charged space, now that it was just he and the ol' man.

Aris sank into the worn fabric of the couch, the familiar rough weave grounding him. The lingering scent of their dinner mingled with the hum of the furnace, and the muted glow of the lamp cast long shadows across the room.

Jed flopped down beside him, a playful smirk on his face as he waved a hand at the window. "Can you believe this?" he said with a chuckle. "We've had enough snow this year to bury the whole house twice over."

Aris let out a quiet laugh, the sound lighter than it had been all evening. "Yeah, winter's really making sure we don't forget it's here." His eyes met Jed's, and for the first time that night, he felt a tentative warmth of connection in the shared joke, the way the words softened the weight of unfamiliarity.

213

The next morning, Aris showed up at the bakery to take the day-old treats and bread that Levi had baked to those who needed it. The schedule they'd made to rotate families in need was working well. Everyone got something each week.

When he stepped through the door, Jed was at the front counter. Levi's form shifted in and out of his view from the retail area as he pulled pastries from the oven and shoved another tray in. The tension in his shoulders dissipated when he didn't see Selene. At least he didn't have to watch what he said. He was always afraid of saying something that would push her away.

Aris paid for the day-old pastries, and Levi bagged the bread. "I have a couple of orders to work on, so I won't be back until later this afternoon. Want me to meet you at the house to work on the booth?"

Levi nodded and opened his mouth to speak, but Jed beat him to it.

"Yup. We'll head up there around four-ish. Barn's unlocked, so you can go right in if you get there before us."

Aris nodded smartly. "See you then." He turned and walked out to his truck.

Jed narrowed his eyes at Levi. "What's with him? Cat got his tongue?"

Levi shrugged. "Maybe Selene chewed him out or something. They've been acting weird toward each other since the bonfire."

"You can say that again," Jed muttered.

Two days later, they finally finished the booth. Levi hooked the trailer to his truck. Selene took hers, and Jed took his, as they all had additional errands to run that afternoon. They followed Levi down to the bakery, where they unhooked the trailer in the rear parking lot. As Levi fit the trailer lock onto the hitch, Aris grabbed the extra boards he'd stowed on the trailer and placed them behind and in front of the trailer wheels to ensure it wouldn't roll.

Levi and Jed said they'd be home in a couple of hours. Selene said her errands would take a little longer. As they headed to their respective trucks. Aris reached for Selene's arm. "Want to get a bite to eat? I'm hungry and would rather have some company."

Selene hesitated. She didn't want to give Aris the impression that she was ready to start hanging out with him, but her traitorous stomach decided to let out a loud growl right then.

Aris laughed. "I guess that's my answer. I'll drive."

She shrugged and said, "Okay, sure. But I have a ton of stuff to do and can't stay long."

"Not a problem. I don't care to eat alone in a restaurant, and I really don't feel like cooking anything right now."

"Where are we going?" Selene asked as she slid into the passenger seat of his truck.

Aris started it and turned the heater on. As he fiddled with the MP3 player connected to the speakers, he said, "I thought we'd try that new diner down this side of LaFollette."

Selene turned in her seat to face him. "That works. Do we have time to make a quick stop at Mountain Mama's?"

"They closed their doors a while ago. I'm not sure what happened, but there's another shop nearby. Pine-something."

"We can check it out. Maybe they'll have what I'm looking for."

They rode in silence for a few minutes before Aris said, "The Pine Branch. That's what it is."

"Are they new? I don't think I've ever heard of them before," Selene said.

"Yeah, they've been here for a couple of years," Aris said as they entered town.

A few minutes later, they pulled into the parking lot. When he got out of the truck, Selene's eyebrows lifted.

"You're actually going into a store like this?" Selene motioned toward the building.

Grinning, Aris said, "You forget that I'm an artisan, too. I do like looking at stuff other people make."

Selene's head whipped around. "Everything's handmade?"

"I think so," he said, opening the door for her.

They spent more time than they planned in the gift shop, and Selene had several bags as they walked out. She stowed them in the rear seat of the truck. When Aris put his bag next to hers, her curiosity got the best of her. "What did you get?"

He pulled a bottle of maple syrup out. "Best around," he said, holding it up before sliding it back into the bag.

They turned into the diner's parking lot and stepped out onto the sunbaked asphalt. Selene hesitated mid-stride, the savory scent of grilling beef and hot, salty fries curling through the air. Her stomach rumbled loud enough to make her glance down, half amused, half desperate for a bite.

A couple of steps later, Aris's stomach let out a rumble, whether to Selene's gut growling or the aroma wafting from the kitchen, he didn't know, but he hoped the place wasn't too crowded. He was hungry.

They sat at the bar and perused the menus the waitress put in front of them. "What's good?" Selene asked.

"Never been here before, but those burgers sure do smell good. I think I'll get that," Aris said, closing his menu.

"They do. I think I'll get the same."

The waitress came by with their soft drinks and took their orders. "It won't be long," she said, smiling.

"Did you have other places you needed to stop?" Aris asked.

"No. I found most of what I needed in that gift shop. The other, I can order online. I really should get back."

He gave her a thumbs-up as he chewed a large bite of his burger. He finally swallowed and said, "This is damned good."

Selene mimicked him as she chewed her burger, giving him a thumbs-up.

Forty-five minutes later, Selene pulled her jacket shut as they walked outside. "Wow, that temperature has dropped."

"That it has," Aris said, glancing up at the overcast sky, lips pressed tight, and brow furrowed as his fingers tapped anxiously against his arm.

218

As soon as they slid into the truck, Aris started it and cranked the heat. "I have to make one quick stop before we head up the mountain. Hopefully, it hasn't snowed that much, and we can make it up the hill."

Selene turned to him. "Was it my imagination that I saw a clear sunny day today?"

"Must have been we both imagined that shit," Aris grumbled.

Selene's phone rang. Glancing at the screen, she swiped the call active. "Hey, Dad."

"Where are you, Little Girl?"

"LaFollette with Aris, why?"

She heard Jed sigh loudly.

"What, Dad?"

"I don't think you're going to make it home. It's been snowing here for a few hours now, and it's like that other storm we got. That road up the mountain is going to be slick, since it was above freezing, and then dropped ten degrees in less than an hour."

"Well, fuck," Selene muttered, glancing at Aris from the corner of her eye.

This time, Jed didn't even chastise her for swearing.

CHAPTER 21

Just as she hung up the phone, the flakes started drifting down from the sky. She turned to Aris. "I heard him. He was talking loud enough. I agree, I don't think we should try to get up the mountain today. This was an unexpected storm, which means the county hasn't even treated the roads. That mountain's going to be a certified cluster fuck."

"Language," Selene growled, channeling her father.

Aris laughed. "We might as well make the best of it. I'll grab what I need in here really quickly, and then we can head out. The closest motel is over in Caryville."

Selene waited in the truck while Aris ran into a small shop that carried blacksmithing materials. He was out in a few minutes.

"Let's stop at Walmart on the way through so I can pick up a couple of things for overnight. I can't stand not brushing my teeth before bed or in the morning," she said as he climbed into the warm vehicle.

"Same," Aris grunted as he backed out of his parking spot.

He turned into the Walmart parking lot.

"Figures, it's crowded," Selene muttered.

Nearly forty minutes later, Selene texted Aris that she'd meet him by the exit doors.

He swiped his card and then punched the numbers in on the credit card reader and took his receipt. As he walked toward the exit, he pulled his phone out. When he glanced up, Selene was grinning.

"You must have been checking out when I texted you."

"I was. Let's get out of here."

They stepped out into a winter wonderland. The snow had picked up and was covering the ground. "Gonna be slow going," Aris muttered.

When they finally reached the other side of Caryville, nearly an hour later, they pulled into one of the motels by the highway. "Wait here. I'll grab us two rooms."

"I can pay for mine, Aris."

He shrugged. "Okay."

They both went into the office. The lobby had several people in it. "I wonder what's going on," Selene commented.

"I don't know, but I hope this doesn't mean it's full," Aris said, glancing at the clusters of people in heavy coats and pulling rolling suitcases. The low murmur of voices blended with the faint jingle of Christmas music from hidden speakers, while the sharp scent of pine from a decorated tree drifted under his nose.

He had the sinking feeling that every hotel in town was packed for the holidays, and a tight knot of worry twisted in his stomach.

"Well, there are three or four more around here," Selene replied, though her voice was quieter than usual, her fingers cold against the strap of her bag.

As they walked up to the front desk, the clerk smiled. "Can I help you?"

"We need two rooms, just for the night," Aris said.

The clerk typed something on the computer. "I'm sorry, but we're booked. The others probably will be, too, because of our Christmas holidays."

"Thanks. We'll give it a shot," Aris said as he guided Selene back out into the cold.

"Well, fuck, that doesn't bode well for us," Selene said.

"No, it doesn't." Aris started the truck and then pulled up a travel website. He typed in the information for hotels in Caryville. "The one down the street shows vacancies."

He put the truck in gear and made his way out onto the street. He turned into the parking lot. "Do you want to wait or come in?"

"I guess I'd better come in, in case they do have an opening."

Selene could barely keep up with Aris as he took long strides across the snow-covered lot. When they entered the lobby, another couple was at the front desk. "Shit," she muttered under her breath.

When the couple finished their transaction, Aris and Selene stepped up to the desk. "We need two rooms for tonight," he said to the smiling clerk.

She typed the information into the computer. "I'm sorry, we only have one left. It's a double queen on the second floor. Would that be okay?"

Aris turned to Selene, who said, "Doesn't look like we have much of a choice."

"We'll take it," Aris said, handing his credit card to the clerk.

After he finished the transaction, Aris took his credit card and two keycards from the clerk. He handed one to Selene. They got into the truck, and Aris drove around the back to the stairs nearest their room.

"I hope it's clean," he said as he grabbed his stuff from the rear seat.

"Me, too," Selene said. She shivered as she grabbed all of her bags and looped them over her arm.

As they moved toward the stairs, Aris asked, "Want me to take some of those?"

"I'm good," she said. *But it's damned cold. Let's just get inside.* She trudged beside Aris, her arms aching with the weight of her bags. The frigid air stung her cheeks. She eyed the looming motel door as Aris slid his keycard in.

Once inside, she put her bags on one of the beds, sighing in relief at getting rid of the weight. But it didn't last long. What a cluster fuck. What started as a nice day ended up being one she wouldn't want to repeat. She hoped that they would be able to get home in the morning. She wasn't looking forward to spending the night in the same room with Aris, and two nights was out of the question. *Well, it might not be. Deal, girlie.*

Aris plopped down onto the love seat and, grabbing the remote, turned the TV on. "Are you hungry?" he asked, his voice rough and uncertain. He shifted, the coarse upholstery scraping his elbows as he tried to get comfortable. Tension pricked along his shoulders as he glanced at Selene. He didn't want to say something that would piss her off more than she already was. It was going to be a long night.

She scrolled through the hourly forecast for the next couple of days. The more she saw, the more her lips tightened. "Damn," she said under her breath.

"Selene?"

"Huh? What?"

"Are you hungry?"

"Uhh…"

Aris rolled his eyes and stood to look through the drawers to see if the motel had room service. He hadn't seen a restaurant, so he wasn't really expecting to find a menu. He pulled out his phone to check for the closest restaurants.

When he found one, he pulled up the menu and cast it to the TV.

"We might be stuck here for two days. This snow isn't going to let up any time soon," Selene said.

When she glanced up, the menu was on the TV. "What's that?" she asked, pointing.

"I'm hungry. I'm going after food. Do you want something?"

"No room service?"

"Nope. This is the closest place," Aris said, nodding toward the television.

Selene reached for Aris's phone. "Give me that."

He handed it to her so she could scroll through the menu. "What are you getting?" she asked, keeping her eyes trained on the menu as Aris scrolled and tapped.

"I don't know yet. I'm just hungry."

They eventually settled on a steak for Aris and a rack of ribs for Selene. Aris placed the order and then left to get it.

While he was gone, Selene put her bags in the closet and her personal items in the bathroom. She also put Aris's purchases in the closet and the bag with his personal items in the bathroom. She was lost without her

Kindle, but didn't want to download a book to read on her phone, since she didn't have a phone charger.

Aris had been gone for nearly an hour. Selene had just lifted her phone to call him when someone knocked on the door. When she looked through the peephole, Aris was standing there with several bags. She breathed out a sigh of relief that he'd made it safely back as she opened the door and relieved him of a couple of the bags.

"I was just going to call and see if you were okay."

"Sorry, I should have texted you to let you know. I wanted to get a phone charger, and had to go to two different places before I found someone with the right one. I hope it fits yours, too."

"Oh, that's great. I hope so, too. Then I can at least download a book to my Kindle app and read."

Aris set the bags on the desk, and Selene followed, also depositing the ones she'd taken from him next to them. Pulling a small bag out of a larger one, he said, "Here's the charger. See if it fits your phone."

While she did that, he took orange juice, four cans of Coke and several bottles of water out of another bag and put them into the mini fridge in the corner of the room.

"It's the right one," Selene said, opening the package.

"I have over fifty percent, so go ahead and plug yours in first." Aris pulled two iced raspberry teas out of another bag and handed one to Selene. "I hope you still like this. These came with the meal."

She took it. "I sure do. Thanks."

They sorted the rest of the boxes from the restaurant so they had their respective orders, and then sat at the small round table in the other corner of the hotel room to eat.

They made small talk about their jobs during dinner, and then cleaned up the mess. Selene changed into the t-shirt and sweatpants she'd purchased at Walmart, and then Aris changed into shorts. She wasn't going to sleep in anything less, at least, not with Aris in the same room. Luckily, she wore wire-free bras, so it wouldn't be uncomfortable to sleep in.

"Anything good on?" Selene asked.

Aris clicked through channels, each one throwing a different wash of light over the bedspread. "Cooking show. Crime show. Commercials." Click. Click. Click. "Never anything good on," he muttered.

Selene squinted at the screen as another laugh track crackled. "Did we just loop back around?"

"I think so." He tossed the remote onto the mattress; it bounced once and slid toward her knee. "We've officially reached the 'infomercials and reruns' hour."

She stared at the frozen announcer on the paused screen, then nudged the remote back to him. "Turn it off. I'm bored just looking at his teeth."

Aris hit the power button. The room fell quiet, the sudden stillness louder than the TV had been. Selene shifted, tucking her feet under her. "So," she said, "tell me more about that client who keeps emailing you at midnight…"

They discussed more of the local gossip before he flattened his lips, wanting to ask the question, but not sure if he should. "Do you think you might move back?" he asked. He was hoping she would—sooner rather than later—but knew that it wasn't a probability.

She shrugged. "Maybe someday."

The conversation slowed to a lull. Selene didn't want to tell him she'd been considering moving back this year. The commute to go into the office a couple of times per month wasn't bad, and her job allowed remote work. She'd never taken advantage of it until she got snowed in the past month, and she found that she was more productive working from home, even with all of the time she spent in the bakery.

Aris flipped through the channels at the top of the hour to see if a good movie was coming on. It was only nine, and it was too early to go to bed.

Selene got up and grabbed each of them a bottle of water and a bag of chips that Aris had picked up while he was out. She opened the chips and put the bag on the love seat between them and handed Aris a bottle of water.

"Thanks," he said. "Hey, you want to watch this?"

She turned to look at what was on the TV. It was Die Hard. Selene laughed and said, "Okay, but only if you don't call it a Christmas movie."

Aris smirked. They'd had this debate many times before. He set the clicker on the small coffee table in front of the loveseat and curled up in his corner of the loveseat. Opening the bottle of water, he put it between his legs and then grabbed a handful of chips.

Selene smirked back and repeated his actions with her own drink. About a third of the way through the movie, she motioned to the chips. "Done?"

Aris nodded. "Yeah."

Selene rolled the top of the bag down and finished off her water. Before the movie was over, she'd fallen asleep, leaning on the arm of the loveseat.

Aris pulled the covers down on one of the beds and then slid his arm under Selene's legs and the other around her back. He lifted her, hoping she wouldn't wake up. Her arms went around his neck, and his eyebrows lifted before he realized that she'd done it in her sleep.

He set her on the bed and covered her. He then pulled the covers down on his bed, but stood there for a minute, not knowing what to do. He absently rubbed the front of his pants, knowing the semi-hard-on he'd had all night had become harder and that it wouldn't go away on its own.

Still rubbing himself, he turned the station to one of the country music stations and turned the volume down.

CHAPTER 22

Selene's eyes popped open. *What the fuck?* She thought she had dreamed that Aris had picked her up and put her in bed. Aris was standing, staring at the TV, but his back was to her. It took her a minute to notice that his arm was angled in front of him and moving.

Shit. What the hell is he doing?

He changed the channel and then swiveled his head between the bed and the bathroom. As he turned toward his bed, her eyes slammed shut so he wouldn't see her watching him. Her heart raced as she heard him sit on the edge of his bed. The light behind her eyelids dimmed as he turned off the light, leaving only the glow of the light from the television in the room.

Selene chanced opening her eyes just enough to see what he was doing. She couldn't miss the lump in the front of his shorts. *No way.* She barely swallowed the moan at the back of her throat as a burning heat ran down her spine straight to her clit.

She resisted the urge to press her legs together, knowing that if she moved, he'd realize she was awake.

When he stripped off his t-shirt, she almost moaned again at the strong muscles in his arms and the line of dark blonde hair that ran from his chest to where it disappeared under his shorts. He crawled under the covers and turned to his side, facing her.

"Goodnight, Selene."

Her eyes slammed shut. *Oh, shit. Did he catch me staring? Hell.*

It took her a minute to realize that he hadn't noticed her eyes were open just a slit before she slammed them closed again. Her heart rate slowed, but she couldn't fall asleep, leaving her awake in the hush of the dim room.

Aris turned over to face away from Selene, hoping his hard-on would go away on its own. He knew that it

234

most likely wouldn't, but he felt weird jerking off with her in the room. He didn't want to take a cold shower and risk waking her up.

God damn. This storm couldn't have held off for just a couple of more hours.

The pressure only kept building, even though he'd turned away from her. He reached over and grabbed his shirt to pull it under the covers. With as little movement as possible, he pulled the front of his shorts and underwear down so his turgid cock was exposed.

Keeping his back to Selene, he quietly rubbed himself. When the burning sensation ran down his spine, and his cock jumped in his hand, he pulled his shirt over it as he turned his face into the pillow to muffle the moan he couldn't hold back as he shot his load into his shirt.

After cleaning himself up, he pulled his underwear and shorts back over his cock and balled the shirt up, stuffing it under the other pillow. *Maybe I can get some sleep.* He didn't dare turn over to see if Selene was still asleep.

Selene's eyes slid open, and it took a few seconds to remember where she was. The room was quiet, and the television was still playing country music. She craned her head to check the time on the clock on the nightstand. Seven. *At least I finally fell asleep.*

She quietly got out of bed and went into the bathroom. After brushing her teeth, she turned the shower on. When the water warmed, she grabbed the shampoo and soap she'd purchased the day before and stepped under the warm spray.

Aris woke up to the sound of the shower running. He sat on the edge of the bed and rubbed his eyes. After a few minutes, he remembered what he'd done last night. He grabbed the shirt and stuffed it into a bag, and then put that into a bag with some of the stuff he bought yesterday.

He heard the shower shut off, so he pulled the new shirt over his head and sat on the edge of the bed to check his messages and the weather.

The bathroom door opened, and the scent of lavender drifted out on the steam from Selene's shower. She was wearing a clean shirt and another pair of sweatpants. These were black instead of the gray pair she had on last night.

"Good morning," he said.

"Morning. The water's still hot if you want to take a shower."

"In a few." Aris continued scrolling on his phone.

When Selene sat on the other bed, he said, "You're not going to like this. This snow isn't supposed to stop until late tomorrow evening. We might be stranded here for two nights."

Selene sighed and tightened her lips.

"A little later, I'll text a friend and ask him about the road conditions. He may know, since he works for the county. He doesn't take care of the road going up the mountain, but he'll know who does. Let's grab some breakfast first."

She nodded. "Okay, that sounds like a plan."

They put their shoes on and headed down to the lobby, where the motel offered a continental breakfast. When they opened the front door, the smell of waffles drifted out. Selene turned to Aris.

"I smell waffles!"

Aris grinned. "Me, too. And I'm glad. I could use something hot."

They went inside and waited for the person in front of them to make a waffle. Once they made theirs, they loaded up with butter and maple syrup. Both of them also grabbed a bottle of orange juice, a blueberry muffin, and some bacon before heading back to their room.

Inside, Selene said, "Not too shabby for a continental breakfast. Most hotels only have baked goods and cereal."

Aris nodded and talked around the mouthful of waffle. "Yeah."

When they finished breakfast, Selene took the plates to the sink between the bathroom and the entryway and rinsed them off. When she finished, she stacked them neatly on the counter for housekeeping to pick up.

"I guess I should text Levi and let him know that this storm might leave us stranded for at least another day," Selene said.

"Hold off until I hear from my buddy. I'll text him now."

"Okay." Instead, she opened the Kindle app on her phone and searched for a book to read.

When Aris's phone binged, Selene lifted her eyebrow as he read the text.

"They won't mess with it until the snow looks like it's going to stop and the temperature comes up a little. It's too cold for the ice melt to be effective. They're hoping…" Aris paused as he scrolled through the long text. "They're hoping for early tomorrow morning."

Selene switched over to her weather app. "It's telling me that the snow won't stop until tomorrow night. I hope it doesn't take that long."

"What's the temperature tomorrow?"

"The high is twenty-nine."

"He said the high has to be at least twenty-seven for a few hours for the ice melt to work right."

Selene set her phone down. "I'll go down and see if we can get the room for another night. Since you paid last night, I'll get it for tonight."

Aris nodded. "Okay."

She grabbed her keycard and shoved it and her phone in her pocket.

Selene approached the front desk. When it was her turn, she said, "We need to reserve the room another night. Um, if there is another one open, I'd like to reserve that one, too. We're stuck sharing a room when we are only friends."

The clerk typed something on the computer. "You got lucky. Someone had reserved it, but canceled due to the storm. The bad news is that we don't have another room open."

"No problem," Selene said. She handed over her credit card to pay for another night.

As she walked away, she heard the clerk tell the couple behind her that they had no vacancies. She almost turned back to offer to share their room, but that meant she'd have to share a bed with Aris.

No. No, no, no. Not happening. It's bad enough we have to share a room. Though he is acting nice. Her mind flicked to him jerking off, and her face pinked as her core heated.

She knew that most hotels would open their lobbies if people were stranded with nowhere else to go, so she didn't worry about the other couple. They'd have a warm place to stay. Uncomfortable. But warm.

Aris glanced away from the TV when Selene walked back into the room.

"We got lucky. They had a cancellation for tonight. But they didn't have an extra room."

"I didn't figure they would," Aris said. "The town is pretty well shut down."

"When I was out there, I checked the road. It's got a packed layer of snow on it, so we can drive for lunch."

"Okay. What we can do is grab a hot lunch and then some sandwiches for dinner, that way we won't have to go back out later. Less chance of getting stuck or wrecking."

"That makes sense," Selene said, nodding.

Aris walked over to the window and pulled the shades aside. "It's not getting better, but it doesn't look like it's getting worse." He glanced at his watch. "It's only nine. We'll keep an eye on it, and if it looks as though it's going to get worse, we'll go out and grab food and snacks."

Selene nodded and stuck her nose in her book. After a few minutes, she said, "I have an idea."

Aris turned toward her and lifted his eyebrow.

"If that dollar store down the street has a small microwave, we can grab that plus some food we can heat up, and then we don't have to worry about whether all the restaurants will close."

"That's a good idea. Let's go now, just in case," he said.

They bundled up and headed out into the blinding snow.

They pulled into the dollar store a couple of miles down the road. "Well, that's a good sign. It's open," Aris said.

"Yeah," Selene said as they got out. "Now, if we're lucky enough, they'll have one of those small microwaves."

They made their way back to the small appliance section of the dollar store that wasn't really one, since just about everything cost more than that. They didn't find a microwave, but did find a small toaster oven that would work. Aris put it in the cart.

Selene led him over to the aisle with the kitchen stuff. She grabbed two cheap plates, a roll of aluminum foil, two forks, knives and spoons, and a pack of plastic containers to hold any leftovers they may have.

On the way over to the food aisles, she grabbed a small bottle of dish soap. She turned to Aris. "Do you need anything else before we hit the food aisle?"

"I think I'm good. It's not like we're going to get these clothes sweaty or dirty, so I can wear them tomorrow, and I have my shorts I can change into at night."

"I have both pairs of those sweats, so I'm set, too."

They browsed the food aisles and picked up some canned vegetables, bread, butter, mini salt and pepper shakers, beans, a pack of hot dogs and several frozen dinners. Aris estimated the small freezer would hold three or four, but they could leave frozen food in the truck.

Selene also picked up a package of ham and some American cheese.

Aris grabbed a small container of mayo. "Okay, snacks," he said.

"We still have half of a bag of chips." Selene picked up cheese curls and some chocolate.

Aris grabbed Wheat Thins, a jar of dip, and a package of chocolate chip cookies.

By the time they got back outside, the snow was falling harder, and small flakes turned to heavy clusters that stung their faces and clung to their coats. The wind pushed against them, bending the branches overhead until they creaked. Their boots crunched in the deepening drifts as they made their way back, grateful they had decided to bring food back to the motel.

The air smelled of pine and cold metal. Through the white haze, the motel's windows gave off a steady yellow glow. The lights were still on, though they half expected them to fade any second.

Back in the room, the hum of the heater filled the silence. Selene lined up the food cans on the shelf above the mini-fridge, taking a little too long to straighten each label. Aris flipped through channels, the flicker of light from the television washing over the drawn curtains.

Every so often, the screen flashed static before settling again. Selene sat on the edge of the bed with her phone, pretending to read, her thumb hovering on the screen but not moving. The thought of being stuck here another night sat heavily in her chest. Outside, the wind pressed against the window, as if testing how long the glass would hold.

Aris paused on a local news channel, the broadcaster's voice muffled by static. "Looks like we're supposed to get several more inches overnight," he said, glancing over but not meeting Selene's eyes.

Selene shifted, pulling her knees closer. "Did they mention the roads?" she asked, her voice tight. Her eyes stayed glued to her phone, but the screen had dimmed.

"Just 'hazardous conditions'—same as earlier." Aris tossed the remote onto the blanket, the faint thud seeming louder than it should have.

Selene tucked her hair behind her ear, studying the cans stacked in a neat row. "Maybe we should ration the food a little more. In case we're here longer than we planned."

Aris nodded, drawing in a breath like he was about to say something else, but the heater kicked on, drowning out whatever words might have followed.

The wind rattled the window again, and Selene watched as Aris quietly rearranged his pillow, the space between them thickening with each minute the storm lingered outside.

CHAPTER 23

Selene smeared mayo on four slices of bread while the soup heated in a small pan in the toaster oven, her hands working on autopilot. Aris continued flicking through channels, not finding anything interesting on TV. His eyes darted from the swirling snow in the window, then back to Selene. His foot tapped erratically under the table, betraying nerves he couldn't control.

She carefully poured the hot soup into two mugs and placed a mug and a sandwich on each plate, adding some crackers. They already had their drinks, so she slid a plate in front of Aris and sat on the other side of the table with hers.

Aris set both hands flat on the table, knuckles white. He drew a shaky breath, tried twice to begin, and failed both times. When he finally spoke, his voice was rough, quieter than she'd ever heard it.

"Selene, I... I know I tried to apologize before, but I keep thinking about it, how I just disappeared." He swallowed, squeezing his fists tighter. "It wasn't just a fight. I left. No calls, no texts. You were my best friend, and I treated you like shit. I was so mad at you back then. I know it's no excuse. I can understand why you're still mad at me. Ten years, and I tried acting like it never happened."

He ran a hand through his hair, eyes not meeting hers. "I'm sorry. I was scared you'd hate me if I reached out, and sometimes I think I deserved it. Still, every year, I wanted to pick up the phone and talk. I missed everything. Your birthday, your wins, even when things didn't go right. All of it. You mattered to me, and I didn't show it. I messed up, and you didn't deserve any of it. I wish I'd done better by you."

Silence pressed between them. Selene's spoon scraped softly against the ceramic as she nudged a piece of carrot through her soup, her hand just a little unsteady. Aris blinked hard and dropped his gaze to the worn tabletop, a sheen in his eyes that caught the lamplight before he looked away.

Selene let the spoon slip from her fingers; it landed with a muted clink against the mug. She settled back in her chair, her eyes drawn to the shape of his hands, the way his shoulders curled inward.

Fragments of their childhood flickered through her mind. Mud-splattered kicks under summer trees, Aris's flour-dusted arms at the bakery, the bonfire's warmth on both their faces, the clatter of shopping carts just yesterday. The present swirled with all those old, unfinished threads weaving silently between them.

She slid her hand across the table, not quite touching his, but letting it hover near enough to close the gap. "You really hurt me," she said quietly, her voice hitching just once.

Aris's fingers closed into a fist, then slowly relaxed, knuckles brushing the edge of the table near her hand. "Yeah," he said, voice rough. "I know I did. I don't expect you to just... get over it. I just wanted you to hear it. That's all."

He watched her, swallowing, the apology lingering in the space between their hands. "If it takes time—if it takes anything—I'll wait. I just don't want to mess it up again."

Selene continued pushing her soup around, her appetite nearly gone. "I-I… can't, Aris."

He slid his unfinished lunch away and stood up to look out of the window. The heater sputtered and whirred, working overtime against the creeping chill. Outside, the snow pressed steadily at the window, its rhythm muted by the thickness of the commercial windows.

One tear slid down Aris's cheek. *We're stuck, and I can't even get through to her.* He never thought she'd completely reject him. He was hoping they would become friends again, and then maybe more. He knew she wanted it—he didn't imagine her almost kissing him at the bonfire. Until Levi unknowingly interrupted the moment. *Thanks, Levi.*

It was several minutes before he trusted his voice to stay steady. Keeping his back to the room and Selene, he asked, "Do you remember that camping trip? The one where you burned the corn because you didn't soak the husks and put it right over the flames?"

Selene laughed—a real one, caught off guard and wry. "You never let that go. Dad still brings it up at every family reunion."

Aris turned and leaned against the wall next to the window, more relaxed than he'd been all week. "When that fire caught those husks, it got so big that it burned the steaks before any of us knew it. Never had burned steaks since."

"That's because you never let me cook after that," she countered, turning her mug in slow circles. "You acted like I'd melted your taste buds permanently."

He grinned, a little sheepish. "I kind of liked that trip. Even with the rain, the bears. I… I missed stuff like that."

When she didn't respond right away, Aris's eyes lowered, staring at the bland commercial carpet found in cheap motel rooms along the side of the highway, and not really seeing it.

Selene let the moment sit for several long heartbeats, then nodded, quieter now. "Me too."

The old ache that she'd managed to hide away ever since they'd last argued came circling back, even though she'd sworn that Aris would never have that power again. Not after all those years, not after she'd patched together new routines and learned how to walk around the empty places he'd left behind.

And yet, that morning, she'd found herself laughing at one of his careless jokes. Yesterday, she'd caught a look on his face that made her remember every late-night secret and terrible pun. Now here she was, wishing things could be different, letting the thinnest hope thread through the cracks she'd spent so long building up.

"Stupid," she thought, shaking her head. *You're just going to get hurt again. He'll leave; you'll fall; you'll be the only one picking up pieces. You should've shut him out, kept things tidy and safe.* But the walls were already

249

shifting, already weaker. The effort to keep them up left her exhausted. She tried to steel herself, to shut every window against the storm outside and the one he brought back into her body and soul. *Stop letting him in.*

Aris stayed by the window, silent, watching a snowplow crawl past in the distance. Selene's mug was cool in her palms; she drank the broth despite the bland taste, more for something to do than for comfort. The room stretched tight with the things unspoken, the drone of the television the only counterpoint to the hush.

A low rattle sounded from somewhere in the vent, and the power flickered. Selene startled, blinking as though waking from a trance. She glanced around the small table—a few cracker crumbs, half-eaten sandwiches and mugs of soup, a broth stain on her napkin. Habit made her reach for a paper towel to blot it up, her movements slow but steady.

"Storm's getting worse," Aris said eventually, his voice level again, but subdued. He rapped his knuckles gently on the glass, eyes tracking the swirling flakes. "Hope the power holds."

Selene managed a faint smile, her gaze distant. "At least the motel has generators. I hope."

She wrapped the half-eaten sandwiches in aluminum foil and put them in the fridge, knowing Aris wasn't going to eat any more. They'd finished their soup, so she gathered the dishes and brought them to the bathroom sink to wash.

Aris stayed near the window a bit longer. The moment between them held, fragile as spun glass, but something softer was threading through from old familiarity—a tentative truce, drawn out by the snow's relentless hush.

As Selene rinsed the mugs, the dull scrape of ceramic on enamel mingled with the subdued sounds from the television. The world outside was white and featureless, but inside, life limped forward—the quiet cleanup, flickering lamps as the power managed to hang on, and the faintest warmth of shared memory lingering between them.

She finished washing the dishes and stepped back into the room. Aris was lying on his bed with his back to her. Selene climbed onto her bed and picked up her phone to continue reading the romance she'd downloaded.

When she realized she'd read the same paragraph four times, she set the phone down, letting the disrupting thoughts come to the front of her mind.

Why not? Because he's just going to hurt you again. But it's been ten years. People change. Not that much. You can't let him back in. Just as friends. You know he wants more. He always did. Admit it, so did you, but for whatever reason, neither of you acted on your feelings in high school.

Selene wondered what path their lives would have taken had they acted on their feelings all those years ago. Would they be married today? Would they have broken it off, ruining their friendship? *Not that it didn't get ruined anyway.* Would she be stuck in Knoxville, trying to avoid him for all those years?

"Damn it," she muttered under her breath as she stood and paced the floor from the door to the window and back again.

Aris watched with red-rimmed eyes as she turned at the window to pace toward the door. He quickly wiped his eyes and buried his face in the pillow so she couldn't see how much she affected him.

CHAPTER 24

Selene glanced at the clock on the nightstand between their beds. Almost five. Aris hadn't moved, but she could tell he wasn't sleeping. She put her phone on the charger and moved over to the small fridge. Grabbing one of the frozen dinners, she read the back of the carton for cooking times and put it into the toaster oven.

When the timer went off, she carried it over to the table. "Aris, come on and eat."

"Not hungry." His reply was muffled.

"Have it your way," she said, grabbing a fork.

Aris knew his eyes were still red and swollen, the skin beneath them hot and tight in a way he couldn't ignore. He kept his back turned, avoiding Selene's gaze, not wanting her to see the mess he'd become. Each pulse of hurt made his vision blur at the edges.

The thick, chilly air pressed against his cheek, prickling his skin and blending with the scent of fried chicken that permeated the room. Every noise—the newscaster's voice, the scrape of Selene's fork, the humming of the heater—amplified, each tear stripping his nerves raw.

He tried to steady his breath, but the ache behind his ribs left him feeling hollow, unanchored. The loss churned through him, a heavy, sour weight low in his chest. Losing Selene again—really losing her—wasn't supposed to feel this sharp. It was more than before. Every memory pressed against him from the inside, too big to contain.

Suddenly, his stomach growled—sharp, insistent, a twisting emptiness that echoed in the awkward hush of the room. The sound was embarrassingly loud, betraying him before he could control it. Aris clenched his jaw, mortified, as the rumble faded into silence. Even the mundane urge for food felt jarring now—a reminder of how everything ordinary had changed.

Stuck in the room with her, he couldn't run. *Yeah, like you always do. Shut up. It's true. Even now, when it gets to be too much, you make an excuse—any excuse—to get away from her as fast as possible. Fucking coward. No, she doesn't want to be around me. Right, because you're a fucking running coward.*

Fresh tears ran down Aris's face as he ran headlong into his demons with no way to escape.

Selene stabbed a piece of chicken hard enough to scrape the plate. Her jaw tightened against the flicker of guilt that edged in, unwelcome and sour—what right did she have to feel bad for him? She hadn't walked away. She hadn't vanished. And yet, seeing Aris curled up, the way his stomach growled so loudly in the echo of their silence, made her chest pinch just enough to sting.

She scowled at herself, furious for letting any crack show in the walls she'd built. He was the one who left, who came back wanting normal like nothing had happened. She pressed her lips together and started cleaning up, stacking containers with more force than needed, hands moving faster as anger nipped at her heels. The way he wouldn't eat, wouldn't even turn around—it was just another reminder of how deep the mess ran.

The need to escape surged. Selene dumped the trash, yanked on her coat, and shoved her boots onto her feet. "I'm just going downstairs for a minute," she said, almost daring him to question it. Without waiting for his answer, she opened the door. The cold hit her like glass, and the

255

wind whipped harsh, blinding snow into her face—precisely what she needed.

Before Aris could say anything, the blustery, frigid air blew in so fast that the heater couldn't keep up. "God damn it, Selene."

Figuring she wouldn't go far, he buried himself under the blankets. He knew he should eat something, but he didn't feel like eating, despite the complaints from his stomach.

When she wasn't back in what seemed to be over an hour, Aris sat on the edge of the bed. "Where the hell could she be?" He hoped she wasn't frozen somewhere outside, but there wasn't a lot to do in the lobby, and that was the only place she could have gone.

The wind shrieked against the motel's thin walls, rattling the door and scraping cold whistles through every crack. Suddenly, a deep, metallic boom split the night—so loud it vibrated through the laminate floor and made Aris's teeth ache. The room shuddered.

Shadows shifted, and for a heartbeat, every hair on his arms stood straight up. The air buzzed sharply with the acrid tang of burning wires, and the hum of distant machinery stuttered into silence.

The lights flickered, then, after several long seconds, they snapped back on. The heater kicked in with a rattling shudder, blowing out a stale rush of warmth and masking the metallic chill in the air. The generator's pulse throbbed in the distance, breaking the silence.

Aris checked the clock, the red digits bleeding into the shadows. The minutes crawled by in small, dragging intervals. He listened for Selene's footsteps, for the sound of the door, but only the wind pressed against the glass. Worry crept under his skin—tightening his chest, making every creak in the room sound too loud, too close. The ache in his palms grew as he waited for her return.

"Fuck!" He knew he'd have to go out and try to find her. He hoped she was still in the lobby. Pulling his boots and coat on, he grabbed his truck keys. As he stepped out of the door, his foot hit something solid, yet soft.

"Damn it, Selene! What are you doing out here!? How long have you been sitting here? Fuck my life. You're a God damned ice cube." Aris clipped his words, the wind whipping them into fragments.

His fingers latched around her arm, the grip solid and stinging warm against her numb skin as he yanked her off the snow-choked concrete. Frost bit through her jeans and jacket; icy granules clung to her boots.

When she tried to stand, Selene's legs barely obeyed. Pins and needles shot up her calves, threatening to buckle her knees. Her breath came out in sharp bursts, each inhalation tinged with the tang of snow and exhaust. She stumbled, boots crunching and skidding, heart thumping loudly beneath layers of thick, damp fabric as Aris steadied her with a muttered curse against the howling cold.

Once inside, he slammed the door closed behind her and stripped her jacket off. Pushing her down onto the bed, he pulled her boots off and then peeled her socks off. He breathed a sigh of relief to see that her feet had only a slight blue tinge and weren't frostbitten.

"You have to get out of these wet clothes, Selene. You'll never warm up. Jesus Christ, woman. What were you thinking?"

When she didn't move, Aris placed a hand on each side of her face, forcing her to look at him. She was shivering so much that she couldn't speak. Not that she wanted to.

"Are you going to change, or am I going to have to peel your clothes off and put dry ones on you myself?"

Selene's piercing green gaze softened as she took in the worry etched in his swollen, bloodshot eyes, but still, her shivering wouldn't let her move.

"Fuck." Aris lifted the bottom of her soaking t-shirt. When Selene didn't lift her arms, he lifted each one, sliding the shirt off. He left the deep purple scraps of lace covering her breasts in place.

He pushed her back on the bed and slid her sweatpants over her hips, rolling her from side to side to get them past her hips. His cock hardened at the matching lace panties she wore. Biting back a curse, he threw her wet sweats on the floor with the t-shirt and then pulled the covers over her.

Aris grabbed the heavy bedspread from his bed. He climbed into her bed and pulled her against him, and then covered both of them with the blanket. It was the only way he knew to warm her fast enough, as the motel automatically cut the heat down to sixty degrees for all rooms to help conserve generator fuel.

He knew she couldn't feel his erection, but as soon as she warmed up, she would. No matter what he thought about—even the most painful thoughts of never seeing her again—it wouldn't go down.

Selene's breath evened out soon after she stopped shivering.

Good. Maybe she won't realize it, or if she did, she won't remember. Aris's face reddened, hoping she wouldn't remember. He knew he should move to his own bed, but he couldn't. He fell asleep pressed against her, his arms holding her to his needy body.

CHAPTER 25

Selene woke, tangled in strange warmth. The unfamiliar weight pressed against her side, making her heart thump unevenly. The scratchy motel blanket bunched at her waist, and the air smelled faintly of fried chicken and, more strongly, Aris's cologne.

Disoriented, she lay still, listening. Slowly, yesterday's memories unfurled—snow, the power flicker, Aris's apology. But something heavy anchored her to the mattress. *Oh, shit. What's Aris doing in my bed?*

She shifted, trying to glimpse the red glow of the clock through the gap between the two beds, but Aris's arm slung over her waist, pinning her. His breath ghosted across her neck, calm and rhythmic, brushing warmth beneath the chill in the room.

She tensed and tried to ease away, but he tightened his hold around her, muscles flexing as he burrowed deeper into sleep. The soft, steady and deep sound of his breathing filled the hush. Selene stared at the cracked ceiling, pulse humming fast, trapped by the gentle weight of his arms.

Suddenly, she noticed that her arms and shoulders were cold where she'd thrown the blankets off. *Why the hell is it so cold in here?* Then she remembered. The power had gone out. Suddenly, she could hear the thrumming of generators in the distance and knew the motel had locked the temperature in all of the rooms.

As she pulled the covers back over her shoulders, Aris moved slightly, and his breathing changed.

"Selene," he mumbled.

She stilled, hoping he would go back to sleep.

"No!" Aris's breathing turned heavy. He called her name once more, and then his breathing settled.

Selene felt the subtle twitch of Aris's arm—gentle, aimless, unmistakably the grip of someone lost in a dream. She eased her body onto her back with practiced

262

slowness, the mattress creaking quietly beneath her. His face hovered just inches away, the shadows caused by the dim light from the television dancing over his rough stubble and relaxed features. Each breath sent a soft warmth washing over her lips.

Aris moaned, a low, vulnerable sound muffled by the pillow. He pressed closer, the heat of his body blanketing her side, and she caught the musky blend of his cologne and his skin.

Her breath caught, sharp and shallow, as the unmistakable press of his body grew insistent against her hip. Heat radiated through the bedspread that was between them, every nerve sparking beneath his shifting weight. Aris moaned again, the sound low and raw, escaping him as he burrowed closer, lost in whatever dream held him. A flush crept across Selene's skin, prickling at her neck and sending tingles down her spine and into her core, causing her muscles to quiver.

Holy fuck.

A moan escaped before she could swallow it as her quivering muscles clamped down on nothing, causing her to press her legs together. She resisted the urge to rub her clit, knowing it would wake Aris. She finally fell into a deep sleep.

When Aris finally woke up, something was different. He finally realized that he couldn't hear the wind howling. He turned his head just slightly and was face-to-face with Selene. Between his morning wood and having her in his arms, his cock was harder than it had ever been. *At least, that's how it feels.*

Selene had her arms wrapped around him, and his around her. He tried to slip out of her grasp without waking her. He knew she wouldn't appreciate feeling his cock poking into her belly. It surged with that thought. He lifted his arm and shifted in the bed, but Selene's arm grasped him tighter.

Shit. She's awake.

"Aris," she moaned as her lips found his.

He moaned into her mouth as his cock jumped, and he opened to allow her tongue access. Their tongues dueled for several long heartbeats before he broke the kiss.

"Oh, fuck." He untangled himself from her and moved away. "I'm sorry, Selene. That—"

"Shh. Come here." She pulled him closer, but he was like a big, solid wall that wouldn't move.

"You don't know what you're doing, Selene," he whispered.

"Yes, I do. I need to feel you inside me. Now."

264

"Selene," he moaned. "Oh, God. I can't do this."

Her eyes caught his as she turned to look at him. "Aris." She flipped the covers off, and his hips shoved forward against the air when the odor of her sex wafted in the air. She slid her hand down to her waist and under the thin elastic of her panties.

When her fingers found the hard bump between her legs, she moaned, "Aris, I really need to feel you in me. Now."

Her hips jerked against her hand, and she cried out as an intense wave washed over her. She moaned his name over and over.

Aris grabbed his cock. He was going to cum just watching her moan his name while she got herself off. "Jesus, Selene. You're going to hate me. You're going to hate yourself if I fuck you. Ohhh, fuck!" His curse ended in a long, low moan as ropes of hot white cum spurted out of him.

"No, I'm not, Aris. I know what I'm doing." She slid down the bed and licked the cum off the tip of his cock, and then drew him in her mouth. She ran her tongue over the tip and then around the ridge.

Aris moaned as he felt himself harden again.

She pulled him into her mouth until he hit the back of her throat. As she lifted her head, she tightened her lips and sucked him. As she took him in again, her hand found her clit. She moaned around his cock, and the humming caused his hips to jerk into her mouth.

He pushed her away. "I need to be inside you." He flipped her onto her back and shoved her legs apart. The head of his cock tickled her entrance as he stared into her eyes. "God, baby, are you sure?"

"Now, Aris," Selene begged as she wrapped her legs around his hips, pulling him into her.

The head of his throbbing cock breached her entrance, and he couldn't hold back. His hips slammed against her as he buried himself inside her warm, moist pussy. He slammed into her over and over as her hips met his, stroke for stroke.

She arched her back as the heat rippled through her. Each time their bodies met, a moan escaped her lips, soft at first, then sharp and breathless. Her fingers dug into his skin, feeling the flex of his muscles, and her nails left crescents along his shoulder blades.

Aris knew he couldn't hold off any longer. He reached between them and roughly thumbed her clit. He moaned loudly when she stiffened and cried out his name as tingling waves crashed through her.

Her muscles gripped his cock, drawing him deeper with every pulse. He gasped, the sensation overwhelming, unable to hold back even if he tried. His voice broke open, shouting her name as jolts of pleasure surged between them. For a moment, everything stilled, the sheets tangled around their legs, the air thick with the smell of their sex, his forehead pressed against hers as their hearts raced in perfect sync.

He braced himself on his elbows so as not to crush Selene with his weight, the muscles quivering under the strain. "I can't move, but I have to, or I'm going to crush you." Aris took a few more deep breaths before rolling them both to their sides, his partially spent cock still inside of her.

Selene sighed softly as fingertips traced lazy circles over the warm, slightly damp skin at the nape of Aris's neck, the scent of sweat and skin lingering in the heated air. The aftershocks of her orgasm clenched his flaccid cock, making him moan. Her uneven breath mingled with the lingering pulse between their bodies. "Never in my life, baby," she said on a soft breath.

Selene's fingertips traced lazy circles over the warm, slightly damp skin at the nape of Aris's neck, and the scent of their combined sweat lingered in the heated air. Her breath, still uneven, mingled with the lingering pulse between their bodies.

Still catching his breath, Aris whispered, "Not in mine, either. I think you have officially ruined me for anyone else."

Pulling his head closer, Selene kissed him, pressing her tongue against his lips. He opened to give her access, their tongues slowly dueling. She moaned into his mouth and broke the kiss as her hips moved against him of their own accord. Her thumb traced lightly over his shoulder, and a teasing smile played at her lips.

"That was definitely not what I expected when we checked in here," Aris said quietly.

"Mmm," Selene moaned, more intent on the sensation between her legs as her hand slid down his shoulder to press against his ass, keeping him in place as she ground her clit against his pelvis with short, gentle strokes of her hips.

"I've thought about this for a long time. Us. I wondered if I'd ever get the chance to really know you again."

"I've wondered about how it would be with you over the years. What might have happened if that fight didn't break us apart," she whispered, smiling softly.

Aris met her gaze, his eyes vulnerable. "I don't ever want things to go back to how they were. I want this. This honesty. You. Just the way you are."

He almost let those three little words slide off his tongue, but held back, not sure how she felt. His cock pulsed inside of her, trying to come back to life.

"Aris," Selene moaned, drawing his name out, when she felt him growing inside of her. Her eyes shone with the emotion she couldn't verbalize, as she didn't even know what it was. "I—"

268

His arms tightened around her as he rolled them so he was on his back and she was straddling him. He reached up and filled his hands with her breasts, his thumbs rubbing her sensitive nipples.

She arched her back, trying to give him more access, but it changed the pressure on her clit. She fell forward, her hands supporting her as she moved her knees farther apart.

Aris's hands landed on her hips, his fingers digging into her ass as he met her demands. "God, baby, don't stop," he moaned.

"I need—" Selene drew her knees together as she sat up. Her hand moved to her clit, rubbing furiously as she rode him.

His hands clenched her hips, his eyes on her fingers as they ground against each other. His cock throbbed inside of her, and he groaned, trying to wait for her. "Selene," he groaned.

"Now, baby, now!" she shouted, ending in a drawn-out moan as she spurted on him and then slammed down on him as her muscles clenched him over and over.

He shouted her name as he stiffened and shot his load into her dripping pussy.

Selene fell forward, burying her face in his neck as her hips ground against him, and her muscles continued pumping everything he had out of him.

CHAPTER 26

The next morning, Selene made coffee, bacon and scrambled eggs in the toaster oven. At two in the morning, when they had finally drifted off to sleep after making love several times throughout the day, the wind was still howling, but by seven, when she woke up, the blizzard had moved on. It was still snowing, but the small flakes drifted lazily down.

Aris woke to the smell of breakfast. "Good morning, babe."

"I think it's going to be a good day," Selene said, smiling. She was sore, but it was worth it. She'd have a good soak in the tub when she got home, and that should help some. She didn't dare put her bare ass in a motel tub. There's no way housekeeping would clean the tub as well as she did at home.

Aris got up and took a shower, putting on the same clothes from the day before. He was halfway through his shower when he realized what was different. He quickly dressed and strode over to the window. Pulling the blinds aside, his eyes widened at the calmness outside.

He grabbed his phone and sat on the edge of the unmade bed he and Selene had shared.

She laughed, knowing he was checking the weather. "It's supposed to stop snowing by this afternoon. I'm hoping they start working on the road up the mountain this morning."

"Me, too," Aris said as he walked up behind her and wrapped his arms around her waist. "Is that breakfast about done? I worked up an appetite last night."

She elbowed him to move him out of the way. "You'll eat sooner if you let me move around."

He gently bit the bottom of her ear and kissed her cheek. "Okay. Just hurry."

Selene handed him a mug of coffee. "Sit."

"Yes, ma'am."

She rolled her eyes. "Don't start."

"Yas'm."

"You're pushing it, buddy." Selene turned to hide her grin.

Aris laughed and took his coffee over to the table.

Within a couple of minutes, Selene had plated their breakfast. Just as she took the first bite of bacon, her phone binged. Aris unplugged it and handed it to her.

It's a text from Dad.

JED: It finally stopped snowing. The town plows are out, but we won't be able to make it out of the yard for a couple of days. We got nearly three feet of snow, and it's not going to melt in a day.

SELENE: We're still stuck in Caryville. Aris's friend is supposed to text us when they start clearing the road up the mountain.

JED: Might as well stay there. You won't make it home.

SELENE: Maybe.

She set the phone down and attacked her eggs. After she took a bite and swallowed, she said, "That was Dad. They got almost three feet of snow. They're snowed in for a couple of days, but the plows are out clearing the roads in town."

Aris's phone binged. He quickly read the text out loud from his friend, who worked for the county. "Beginning to plow the mountain road. Slow going. Will update later."

"I can imagine it would be slow-going with all that snow. They got more up there than we got down here," Selene said. She held up her arm, marking the depth of the snow she had checked earlier with her other hand. "We only got about two feet here."

Aris stomped the snow off his feet before he walked into the motel room. He'd gone downstairs to see if maintenance had a shovel, and then shoveled the steps and walkway in front of their door. When he'd finished, he'd decided to clear the rest of the second-floor walkway—or at least until he got too cold.

When he stepped inside, Selene had a cup of hot coffee waiting for him. She handed him his phone. "You got a text while you were outside."

He sipped the coffee for a minute, and then swiped his phone active. Taking another sip of coffee, he said, "This is good. Hot. Just what I need."

Setting his cup down, he read the text. "Halfway up the mountain. Expect you to be able to reach town by five p.m." He sent his buddy a thumbs-up and turned toward Selene. "You're not going to be able to make it to your house. The hill is too steep. But my truck will make it to mine. Do you want to stay here another night or stay at my place?"

"I'll stay at your place. Since they've cleared the town, I can open the bakery in the morning."

"That works. Let's start cleaning this stuff up." They packed the dishes in the bags they came in, put the toaster oven in its box, and made sure everything else was ready. Selene piled everything on one of the beds while Aris gave the room another walkthrough to ensure they didn't forget anything.

Once they had everything, Aris carried several armloads of bags down to the truck. He had gone downstairs earlier to pay for late checkout. They could leave anytime before three in the afternoon without having to stop at the lobby.

The sun finally broke through, its pale yellow glare bouncing off drifts of snow and sending sharp reflections flashing across the windshield. The air stung with cold, but after days of bitter wind, it almost felt soft against his cheeks as Aris stepped outside.

In the cab, the seats were stiff with chill, and his breath clouded the glass until the heater kicked in, filling the space with the dry, metallic scent of warming air. He let the engine rumble until the rest of the snow on the windshield melted. He put the truck into four-wheel drive. When he finally shifted gears, the tires crunched over icy patches of gravel, navigating a path out of the parking lot traced by half-plowed snow.

The roads were slushy, so everyone who dared to venture out was driving slowly. It took twice as long as usual to get back to LaFollette. Once there, they stopped to grab subs to bring home with them.

Before Aris turned onto the main road going up the mountain, he made sure Selene had her seatbelt on. He switched the radio to a local country station, turning the volume low. The road out of town wasn't bad at all, and he hoped it would be as good all the way up the mountain, but wasn't expecting it.

Once they reached the first pull-off at the bottom of the mountain, Aris turned into it. "Let's put the chains on, baby. You come on over here and pull forward when I tell you to," he said as he slid out of the truck.

Selene nodded, and instead of getting out and going around, she climbed over the center console. When Aris got the chains set, he whistled loudly and held his hand up, using the tips of his fingers to motion her forward slowly. When the chain hooks were behind the tires, he motioned her to stop.

Aris hooked the chains on both rear tires, installed the bungee cords and checked to ensure everything was tight. He climbed back into the cab and held his hands to the heater to warm them up. "We may not even need them, but it's better to put them on here than it is on a hill."

"I hear that," Selene said.

Aris drove slowly up the mountain, watching for patches of ice. The county had done a decent job of cleaning the roads and had put down a layer of sand along with the ice melt to give vehicles more traction.

When they finally made it to Evermist, they found that the roads still had a foot of snow on them, as the small town didn't have the resources to continue plowing.

"I guess I won't be opening the bakery tomorrow," Selene said.

"Nope. You sure won't. I'm sure I can keep you busy," Aris said with a lecherous grin.

"Okay, dirty boy."

When they reached his road, they found the plows had left a bank of snow. "Ready for some fun?" Aris asked.

"Just as long as we don't get stuck."

Since he couldn't hit the bank at an angle, he turned the truck around, backing across the main road so it was facing the large pile of packed snow head-on. He shifted into first gear and drove slowly up the snowbank. The weight of the truck crushed it down some, so he made it over it easily. On the other side, the snow wasn't quite as deep as he figured, thanks to the wind that blew some of it off his road.

He knew that he might hit spots where it was over three feet deep if it drifted, so he kept his speed below ten miles per hour. They finally made it to his house nearly five hours after they had left town. Aris turned the truck off. "Safe and sound."

He reached into the back seat and handed Selene her purse, the bag with the subs, and the bag holding the rest of the drinks and canned goods. "We can leave everything else in the truck until tomorrow. Stay here for a minute."

He hopped out and, taking long steps through the deep snow, made his way to the front porch. He unlocked the door and made sure the blizzard hadn't frozen it shut, then grabbed the shovel. He cleared a path on the porch, the steps, and then a path to the truck. Since he had parked only a few feet from the house, it didn't take him long, and Selene slid out, making her way carefully up the steps while Aris shoveled out the other side and rear of the vehicle.

He stomped the snow off his feet and pants, and took the bag of canned goods from Selene. "Let's go eat. I'm hungry."

CHAPTER 27

Once they finished their subs, Aris went into his room to find a pair of sweats and a warm shirt for Selene. He also laid out a pair of his boxer shorts and a t-shirt she could use to sleep in, if she wanted.

He put a bag of popcorn in the microwave and brought two sodas into the living room. Selene had found a movie for them to watch. Once the popcorn finished popping, he added extra melted butter and salt and shook the bag before pouring it into a large bowl.

He pulled Selene off the sofa, handed her the bowl, and then sat down, stretching his legs toward the other end. Aris grabbed her by the hips and pulled her into his lap. "Comfortable?"

She leaned back against him. "Yeah. This is nice."

He reached over and dragged the coffee table a little closer so they could both reach their drinks.

When the movie was over, Selene went to stand up, but Aris held her down. "I don't want you to move yet," he whispered and then nuzzled her neck.

She could feel his hard cock pressing into her backside. When she adjusted herself in his lap, he groaned. His hands found their way under her shirt. He smiled when he found she was braless and gently pinched her nipples.

"Jesus, Aris," she moaned as she wiggled her hips against him.

He grabbed her around the waist and twisted so his feet were on the floor, and then lifted her off him. Aris slid her sweats and panties down. "Take these off," he said lowly as he took his off.

He moved to the edge of the sofa and, while grabbing her hips, leaned against the back as he pulled her into his lap. Guiding her, he lined up the head of his pulsing cock with her entrance.

Selene lowered herself onto him, moaning as he filled her. She rotated her hips as her legs lifted her slightly on every stroke.

"I need more," Aris growled, pushing her up and then turning her so she could straddle him. As soon as she lowered herself onto him, his hips bucked into her.

Selene's hands tightened on his shoulders, her steady, firm grip pressing her fingers against his skin through his shirt. She drew in close, grinding her hips against his pelvis, and as he shifted back on the sofa, the cushions released Aris's scent mixed with his cologne, making her pulse stutter and thoughts blur.

Aris felt her building, so he stood while holding her as she ground against him as he walked around to the back of the sofa. "Down," he growled. When she put her feet down, Aris turned her, bending her over the rear of the couch and entering her from behind more forcefully than he meant.

Her fingers dug into the fabric at the back of the sofa, turning her knuckles white as she met his every thrust with a high-pitched whimper. Heat radiated from his body, sending a jolt up her spine each time he hit her cervix.

He knew he wouldn't last much longer, so he moved her hand to the nub between her legs. As she rubbed herself, her cries became louder and more breathless.

Aris yelled her name as he stiffened against her, pumping his load into her.

"Oh, fuck, Aris!" she yelled as he sent her over the edge, her muscles clamping his cock for several long heartbeats.

Selene leaned heavily across the back of the sofa, trying to catch her breath, as Aris leaned against her back.

"If I move, we're both going to end up on the floor," he panted.

"I don't think my legs are going to hold me anymore," she said lowly.

"Aw, hell." Aris wrapped his arms around her and sank to the floor with her in his lap.

Selene turned, wrapping her arms around him. "Aris," she whispered.

"I know, baby, I know."

The incessant ringing woke Aris from a dead sleep. He fumbled for his phone, but it stopped ringing when he finally found it. He glanced at Selene, who was still asleep. When the phone rang again, he quietly cursed. "It's too damned early for anyone to be calling," he said grumpily when he answered without looking to see who it was.

"You sure wouldn't make a good baker, then," Levi said.

"Fuck off, Levi. What do you want?"

Selene could hear her brother laughing through the phone.

"Tell my sister, who won't answer her phone, that she needs to get her ass here and help finish the booth. In fact, you can get your lazy ass over here, too, so we can take it off the trailer."

"Hell, I've been out of it. It took us forever to get up the mountain last night. How did you get out of your driveway?"

"Ol man Pritchard came by with his scraper blade on the back of his tractor early this morning. Once he got enough snow scooped out of the way with the bucket, he was able to scrape it smooth, leaving several inches of snow as a layer for traction. We put chains on Jed's truck and were able to make it down the driveway. We even tried going back up and didn't even get stuck."

"He must have wanted his early morning bakery fix bad enough to plow you out. Is the town open today?" Aris asked.

"Nope. Mrs. Miller called and said a bunch of 'em were staying closed so they could finish getting ready for the festival finale since these storms put a kibosh on it for several days. We have two more days to finish up, then the three days of the festival, which will close down at two in the afternoon on Christmas Eve."

"Okay. We'll be there in a bit."

Aris threw his phone on the end of the bed and snuggled up to Selene.

"I guess that means we have to get ready," she said sleepily.

"Yeah, but I didn't define 'a bit.'" Aris snaked his hand over her hip and found her clit as he kissed and sucked the back of her neck and shoulder.

After spending all day at the bakery—part of it working on the booth—Selene was in her room, going through boxes in the closet. She was surprised to see they were still there after all these years. Her mother had always said they'd be there when she wanted them, but she never thought of going through them before.

They'd have to go through her mother's things eventually, so she might as well start with her own room. She could go through the attic next. That would give her father time to come to terms with cleaning.

While she was thinking she might want to move back to Evermist, she'd been considering the move even more since her and Aris's relationship changed. As she went through boxes, she made different piles. One to definitely keep, a "maybe" pile, a "donate to the church" pile, and a "throw it away" pile.

Pictures, scrapbooks she'd made throughout her school years and other mementos went into the maybe pile. She'd go through them later to decide if she would keep them. She probably would.

By the time she'd finished her room, it was time to make dinner. She glanced longingly at the piles on the floor, but she could go through them later. Grabbing a trash bag, she put everything in the "throw it away" pile into it. Those items were either broken or so worn that they wouldn't do anyone any good.

She was able to fill a large trash bag with donations to the church. Selene moved the other piles out of the way in case she didn't get to them tonight.

As she pulled ingredients out of the fridge to make a meatloaf, the back door opened, and Levi and Aris strolled in. "Are you staying for dinner, Aris?" she asked.

"If you'll have me."

"Of course, we'll have you, boy! Come on in here and keep me company," Jed bellowed from the other room. Aris rolled his eyes and did as Jed asked.

"Need help, Sis?" Levi asked.

"You can peel some of those 'taters for us." She opened two cans of creamed corn and put them in a pot, added a scoop of butter and a little salt and pepper.

While Levi peeled and cut the potatoes, she chopped green peppers, onion and celery for the meatloaf. She added that, plus salt, pepper, garlic powder and a little onion powder to the burger. Then, she mixed a can of tomato sauce, some Worcestershire sauce, liquid smoke and two eggs and added it to the meat mix. Finally, she poured in some Italian-style Panko bread crumbs and mixed everything. She had enough for two loaves, but since everyone was hungry, she made individual loaves and placed them on a cooling rack in a baking sheet so that they would cook faster.

She topped them with ketchup and slid them into the already-warm oven while Levi rinsed the potatoes and put them on to boil.

Levi peeked around the corner to make sure Aris and Jed were still in the living room. He motioned her into the pantry and whispered, "What's going on with you and Aris?"

"What do you mean?"

"You're not biting each other's heads off."

Selene shrugged. She didn't want to tell her family about her relationship with Aris just yet. She didn't know if it would last. She hoped so, but it was too new, and there was still a lot of old hurts buried deep inside both of them. "I guess we became a little friendlier toward each other after being cooped up in the same hotel room—"

"The same room? Holy shit, Sis." His eyes shifted toward the living room, even though he couldn't see Aris, and then back to her. "You fucked him, didn't you?"

Levi held his hand up. "Don't try to deny it. I couldn't quite put my finger on it, but that's what's different with you." His right eyebrow lifted as Selene huffed at him.

"None of your business, Levi."

He laughed. "You just told on yourself. Now I know for sure."

"You don't know shit," Selene snarled under her breath.

Levi pulled her into his arms. "Yeah, I do. I'm glad. You two belong together. Maybe Aris won't be such a stick in the mud now."

Selene pulled back. "Don't say a word, Levi. I don't know if it happened because we were bored or because…" Her voice trailed off.

CHAPTER 28

Aris finally headed home around seven, and Selene padded down the hall to her room, the soft creak of the wooden floorboards mingling with the scent of aged paper and dried flowers. She lifted one of the piles of boxes and put it on her old desk.

Grabbing one of the many scrapbooks, its worn leather cover felt cool and soft under her fingers. As she turned the brittle pages, the faint rustle made it seem as if the book was sighing. Her fingers lingered over the faded photographs and fragile mementos. Ticket stubs. Flowers that Aris had given her, which she dried. Photos of them together. Pictures of her parents and Levi.

Pictures of her friends that she'd lost touch with several years ago. She'd tried to keep in touch with them, but they all had eventually drifted apart.

As she turned to pages filled with snapshots from her junior year, a rush of warmth fluttered in her chest. There was Aris, smirking beside her at a school dance, his laughter a memory almost audible in the silent room.

The photos brimmed with sunlight and shared secrets, each image catching a little piece of the careless joy that had colored that year. But as she moved forward in the scrapbook, the photographs shifted.

Senior year bled onto the page, and with it, Aris's presence vanished. The group shots seemed emptier, the smiles more strained, the colors a little less bright. A hollow ache settled beneath her ribs, a dull contrast to the golden glow of the year before. She traced the edges of these pictures, her fingers hesitant, mourning the invisible outline where Aris once stood, feeling how sharply nostalgia could tip into something like loss.

Tucked inside the pages, almost hidden under a loose snapshot, she discovered a folded scrap of notebook paper. She carefully opened it, not wanting to damage the fragile paper. She already knew what it was before her eyes landed on Aris's hurried handwriting.

290

The words dated back to that raw, confusing week when they'd had that big blow-up in the summer of her junior year. Her chest tightened as she read his impulsive apology, each line bringing back memories she thought she'd buried.

The note trembled in her fingers as a wave of nostalgia washed over her, combined with the ache of lost time. It's a note that she'll keep, but won't show Aris. At least not yet. She wondered if he even remembered writing it.

By the next afternoon, Selene, Jed and Levi had finished the holiday booth. They'd set it up about halfway between the square and the bakery so it would be closer to the festivities. They'd been in the bakery since, and it was now well after eight at night. Jed and Selene were helping Levi prepare all of the dough they'd need to start baking in the morning.

They would all take turns at the stand so they could all enjoy the festivities. They would also rotate baking duties and time in the bakery, since it would also be open.

Aris would showcase some of his knives and other handmade steelworks in one part of their booth, and would watch the booth if at least one of them couldn't be there.

Earlier that day, Jed had noticed that the outside light in front of the bakery had blown. He'd muttered several impolite words about having to deal with another problem when he was busy inside. He'd changed the bulb, but the light still wouldn't work.

Selene had just put another batch of Christmas Danish in the oven when the back door blew open.

Aris stepped inside and set his toolbox on the floor. "That wind's picking up. I sure hope this shit holds off until after Christmas."

"Language!" Jed bellowed as he stepped out of the walk-in cooler. All three laughed at him as he stepped into sight with a scowl on his face. "Ah, you brought your tools. Thanks, Aris. I changed the bulb twice, thinking the first new one was blown, too."

"It's probably in the switch if everything is working." Aris raised his eyebrows at Jed.

"It is. The other outside lights are working, as are the outlets on that wall."

"Well, let me get to it." Aris chanced a glance at Selene and winked as he turned away from Jed and Levi.

She pulled the finished Danish out of the oven and slid the next tray in. "Last one. Finally," she muttered. She didn't know how Jed and Levi did this with just the two of them.

Levi leaned against the counter, rubbing his hands together. He'd just come out of the walk-in cooler after arranging the space to fit another tall dough cart. All he had to do in the morning was bake.

Selene kept glancing up at Aris as she piped the glaze onto the Danish. Out of the corner of her eye, she noticed Levi smirking at her. "Shut up, Levi."

"I ain't said a word." He chuckled and winked at her.

Selene rolled her eyes. "You don't have to."

"Want me to get Dad out of here so you two can have a few minutes?"

Her head swiveled toward her brother and then to her father, just coming down the hall from the office and back to Levi. Before she could say a word, Levi said, "Hey, ol' man. How 'bout we go up and start dinner and give Selene a break from cooking for once? She's got about a half-hour to wait for this last batch to come out of the oven. We can add the filling and glaze in the morning. We should have dinner done by the time she gets home."

"I am kind of hungry," Jed said. He turned to Selene. "Are you sure you're going to be okay?"

"Yeah. It'd be nice to get a break from cooking. And I'll invite Aris, so cook enough for him."

"We generally do," Jed said. "Well, let's get going so dinner will be ready by the time she gets there." He nodded toward the back door, and Levi followed him out.

Aris walked into the kitchen. "Where's Jed?"

"They went home to start dinner. I have to wait until these finish baking, and then I'll head up, too. Are you coming for dinner?"

The corner of Aris's mouth lifted. "Really?"

"Yeah." Selene stepped closer and brushed the back of her hand along his cheek.

"How long do those have?" he asked lowly.

"About five minutes."

Aris stepped closer to her, gently pushing her against the counter. For every step backward she took, he pecked her on the lips. When she reached the counter, he ground his hard cock against her. "I've been needing to do something about this for a couple of days now," he whispered.

Selene wrapped her arms around his neck and ran her fingers through his hair. "Oh, yeah?"

Aris kissed her. "Yeah," he said and then kissed her again, this time, pushing his tongue between her lips. She moaned into his mouth as she opened for him. As their tongues duelled, Aris ground his hips against her. Selene

294

heard a moan, but this time, she couldn't tell if it came from her or him—or both.

The buzzer on the oven went off, causing both of them to jump. "Damn it, that scared the shit out of me," Selene said.

Aris laughed. "Me, too."

He moved so Selene could take the Danish out of the oven.

As she took the first tray out, she said, "We have to wait about twenty or thirty minutes for them to cool before I can put them in the cooler. Do you want to head up to the house?"

"And miss some alone time with you? Not a fucking chance."

Selene slid the hot Danish onto a dough rack to cool and turned back to Aris. "Now, where were we?"

"You don't have to be out here while they cool, right?"

"Right."

"I locked up the front already." He took her hand and led her down the hall toward the office. Once inside, he pulled his shirt off and then hers, and then pressed her against the closed door as he pushed her bra out of the way and filled his hands with her breasts.

When he leaned down to take one in his mouth, Selene arched her back, giving him more access and moaned. Her hands found the buttons on his jeans and fumbled them loose. She could feel how hard he was behind the button-fly. She hooked her thumbs in the waist of his jeans and underwear, and slid them down past his hips as he sucked on one breast and then the other, giving them equal time.

She took him in her hand and rubbed up and down his shaft.

"Fuck! You gotta stop, baby. I'm right there. I'm gonna cum all over you if you don't stop."

Selene groaned at the loss of his warm mouth on her breasts as she unfastened her jeans and slid them off her hips, kicking them away. She put one leg around Aris's hip. "Take me right here, right now, baby."

Aris raised his eyebrows and then grinned as he lifted her other leg and backed her against the door. Her arms went around his neck, and he put one hand on the bottom of her ass to help support her and the other on the door.

She clamped her legs against his hips as she pushed herself up so the head of his cock was at her entrance. "I'm so ready for you, Aris."

As she lowered herself onto him, his hips jammed against her. They both moaned loudly as Aris tipped his head back. He slammed into her again and again. "I'm not going to last, babe," he ground out as he pounded into her.

Her hands clawed the back of his neck and shoulders, fingertips pressing urgently into his skin as if anchoring herself to him. The room was thick with the scent of sweat and longing, air humming with the low thrum of their mingled breaths.

"I'm right there, Ar…is," she gasped, her voice breaking into a trembling plea, his name falling from her lips almost as a whimper. Beneath her touch, she felt the pulse of his heartbeat, a frantic tempo matching her own.

As her muscles tightened around him, a sharp rush of emotion washed through her. Fragile. Raw. Dizzying pleasure tangled up with a surge of desperate, aching love. For a breathless moment, the world outside the shadows of their bodies disappeared. All Selene knew was the shiver in his shoulders beneath her hands, his deep moan echoing in her ear, and the bright and unbearable sense that she was both lost and found, right there with him.

Aris slammed against her one more time and then shuddered beneath her as Selene's nails raked his skin, sending a hot pulse through his veins. Her breath against his cheek and the fragile, desperate way she said his name ignited something fierce inside him.

The warmth of her body consumed all of him, the electric tension of her muscles clamping around him. Each sound reverberated through him, dissolving the distance between longing and fulfillment. In that breathless instant, Aris surrendered to the raw intensity,

297

aware only of Selene's closeness, her scent and touch anchoring him, and the wild, dizzying joy and ache that marked the space where they truly met. He stiffened and shouted her name as he emptied himself into her.

CHAPTER 29

Levi pulled the eight pork chops he'd thawed the day before from the fridge, their cold, marbled surfaces glistening faintly in the kitchen's warm light. After spreading them out on a cookie sheet, ground a shower of salt and cracked black pepper over them. Sometimes, the dusty punch of garlic and sweet pungent onion powder would join the mix, but tonight, the air carried the wisp of pure pepper heat.

Grabbing the leftover mashed potatoes, he noticed their creamy, slightly lumpy texture as they plopped into the pot. He splashed cold milk in, and the faint scent of butter mingled with a subtle tang of salt.

Finally, he grabbed the French-cut green beans and added them to another pot. He set the griddle across two burners on the stove and turned the heat on. The six slices of thick-cut hickory-smoked bacon that he cut into quarters sizzled as he threw them on the hot griddle. When the bacon turned translucent, he added it to the green beans.

Now the hot griddle was ready for the chops. He arranged them on it and lowered the heat a bit, since the meat was over an inch thick.

"Dad, wanna set the table?" Levi asked as he stirred the potatoes and green beans.

Jed snickered. "That's a far cry from when you were younger, and I had to fight with you to set the table while *I* cooked."

Levi let out a guffaw. "You mean while mom cooked and you watched TV, but yelled at Selene and me when we pretended not to hear mom."

"That's not the way I remember it," Jed said as he shoved Levi's shoulder with his.

Just then, Aris and Selene came stomping up on the porch.

"Good timing," Levi muttered as he put the vegetables in a bowl and set them on the table. He flipped the chops one more time to ensure both sides were evenly browned, and then piled them on a tray.

"Damn, something smells good!" Selene exclaimed.

"Language," Jed growled.

"You do that just to piss him off, don't you, Selene?" Aris asked, laughing.

"Language," Jed tried to growl, but snickered instead. "Get yourselves in the kitchen. Dinner's on the table."

During supper, they discussed how they would rotate manning the booth so everyone would get a chance to enjoy the Christmas festival and rotate into the bakery to warm up. They also decided that Christmas dinner would be around two in the afternoon and that Aris would bring the Cornish hens he had in his freezer, and the Weavers would provide everything else, but they would all help in the kitchen on Christmas morning.

Aris turned to Jed. "Are you sure you want me here? I mean, it's the first Christmas without Jeanna."

"Yes, son. You're always here, and this year shouldn't be any different."

Aris glanced at Levi and Selene, and both nodded.

"In fact," Levi said, cutting his eyes toward Selene. "Why not just stay here when we come back from the

Christmas festival, since you're always here Christmas morning anyway?"

"Uh—"

"You can crash on the sofa like you've done a million times before," Levi said when Aris hesitated.

"I'll think about it. Those hens need to thaw anyway, so I'll need to bring them up on the twenty-third, so they'll be here either way."

After dinner, Aris headed home. He had to finish that special project. All he had to do was polish and engrave it.

Levi and Selene made a couple of casseroles that would be easy to reheat the next few nights, so they wouldn't have to cook. By the time they got everything cleaned up, it was past eleven, and they had to get up by four in the morning, so they headed to bed.

Before they knew it, Jed was banging on their bedroom doors for them to get up.

As Selene padded down the hall in her socks, she could smell breakfast. She smiled, glad that her father seemed to be back to normal. He hadn't cooked breakfast except for once since Jeanna had died.

She pounded on Levi's door as she passed it.

"I'm up, I'm up," he groused as he opened the door.

Selene set the table as Jed piled bacon, sausage, scrambled eggs, biscuits and gravy into bowls and plates.

Aris opened the front door and walked in.

"It's about time you got your ass here," Jed groused. "Just in time for breakfast. I thought I cooked all this food for nothing."

Selene and Levi twisted their heads in synch toward Jed. "And what are we? Fucking chopped liver?" she asked.

"Language," Aris growled.

Both of them laughed and lifted both middle fingers at him.

Jed shook his head. "Y'uns are too much. Eat. We got shit to do."

Aris hung his coat on the back of his chair. "I'm not arguing. I'm hungry."

That afternoon, Selene watched the booth while Levi was in the bakery, baking, and Aris was working the front. It was almost time for them to switch places.

After several minutes, Levi finally arrived at the booth. A burst of cold air swept in behind him. "You going to check out the festival?" he asked.

Selene nodded. "Yeah. I should have just about enough time to visit every booth before I need to be back."

"Have fun," Levi said, his voice warm and scratchy from the heat of the ovens. He rearranged a tray of cookies.

Selene grabbed her purse, the familiar soft leather caressing her hand, and waved as she strolled down the row of festival booths. Lively bluegrass banjo mingled with the sounds of hammered dulcimers as a group of local musicians turned standard Christmas tunes into rollicking jams, every note tumbling with mountain energy and the easy warmth of front-porch gatherings.

Sweet harmonies floated across the chilly air, blending with laughter and the faint jingle of bells, until the old carols had become something wild and joyous, alive with the heart of Appalachia.

The air was thick with the scent of warm sugar and cinnamon. "You have to try the apple butter," one vendor called, holding out a cracker topped with a golden smear. She smiled, took it, and nodded as the sweetness hit her tongue.

Every few steps, a new patchwork of color flashed, from handwoven quilts to baskets of red apples and glass jars reflecting the bright afternoon light. Knots of people chatted near tables heaped with various food-truck fare for lunch.

Each table carried its own charm—jars of jelly catching the sunlight, crocheted blankets stacked in neat piles, wooden signs painted with sayings that made her grin. A breeze carried laughter from down the lane, and she turned toward the sound.

A crowd had gathered around a donut-eating contest. The donuts swung on strings, dusting the air with sugar as kids tried to bite at them without using their hands. "Go, Tyler!" someone shouted. The smallest boy managed to grab a bite, and powdered sugar clung to his cheeks like snow.

One teen had a steaming cup in his hand, and for every bite of donut, he'd take a sip of mulled cider. Selene laughed, thinking that would be something that Jed would do. Other contests included axe-throwing, archery and many of the standard carnival games that people built themselves.

The town hall was ready for Santa, but he wouldn't arrive until the last day. Selene made her way down the other side of the road so she could visit the rest of the booths.

On the way back, she stopped to get a cup of hot cocoa. A candy cane poked out of the whipped cream. When she licked the cream, she moaned, "So good." They'd used homemade instead of the stuff in the can, or worse yet, the stuff in the tub.

At four, Levi came down to relieve Selene while Jed worked in the bakery. "Where's Aris?" he asked.

"I thought he was with you guys," Selene said.

"Here's Aris," he said, speaking in the third person as he came around the corner. "I just had to finish something up really quickly. And now, since it's Jed's turn to sit here, do you want to walk with me?"

Selene nodded. "Sure, why not. But only for a bit. I need to help close down the booth and then the bakery."

They wandered from the booth into the heart of the Christmas festival, where the night shimmered with soft gold, green and red. The snow under their feet was tamped flat by hundreds of footsteps, crunching faintly with every step. A hush seemed to settle around them despite the hum of laughter, the clinking of mugs, and the rustle of coats brushing past. The scent of caramel and pine carried on the air, wrapping them in warmth against the cold.

Aris walked close enough that his sleeve brushed hers now and then, creating a quiet, steady rhythm that drew her awareness to the space between them. Lanterns and Christmas lights swayed from the eaves of nearby stalls, casting dancing lights across his cheeks. Then he noticed a tiny sprig of mistletoe hanging above a booth's sign, framed by twinkle lights.

"Look," he said softly, nodding toward it. His eyes met hers with a spark that made her pulse skip. He stepped closer, lifting a hand until his fingertips brushed under her chin. The gesture was slow, careful, as if asking a wordless question. Selene's breath caught; the cold air turned sharp and sweet. Then his warm lips found hers, and lingered just long enough for the world to fall away.

When he pulled back, her lashes fluttered, releasing a breath she hadn't realized she'd been holding. Her smile trembled into a soft laugh. "You really couldn't resist, could you?" she whispered, voice still unsteady but light with wonder.

Aris grinned, his thumb brushing her cheek where the warmth still lingered. "Would've been bad luck to miss it," he murmured.

They lingered for a quiet moment after the kiss, listening to the music faintly drifting down the street. Selene recognized the lazy swing of a holiday tune from the saxophone and softly sang the words. Around them, people moved on, unaware, while soft flakes began to fall again.

Selene slipped her hand into Aris's almost shyly, her glove brushing against his. He responded without hesitation, his fingers closing around hers, easy and warm. The crowd thickened as they turned back toward the bakery booth, weaving through the throng. A string of colored bulbs traced over the roofs, pulsing faintly like the heartbeat she still felt in her chest.

"It's hard to believe next week we'll be going back to our old hours," she said after a few seconds, her voice still soft.

He chuckled, the sound low and rich. "You say that like it's a bad thing."

"It kind of is when you're the one who agreed to rotate early baking days with your brother," she teased, glancing sideways at him.

Aris stopped in the middle of the street. "Wait. What did you say?"

"You heard me." Selene grinned and tilted her head.

"Yo-you're staying here?"

Selene started walking again, pulling him from the spot where he froze. "Hmm… most likely. I haven't made a final decision yet, but if I do, that's the plan."

The bakery's booth glowed ahead. Selene could already see Levi leaning over the counter, pretending to reorganize pastries. Aris slowed beside her, reluctant to break the hush between them.

"Thanks for the walk," she said, voice barely above the murmur of the crowd.

He met her gaze again, the same quiet spark still there. "Any time," he replied. "But next time, I'm finding the mistletoe again."

Her laugh brightened the cold air, and they stepped back beneath the glow of their booth—the scent of sugar, cinnamon, and something unspoken still lingering between them.

The hum of conversation rose around the counters again. Trays clinked, Jed called out for more peppermint tarts, and the sound of sleigh bells jingled faintly with each whisp of wind through the open flap.

Levi glanced up the moment they walked in. His grin came on quick, knowing and wide. "Took you long enough," he said, leaning an elbow on the counter.

Selene rolled her eyes at him. "Just walking, Levi, just walking."

"Mm-hmm," Levi said. His gaze darted to Aris, then to the faint blush still pinking Selene's cheeks. "Must've been a pretty interesting route."

Aris chuckled, unbothered, his tone even. "Let's just say we found a nice view."

Levi snorted but didn't press. Instead, he tossed Aris a towel. "Good. You can help with the cleanup, Mr. Scenic Route."

Selene ducked her head, trying to hide her smile as she moved behind the counter, tying her apron back on. Aris took the towel, brushing his shoulder playfully past hers as he passed. The simple touch was slight, but the jolt of warmth it sent through her said enough.

309

They worked quietly for a while, wiping counters, stacking boxes, resetting trays for the morning rush. Outside, the festival lights blinked lower as the crowd thinned.

When Levi stepped out to lock up the side displays, Aris leaned close to Selene's ear. "Next time we'll take the long way back," he murmured.

Her hand stilled on the counter. "Next time?" she asked softly.

He smiled, eyes tracing hers, the faint scent of sugar and pine between them. "Definitely."

She laughed under her breath, turning back to box the last few cookies, her heart still unsteady in the best kind of way.

CHAPTER 30

The next morning, Selene and Levi had just stepped into the kitchen when Aris walked in the front door. "Hey, Aris. We're a little later this morning. Jed isn't even up yet," Levi said.

"Want some help with breakfast?"

"No, thanks. We got it. Good morning, Aris," Selene said as she pulled sausage and ingredients for French toast out of the fridge. She cracked six eggs into a bowl and added cinnamon, sugar and nutmeg.

"So that's your secret ingredient."

Selene turned toward him as she mixed the eggs. "What secret ingredient?"

"I never could figure out why your French toast tastes different. It's the nutmeg. I don't put that in mine."

"I don't know many that do," she said, turning back to the stove.

Jed stumbled into the kitchen. "Why didn't anyone wake me up?"

"We all just got up, too," Levi said. He added, "I think being in and out of the cold all day made us tired. Well, all except Aris. He was here on time."

"I set an alarm, something I rarely do. But I know the cold does that to me and didn't want to oversleep," Aris said.

Selene flipped the sausage and pointed at Levi, then the cabinets. He grinned. "Your mouth busted, Sis?"

"I shouldn't even have to ask. You should have done it by now, you heathen." The light in her eyes showed she was picking on him.

Levi reached over her head to take a stack of plates out. "Be nice or—"

"Or what?"

"You'll have to see."

Selene laughed. "Well, that's about the lamest threat I've ever heard." She cut a slit in one of the sausage patties to ensure it had finished cooking, and then piled them on an oven-safe plate. She put them into the oven to keep warm while she made the French toast.

They could usually eat four slices each, so as the first eight came off the griddle, she piled them on a cookie sheet and stuck them in the oven with the sausage.

"Aris—"

"On it," he said before she could finish her sentence. He stood and got the butter and maple syrup out of the fridge. He reached into the baking cabinet and took out the container of powdered sugar.

Selene flipped the last of the French toast, added them to the platter, and then placed it and the sausage on the table. "Dig in, guys."

The morning light spilled through the front windows in a wash of gold, catching on the dusting of flour that hung in the air. The bakery was fragrant with sugar and butter. Sweet rolls cooled on the racks, cinnamon melting into the warmth. Outside, faint music floated in from the

313

festival. The sound of a fiddle skipped through a carol, and laughter wrapped in winter air.

Selene stood at the large wooden counter, sleeves rolled, hands deep in dough. She worked through it with practiced motions, folding, pressing and turning it. Her rhythm was steady, and the silence between her and Aris was heavy but not uncomfortable.

He leaned against a tall stool nearby, watching her shape the next tray of rolls. His hands were streaked with soot from the forge earlier that morning, faint marks still clinging to his knuckles no matter how often he scrubbed. The fiery smell from his coat blended with the sweetness of the bakery.

"Levi said the booth's been busy all morning," Aris said, his tone light. "Guess people like the frosted star cookies you baked."

Selene smiled faintly, brushing flour from her wrist. "Maybe. Or maybe it's just the last-minute rush before everyone shuts down tomorrow."

Aris studied her for a moment and shrugged to himself. *Might as well get it over with and ask her.*

"So... have you decided yet?"

She paused, hands stilling on the dough. The clock on the far wall ticked, slow and deliberate. "About staying here?" she asked, though they both knew what he meant.

He nodded. "Tomorrow's Christmas Eve, Selene. You said you'd tell them before the holiday."

She breathed in slowly, the scent of yeast and sugar filling her lungs. "I know." Setting down the dough, she wiped her palms on her apron, leaving faint white prints. "Knoxville's comfortable. It's what I know. But here—"

She glanced toward the window, where snowy rooftops framed the distant glow of the festival lights. "Evermist feels alive in a different way. Like it's still making room for things to happen."

He tilted his head, a half-smile ghosting across his mouth. "Things like finding mistletoe in the middle of a crowded festival?"

That earned a quiet laugh, soft but real. "Maybe that's part of it." She turned back to her tray, slid it into the oven, and closed the door with a muted clang. "What about you? How's the forge holding up with all the last-minute commissions?"

"Busy," he admitted. "I've been working on something new—ornamental pieces this time, not just tools. Thought maybe I'd make a few for the winter market next year." He couldn't wait to give her the one he made for her.

Selene looked up at him, a flicker of pride in her expression. "You'll have to show me when you finish some."

"Only if you're still here to see them." His voice was quiet now, eyes steady on hers.

For a long moment, neither spoke. The oven hummed softly. Outside, bells chimed, their echoes fading into laughter somewhere down the street. Then Selene drew a breath and leaned back against the counter. "I haven't decided," she said at last. "But I'm close." Her gaze lingered on him a beat longer than before. "Maybe tomorrow I'll know. It's a big decision."

He gave a slight nod, the corner of his mouth lifting again, though something unspoken lingered in his eyes. "I should go relieve Levi. Are you staying and working with him, or is Jed coming back?"

"It's my turn to walk around the festival, but I might just stay here or help you in the booth. I don't feel like walking around now, but will this afternoon."

Aris nodded. "Okay. See you in a little while, then."

Selene smiled as he turned toward the door, the scent of iron and fire trailing faintly after him. She watched him go, the warmth of the oven brushing her cheek, and wondered whether the thing she was baking wasn't just bread anymore, but the beginning of whatever came next.

At two-thirty, Selene sold the last dozen cookies, and the few muffins that were left went shortly after. Since the booths usually shut down by three or three-thirty, they hung the "Closed" sign. By the time they baked more, it would be close to the end of the festival anyway.

Instead, they all decided to take a break and walk through the festival once more. Jed closed the bakery, too, so he could go with them. They'd spend an hour or so enjoying the festival, and then head back to the bakery to mix the dough for tomorrow's baking.

The four of them bundled up and walked down one side of the street, past booths selling roasted chestnuts, caramel apples, homemade jams and fudge. They stopped at a booth selling hot chocolate and got a hot drink with a candy cane and whipped cream.

They passed the crafters' booths with handmade ornaments and holiday decorations, jewelry and seasonal gifts. When they got to a booth that was selling candles, Selene bought a Christmas tree-scented one and her favorite lavender soap. They passed more booths selling toys for children of all ages, crocheted and knitted goods, and the man selling woodburned signs and home décor.

Jed stopped and rubbed the side of a shiny bowl with a swirled wood pattern. "What kind of wood is this?" he asked the seller.

The seller stepped over and picked up the bowl. "It's a combination of black walnut and mahogany," he said, pointing to the black and reddish woods. He went on to explain how he fused the two types of wood into a block and then created the bowl on a lathe.

"It's beautiful, Dad," Selene said. "You should get it."

"Maybe on the way back." Jed set the bowl on the table.

As they walked toward the next booth, Jed said, "I need to hit the little boy's room." He pointed to the porta-potties set off to the side.

"Okay. We'll wait here for you," Levi said.

As soon as Jed was out of earshot, Selene dug some money out of her purse. "Aris. Go back and get that bowl for Dad." She handed him the money. "Hurry before he comes back."

Levi grinned and nodded, so Aris took the money and jogged back to the booth. When he got back, he handed the bag to Selene. "I had them pad paper around it so you can't tell what it is."

"Good thinking," she said and shot him a genuine smile. "Thanks," she whispered just as Jed stepped into sight.

They continued past some DIY booths where people of all ages worked on beading, building snowmen out of marshmallows and other bits of food, a Christmas card-making booth and more.

318

At the end, near the town hall, they stopped at a photo booth where all four of them crammed inside. Then, Aris wanted a photo of him with Jed, Levi and Selene. They also got a picture of Levi and Selene. Aris knew the owner of the booth, so he said he'd pick up the photos in a couple of days.

They crossed the street in front of the town hall and walked toward the bakery, passing game booths, including a Santa hat ring toss, a snowball toss, penguin plinko, reindeer bowling and more. Aris stopped at the jingle bell toss and paid the woman for several chances.

She handed him ten bells. He had to throw them into cups set up like bowling pins without knocking them over to win a prize assigned to that cup. On the first couple of tries, he knocked the cups over.

"Is that your secret technique? Knock 'em down before you aim?" Selene quipped, grinning as Aris lined up his third toss.

Jed brushed invisible dust off his shoulder. "Maybe if you close one eye and stand on one foot, you'll hit the back row," he joked after Aris's fourth miss.

Levi shook his head. "I'm counting on fifteen tries. Any fewer and I'll eat my Santa hat," he said, tapping the rim of the cup with a chuckle.

Aris narrowed his eyes and tried again, determined to let their jokes roll off his back. On the ninth bell, he flicked his wrist. The little bell skipped, bounced, and nestled perfectly into the center cup in the back row—no cups fell, no bells bounced out.

Selene whooped. "Finally! He's moving up to professional bell tossing!"

Jed pretended to bow. "The legend of Aris. Undefeated in cup destruction and, now, bell precision."

Levi laughed. "Guess I'll keep my hat. Maybe next year, Aris."

He accepted the prize, a queen-size crocheted blanket made with alternating stripes of forest green, wine and taupe-colored yarn. "Did you make this?" he asked, as she put it in a large bag for him. "I sure did. I hope you enjoy it." She shifted her eyes to Selene and back to him.

"I will. Thank you very much." *What was that look? I hope it's not obvious that Selene and I are together. I hope Jed and Levi—*

His thoughts were interrupted when Levi leaned into him and said, "Yeah, enjoy *snuggling* under that," as he shifted his eyes to his sister.

Aris narrowed his eyes. "I don't know what you're talking about, Levi."

"I'll leave it for now, but you know I know."

The group moved away from the booth, passing other colorful games, still ribbing Aris in good fun as they headed toward the bakery, laughter echoing through the chilly street.

Levi stopped at a money tree game. "Anyone feel like gambling? He handed money to the person running the game. He stood there with his hand curled around his chin, and then tilted his head as he reached for an envelope decorated with a crudely drawn Santa.

The woman running the booth smiled. "My kids decorated all of the envelopes and my husband filled them, so I don't know what's in them, but I bet that's going to be a good one. My daughter said her father had better put something good in that one."

Levi grinned and said, "Well, let's see how he did, shall we?"

"Wait," Selene said. She handed money for three more tries to the lady. "One for me, one for my friend, Aris, and one for my dad." She turned to Jed. "You go first, Dad."

He thought about it for a few seconds and then picked an envelope with reindeer.

Selene nodded at Aris, and he picked an envelope with a snowman. Finally, she chose one with a candy cane on it.

"Okay, since I picked first, I'll open mine first," Levi said. He carefully lifted the flap on the envelope. His eyes widened as he turned to the lady. "You've got to be kidding me," he said quietly.

The woman smiled. "Are you going to show us, son?"

He pulled a slip of paper out. It was a handwritten gift certificate for two hundred dollars to one of the specialty food stores in LaFollette. "Thank you. I love this store," Levi said, his eyes shining.

"My sister owns it," the woman said. "She'll be glad the gift certificate went to someone who really appreciates her store."

Levi grinned. "I can't wait until she opens after the New Year to visit."

"Okay, Dad, you're next," Selene said.

Jed looked at his in confusion. "It says, 'Box 10.' What does that mean?"

The woman smiled and motioned to several boxes under the table. She reached into the one with the number ten on it and pulled out a handmade hat and scarf crocheted with fall colors.

Jed's eyes widened as he took his store-bought hat off and replaced it with the crocheted hat. "Wow. This is a lot warmer than my current one. Thank you!"

"I'm glad you like it. And, yes, they are warmer. We use thicker yarn when we crochet them. The ladies in the crochet and knitting group made several of these in colors for men and women."

Aris got a large French apple pie.

"And you don't need to bring the pie dish back. That's part of it. Enjoy," the woman said.

He grinned. "I love French apple pie. I might not even share it with these yahoos." Everyone laughed and then turned to Selene.

"Well, are you going to open yours, Sis?"

She lifted the flap on the envelope. "Box 5," she read.

The woman reached under the table and moved something in the box, and then paused, looking at Selene. "I know just the one," she said, as she fished around in the box.

She pulled out a carved wood Christmas bulb and handed it to Selene. Around the top, it said, *Evermist… home is where the heart is.* The rest of the bulb was a hand-carved scene of the square with a Christmas tree. The lettering and the details were all hand-burned.

The bottom of the ornament had the month and year. December 2025. At the very bottom, the artist had added his initials. "Oh, this is Jerry's work. I've always admired the patience he puts into each piece. I love it."

She turned the ornament in her hand and then glanced at Aris.

323

Jed caught the look and cleared his throat.

Uh oh. Caught. Aris smiled at Jed. "Shall we head up to your place to heat that shepherd's pie you made yesterday?"

Jed narrowed his eyes at Aris and then at Selene. "We sure should. We have a lot of work left to do after we eat."

CHAPTER 31

After dinner, Levi and Selene cleaned up and washed the dishes while Aris sat in the living room with Jed.

"Oh, hell!" Jed exclaimed.

Selene stuck her head out of the kitchen. "What, Dad?"

"I forgot to go back and get that bowl. Someone probably bought it. Damn."

"Language," Levi growled.

Aris laughed and gave Jed a shove on his shoulder.

Selene tried to hide the half-smile that lifted the corner of her lip, but Jed caught it.

"What did you do, Little Girl?"

"What do you mean? I didn't do a damned thing."

"Language, girl!"

She laughed and threw the dishtowel over her shoulder as she padded down the hall toward her room. When she came back out, she had the bowl in her hand.

Levi leaned against the wall between the kitchen and living room, grinning. "We knew you'd forget about it."

Jed lifted an eyebrow at Levi, and then his head swiveled to Selene.

She handed him the bowl. "Yep. We knew you would, and that it would probably be gone by the time we got back around there anyway. It wasn't out there when I walked past that booth yesterday. I gave Aris the money and had him run back and get it while you were in the bathroom."

Jed grinned. "Such workmanship. That guy has some talent. Thank you, Selene."

"You're welcome. We finished cleaning the kitchen. We're going to head down to the bakery. Do you want to come with or stay here?"

Jed set the bowl on the coffee table and admired it for a few long seconds. "I think I'll stay here. Being out in the cold like that makes me tired. How long do you think you'll be at the bakery?"

Levi stood straight off the wall where he was leaning. "Probably just a couple of hours. We just have to mix up the dough for the apple fritters so it can proof. While we're waiting on that, we can bake a bunch of cookies for tomorrow. We have everything else in the freezer. We made some extra every day for the past week, knowing it would be crazy."

"And we counted on selling more than we have been. The risk paid off. We'll have just enough for tomorrow," Selene added.

"While you guys start on the dough, I'll run home and grab the Cornish hens. They need to thaw in the fridge," Aris said.

"Let's do it," Levi said, putting his boots and coat on.

Aris pulled into the gravel driveway, tires crunching on the frozen snow and dirt, and went straight to his workshop. Once inside, he exhaled a breath that hung in the chilly air as he flicked on the overhead lamp, casting warm yellow light across his workbench.

He carefully worked a few final touches on his special project, the metal cool and slick beneath his fingers. The rhythmic scrape of the file was the only sound breaking the quiet.

When he finished, he wiped his hands and then cleaned and buffed the piece. He dropped it in his shirt pocket, the weight familiar and exciting. He made his way to the house, which was silent except for the radiator humming. His weight caused the floorboards to creak as he walked through the kitchen and down the hall to his office.

He boxed up the special project and then turned to the safe. Cool steel clicked as he spun the dial, opening it with practiced motion. The subdued aroma of old paper and leather drifted out, and he took the item he needed, feeling the smooth outline before slipping it into his pocket.

Aris stepped into the attached garage and then into the insulated, temperature-controlled storage room. Opening a freezer, he grabbed six Cornish hens and put them in a bag. He double-checked that he had everything and then locked the house. As he made his way to his truck, the cold bit at his cheeks and the bridge of his nose. An endless hush coated the air around him.

As he lifted his head against the wind when he pressed the button to unlock his truck, he noticed small, white flakes swirling in the air. They melted on his jacket and kissed his lashes. He glanced toward the sky.

"Damn it. I knew I smelled snow earlier. I sure hope it doesn't turn into a blizzard, or there's going to be a lot of pissed-off people."

Tomorrow was the big day for the festival. Santa would be at the town hall for the kids, and Cody Gene was supposed to give a Christmas concert for the last two hours of the festival. He was stopping on his way to Watauga Lake from Nashville.

Aris pulled into the bakery parking lot and stopped next to Levi's truck. He moved the box with the special project to the floor of the vehicle to keep it out of sight, and then took the item from his pocket and locked it in the hidden storage under the center console.

Grabbing the cold, slippery bag of Cornish hens, he stepped out of the truck. A brisk wind whipped at his jacket, the cold biting through the canvas and nipping at his skin. He looked around at the dark sky and the thin glimmer of frost coiling across the gravel lot. "Hell, they're not even going to get a chance to think about thawing out in the truck." With a shiver, he set the bag back onto the passenger seat.

Aris ducked into the bakery, the rear door sighing closed behind him. The air inside wrapped around him,

329

warm and thick with the scent of yeast and sugar, the sweet perfume of rising dough hovering just above the hum of ovens.

Levi glanced up from behind the huge mixer where he was adding ingredients for sugar cookies, and smirked. "Took you long enough."

Aris grinned, the heat thawing the stiffness from his cheeks. "I had to make a couple of finishing touches on a piece for today." He left it at that, a faint dusting of fine metal shavings on his sleeve, betraying whatever work he'd been doing.

Levi narrowed his eyes, the steamy haze from the ovens blurring the space between them. He got the impression that it wasn't a piece Aris would be selling, but didn't say anything.

They worked for another hour and a half to finish the dough for the sweet treats that Levi would bake in the early morning. They decided that Selene and Aris would come in with him. Selene would roll the cookie dough and add colored sugar and sprinkles, and then Levi would put them in the large convection oven. Aris would take the trays out as they finished and slide them onto a cooling rack.

Once the cookies cooled, they'd package those that didn't need icing, and then the three of them would ice the rest. At the same time, Levi would add apple compote to the fritters and bake them.

330

They wouldn't open the bakery to the public in the morning since everything would close down early. Jed would come in with them to make several pots of coffee for the large airpots. Other vendors had hot chocolate and coffee, so they hoped that the several airpots would last most of the morning.

The kitchen echoed with laughter as Levi, Selene, Jed, and Aris packed the last pastries away, the scent of almond and vanilla swirling in the warm air. Outside, the world was cold and bright.

Levi juggled a tray of cookies, affecting a look of great concentration. "If I drop even one cookie, Christmas is canceled."

Selene smirked, her cheeks red from the heat the ovens put out. "Easy for you to say. Aris baked a dozen extras for disasters like you."

Jed heaved the airpot with a grunt. "I'd rather see you juggle these, showoff."

Aris plunked the next tray into place and shook his head. "He has a strict policy on holiday drama: One cookie down, everyone owes me a cup of coffee."

They packed everything into Selene's and Aris's trucks and drove the short distance to the booth. Others were also setting up. Selene plugged the lights and the space heater in. Within a few minutes, the booth was warm enough to keep them from moving stiffly, and the street glowed with string lights and the scent of pine drifting over from the square's enormous tree. Their breath warmed the air even more as they arranged trays, dodging each other's elbows.

"Careful," Levi whispered, nudging Selene's shoulder as she set down muffins. "You nearly triggered my pastry avalanche."

Selene grinned. "Skill. Try it sometime."

Jed poured himself a little coffee, inhaling deeply. "This is the real reason I came. The cookies are for show."

Aris handed him a tart. "Try not to spill on anyone this year, okay? Santa's watching."

Jed waggled his eyebrows. "What if I want coal?"

Church bells chimed through the frigid air just as a gust carried the smell of Christmas and snow through the air.

Selene sniffed. "I smell snow."

"Don't say that," Jed said. "We need to be able to get back home, and I'm not closing this booth down early."

"You're imagining things," Levi said. "We've had enough snow to last a lifetime."

"It sure is a strange winter. We never see this much," Jed said.

Another gust of wind blew out of the north, cold and biting against their cheeks. The metallic odor of snow swept across their noses. Jed straightened and sniffed the air.

"Oh, hell, not you, too," Levi said lowly.

"Yeah. I smell it. It's strong."

"What's with you two and smelling snow?" Levi asked. I can't smell anything different.

"That's because your snotlocker's busted," Aris said, giving Levi a light shove.

"Don't tell me you smell it, too." Levi narrowed his eyes.

"I did this time. It smells like we're going to get another humdinger."

Selene, Levi and Jed groaned. "Shut up, Aris," they all said at the same time.

Just then, a wiry figure huddled in a faded canvas barn coat with layers of flannel underneath walked toward them. The red-and-black checkered wool scarf covered his neck and the lower half of his face.

Selene nudged Jed. She'd recognized Ol' Man Pritchard's heavy duck canvas pants and waterproof boots that always seemed to have mud caked on them, and the scarf. "Dad, Mr. Pritchard's coming."

"That ol' coot don't know when to stay home. He's after his apple fritter and coffee." Jed moved toward the front of the booth. "Hey, Putt, little cold out, ain't it?"

Selene narrowed her eyes at Aris. He mouthed, "Later." He knew she wanted to ask about his name.

Jed poured a large cup of coffee and handed it to his friend. "You want that apple fritter boxed up to go?"

"Hell, no. I'm gonna stand right here and eat it."

He took the pastry Levi handed him. "Thanks, son." He pulled one of his gloves off, and his rough, knotted hand broke a piece of fritter off and popped it in his mouth. "Good shit. Still a little warm from the oven. Nice and fresh as always."

Putt motioned to Jed. "Let's take a walk."

Jed nodded and filled his insulated cup with coffee. After the two men stepped away from the booth, Putt asked, "How you doing?"

Nodding, Jed said, "I'm doing fine." Because he knew that Putt was asking about Jeanna's death, he volunteered the information. "It's a lot easier to handle her death with Selene and Levi here. And knowing that she was cheating on me..." Jed trailed off.

"Aye."

"Did you know anything about that?"

Putt shook his head. "No. If it was something going around town, I wouldn't have heard. They know I'd tell you."

"I wonder how many knew and never said a word," Jed said lowly.

"I don't guess it matters much. What's done is done, and ain't a thing you can do to change it."

"You got a point, there, old man."

Putnam Pritchard nodded smartly. Jed was more than twenty years younger than him, but he was brought up just like Putt—to think logically. He figured Jed just needed a gentle reminder.

Jed glanced toward the darkening sky as a few white flakes floated in front of his face. "Damn. I hope this holds off enough to get through the rest of the festival. I'm looking forward to watching Cody's performance."

"Cody Gene. Now, young as he is, he's one of us. Brought up right. If he has to cancel, you know you can see him over in Watauga Lake."

"Yeah, I know. I just don't have time to get over there."

"If Selene stays—"

"If," Jed interrupted. "She won't say if she's made up her mind or not. I hope she does."

"She seems to be getting along with young Aris better," Putt said with a grin.

Jed nodded. "I think they're together. She won't admit to that, either. Bet we find out tonight."

"What's going on tonight?"

"Well, he normally eats Thanksgiving and Christmas dinner with us because he doesn't have anyone left. I invited him to stay over tonight since he wanted to come by early and help prep for Christmas dinner."

Putt let out a guffaw, his deeply lined, windburned cheeks crinkling above his bristly gray beard. "Well, if you can stay awake long enough, I guess you'll find out if he sneaks into her room."

"Yep," Jed said as he winked at Putt. "I know how to get her secrets. And she ain't as subtle as she thinks she is, just like Jeanna. She could never hide anything from me, either. Except for that affair."

The men turned around and walked back to the booth. Putt handed his cup to Levi. "Fill'er up, son. Got some tractor work to do."

"Mr. Pritchard, it's Christmas Eve day and the last day of the festival. You should take the day off. Enjoy Cody's concert and the end of the festival." Selene said.

336

"I didn't come this far by taking days off, girlie. You'd do well to remember that. Hard work keeps you from getting too soft when you get to be as old as me."

Selene shook her head and grinned. "I'll remember that," she said as he made his way through the crowds to his truck.

CHAPTER 32

Selene's breath puffed out in visible clouds as she tugged at her scarf, shaking loose the snow melted into its wool. Beside her, Jed arranged the products they had brought down from the bakery. The flakes from yesterday's teasing flurries had thickened overnight, though they were still light and dry enough to float on the slight breeze. The air held that metallic scent that comes before a true snowstorm.

From the town hall across the square came the distant jangle of bells and a low hum of anticipation. Santa's booming laugh cut through the cold air, followed by a child's delighted squeal. The lines were short now—just a few bundled-up families from around town—but everyone knew that by noon, people would start arriving from LaFollette and other surrounding towns. The scents of roasting chestnuts, hot cocoa and pine garland were already mingling with the sugar and butter drifting from the bakery.

Selene ducked beneath the booth's canvas flap, brushing her boots against the pavement to dry the snow clinging to her soles. Jed followed, blowing on his hands. Inside, vanilla, coffee, and the damp wood of the counters hung in the air.

As she arranged paper bags, thermoses of cider, and neat rows of sample cookies, she asked, "Dad, where are your gloves?"

Jed pulled them out of his pocket and grinned. "They slow me down when I'm trying to set stuff up." He held his hands in front of a space heater for several seconds, and then arranged pies, Danish and cookies for the crowd that would soon pile onto the streets.

Aris and Levi arrived with the rest of the baked goodies. As they worked, carrying boxes from the truck to the booth, the snow dusted their hats with flakes, and a curl of steam rose from the pastry boxes stacked in their arms. Aris shook the snow from his coat, laughing as the loose flakes showered Selene.

"It's turning wet and sticky," he said, brushing it away. Outside, flakes clung together as they fell, clinging to every surface—the sign's corners, the booth's counter, even the edges of the pastries when the wind slipped through the flap.

Selene smiled faintly, glancing out at the quiet square. "Let's hope the heavy stuff holds off until after Cody finishes singing," she murmured.

Levi set a tray of cinnamon twists on the counter and leaned close enough for his breath to turn the air between them to mist. "If it doesn't," he said, "there's gonna be a whole lot of disappointed people."

For a few heartbeats, no one spoke. The snow thickened into a gray curtain, soft and relentless, muffling the world beyond their small booth. The sound of Santa's cheer and the mayor's laughter faded into a hush. Inside, the four of them worked side by side, their motions syncing to an unspoken rhythm.

The heavy squall turned into light flurries again. "So, it's going to be that way," Jed muttered.

"Huh?" Levi asked.

"This snow. It's going to do the light, heavy, light, heavy thing."

"Well, as long as it doesn't do it too often and stays light, it shouldn't force everyone to close down," Levi said hopefully.

"I don't know that we'll see as many out-of-towners this year because of it, though," Aris said. "At least not if this snow keeps up. They'll show if they don't think it will get bad, but these squalls might deter some."

"Hmm. Maybe not," Jed interjected. "People will risk more because Cody's coming."

Within an hour, the hush of snowfall gave way to the hum of arrival. Families from LaFollette, Jacksboro, and up the ridge poured into the square. The uneven rhythm of boots crunching snow, laughter echoing off the brick storefronts, and the faint strains of a brass band warming up under the community gazebo created a festive hum.

Children darted ahead of their parents, scarves trailing, their mittens clutching small paper cups of cocoa from the first booth they passed. Vendors called out greetings, and cheerful voices threaded with the crisp edge of cold. The town's Christmas lights glowed weakly in the daylight, their bulbs reflecting blinks of color off the wet pavement as the snow melted beneath so many feet.

Selene and Jed worked quickly, passing out pastries and warm cider to a line that grew faster than they could keep up. Aris exchanged jokes with customers while Levi handed a little girl a gingerbread cookie shaped like a reindeer. Her delighted gasp carried above the noise before she vanished into the crowd, the red bow on her hat flashing once and then gone.

Across the square, Santa's booth had become the day's bright nucleus. His booming laughter rolled through the air as the line snaked around the fountain, winding through puddles of half-melted snow. The mayor, rosy-cheeked and beaming, worked his way along the street, shaking hands and doling out good wishes.

Behind him, a group of high school carolers began to sing, their harmony shaky at first, then settling into something warm and earnest. Each breath they took clouded the air, fading like smoke before the next note rose.

The festival buzzed with motion. Bells jingled with each gust of the wind, children clutched plastic sleds, though the ground was too crowded to use them, and the occasional bark of a dog carried through the din. Overhead, the snow slowed to a lazy drift again, the kind that caught light and lingered before landing.

By ten o'clock, the square had become a moving tapestry of color and scent. Inside the booth, Selene paused just long enough to take everything in. The faces, the music, the white sky beginning to brighten with a hint of sun. Then Levi called her name from behind the counter, and she turned, laughing as she reached for another tray of pastries, the warmth of the crowd spilling through the cold like light through glass.

The brief glimmer of sunlight vanished almost before it began. A hush swept through the square as the gray closed in again. Dense clouds folded together until the world felt pressed beneath a thick woolen sky. The warmth of that fleeting brightness faded, replaced by the dull shimmer of new snowflakes.

Inside the booth, Selene moved quickly, stacking trays of sweet goodies and yeasty bread. The wood counter was slick under her gloved hands. Then came a low rumble that shook the snow-dusted jars on the table. It wasn't thunder—this was closer, deeper. She looked up just as it grew louder, a rolling growl that made a few people turn their heads toward Main Street.

Selene's laugh broke the tension. "Cody Gene," she said under her breath.

Down the road, a line of large pickup trucks with knobby tires came crawling through the fresh snow, their headlights cutting golden tunnels through the gray. The first truck's flag—stitched with a pair of crossed guitars—snapped in the wind. People started running toward the roadside, their boots slapping slush and gravel. The sound of the crowd swelled as phones rose into the air to video the convoy.

Most hoped to get a glimpse of the famous country star. Many had seen him in concert in Nashville or in his hometown of Watauga Lake.

Children balanced on curbs, and parents lifted them to their shoulders. The air buzzed with laughter, camera shutters, and the rhythmic hum of engines idling. The name "Cody Gene" rippled through the crowd like a secret passed from person to person.

The convoy rolled to a stop near the square, not far from the bakery booth. Music poured faintly from a speaker—someone must have cracked open a truck door—and the first few notes of a familiar tune stretched above the chatter. Levi leaned over the counter, a grin tugging at the corners of his mouth as he fished binoculars from his coat pocket.

"We don't have to move an inch," he said, holding them up to his eyes. "Perfect view, perfect sound."

Beside him, Jed smirked and kept loading cookies into paper bags.

"Guys, I'll be right back," Aris said. His voice carried easily in the muffled air. "I want to check something."

"Take your time," Jed said, not looking up. "We're covered here."

Aris tugged his scarf higher and stepped out into the flurries. Every footfall crunched softly in the damp gravel. He passed a cluster of teenagers waving signs painted in red glitter and laughter-spotted breath before veering toward the town hall.

Halfway there, he glanced back. The booth was busy, and Selene was leaning toward a customer, her hair slipping loose from her hat. He turned sharply down a narrow alley where the noise of the crowd softened.

The crowd pressed closer as Cody and his band spilled from their trucks, laughter and cheers rolling up like a tide. The stage crew began pulling cables from tailgates, voices overlapping in a rising rhythm of tuning notes and shouted directions. The air snapped with energy, excitement, frost, and the faint metallic smell of snow that hinted more was coming.

Selene leaned over the counter to serve a customer, her breath trapped in silver wisps. When she glanced toward the square, white snow dusted the band's boots as they formed a makeshift stage under the canopy of streaking snow. A sudden gust rattled the booth, sending fine powder across the pastries.

Levi steadied a tray before it toppled. "Weather's turning again," he said softly, though his grin stayed. "But looks like the show's going on as planned."

Selene smiled back, but her eyes followed the edge of the road where the last of the trucks idled, tail lights glowing faintly through the driving flurries. For a beat, she thought she saw someone standing beyond them—a lone figure near the alley's mouth—then a swirl of snow erased the shape.

Her eyes roamed the crowd, trying to pick out Aris before she realized that she'd never be able to see him in the throngs of people gathering around the square.

CHAPTER 33

Aris stepped into the booth, rubbing his hands against the cold. "Snow's picking up." He glanced across the way at the band. "Doesn't look like they're going anywhere."

"They would be if they hadn't come up here in trucks. There's no way a bus would have made it up here, never mind getting back down now," Jed said. He turned to Aris. "How much snow you reckon we got out there?"

"Hard to tell with it all trampled. Looks like a good couple of inches where it hasn't been disturbed."

"Are you ready to spend a couple of days with us? We'll make it home, but you may not be able to make it down—at least not in your truck if this keeps up," Levi said.

"Yeah. I packed enough for a couple of days, since Miss Snow-Smeller here kept bitching about the air smelling like snow."

"Well, I wasn't wrong, was I?" Selene asked sarcastically.

"Don't remind me," Aris ground out.

When someone tapped the microphone, everyone turned toward the stage.

"Good snowy afternoon!" Cody Gene yelled.

The crowd yelled back.

"Before we get started with our songs, we have a special request. I think y'all know this song."

A cold hush hung in the air as Cody's boots snapped against the stage, the microphone ringing with static as he slid it onto its stand. The crowd drew closer, bundled in coats and hats, breath fogging the space between laughter and anticipation. Cody's voice echoed through the square, creamy and warm as mulled cider, wrapping itself around the festival-goers as he counted off for the band.

The first notes spilled out, ringing over the chatter and the scattered percussion of applause. Aris lingered near the booth's far corner, fingers brushing lightly over boxes stacked in shadow. The music drowned the hush of his careful movement, but his heart thudded in rhythm with Cody's strum.

Selene's brows crinkled in concentration. The tune threaded through memories before falling into place. "I love this song!" Her voice was bright, but she didn't let herself linger as a man stepped through a swirl of snow.

He bought the rest of the cookies—all four dozen, and asked Selene to count two per bag. Her hands moved with practiced speed.

In the commotion, Aris slipped his hand beneath boxed-up knives, heart pounding against rib and palm. He unboxed the special project, unnoticed by all except Levi.

The man paid for his cookies and left, just as Cody's voice drifted into the second verse, rough with feeling and the bite of winter air.

Aris reached into his pocket, smiling the grin Selene could spot from across any room. She flicked a wary gaze toward him, narrowing her eyes. "What are you up to? You only get that shit-eating grin when you're up to something."

Jed, for once, didn't growl at her language, but instead, watched with the hint of a smile.

351

Cody's lyrics floated around them, and Aris joined in, his voice blending in perfect harmony with Cody's. "I think about the years I spent just passin' through, I'd like to have the time I lost and give it back to you."

He held the special project, an infinity symbol held between two ropes made of twisted and braided horse hair. "I love you, Selene." A twenty-four-carat gold clasp joined the two ropes.

The crowd faded into a soft blur, voices pulled distant by the rush in Selene's ears. Her gaze flicked from the small piece of jewelry in Aris's hands, up to his eyes, then back again. As her cold fingers brushed the metal, she turned it gently, tracing the infinite loops as Cody's voice crooned the lyrics.

Her hand trembled slightly as she traced the infinity loop, the cool metal turning warmer with every touch. The inscription shimmered in the winter light, blurring as tears threatened.

Through the chill, her breath caught. On the necklace, the words shimmered:
"No End, No Beginning. Always & Forever – Aris."

A slow, shaky smile spread over her lips, more radiant than the weak sunlight that tried to break through the snow. Words tangled in her throat, so she smiled softly, almost disbelieving.

When Selene finally looked up, her cheeks were flushed, her eyes shining and wide. She didn't speak.

352

Instead, she threw her arms around Aris, nearly knocking him backwards. There, in the heart of the busy festival and Cody's music, she held him close, a tear slipping hot down her cheek as the infinity necklace pressed between them—promise, metal, and love caught in the snowy light. "I love you, too," she whispered.

Aris barely felt the cold now; his pulse thudded in his ears, nearly drowning out the distant chords of Cody's song. He pulled his head back and captured her lips with his. As their tongues duelled, he remembered every careful night in the back room, shaping metal until his fingers ached, willing his love to fuse into the twist of silver.

None of that compared to her touch now, gentle and almost reverent, as she clutched the necklace in her palm and kissed him back.

They finally broke the kiss when Jed cleared his throat. Selene stepped back, her face reddening as she looked closer at the necklace.

Aris took it from her and turned her around so he could fasten it around her neck. "I chose horsehair because it set off the gold plating on the metal."

"Y-you made this?" Selene asked incredulously.

"Yes. I've never made anything this small before. I wasn't sure it would work."

"I'm glad it did," she said, fingering the twisted infinity loop at her throat. "I love it. I love you."

Aris pulled her into a hug again, but it lasted only a few seconds, as a customer walked up to the booth. "Hi, Mrs. Miller," he said. "What can I get you?"

"Well, I wanted some of those cookies, but I heard someone bought all that you had left."

Aris grinned. "Yep. One of the guys from the band's road crew came over and bought them all. We have cinnamon rolls, apple fritters and some muffins left." Aris glanced under the counter. "Oh, and two loaves of cinnamon raisin bread."

Mrs. Miller's eyes lit up. "I'll take two of each of what you have left and both loaves of bread. The pastor and I don't feel like baking over the holiday, and we thought something from the bakery would be even better."

Selene smiled and said, "Thanks, Mrs. Miller. You give Pastor Miller our best," as she bagged everything for her.

Levi handed her the change, but she waved him away. "Consider that a Christmas present from us."

"B-but—"

"But, nothing, young man," she said as she turned and walked toward the church, waving over her shoulder.

He handed Selene the hundred-dollar bill Mrs. Miller had given him. "That's a mighty big tip."

CHAPTER 34

Just before two in the afternoon, Cody announced, "One more, and then we have to hit the road." He set the microphone in the stand and strummed the familiar chords of the singer's biggest hit. It was a two-step written in the style of the 1970s.

Vendors began packing up their booths to take everything home. The squalls of heavy snow had since turned into a wet, heavy snowfall, and the snow was piling up, though not enough yet to stop anyone from getting home. "Looks like it's going to be a white Christmas," Jed said.

"Yup. Does anyone need anything from the little market before they close down for the holiday?" Selene asked.

Everyone shook their heads. "Okay, then. Let's get home." Levi had already loaded the few pastries into his truck. He and Jed got in and waited for Selene and Aris to follow them in her truck. When they arrived at home, they parked next to Aris's vehicle.

When he slid out of Selene's, he wiped his arm across the hood of his truck. "We got every bit of three more inches here than they did in town."

"Looks like you're going to be stuck here until it stops. If we get much more, it'll be a while before it melts," Jed said.

They tromped inside, knocking the snow off their boots on the porch. Aris checked the birds that had been thawing in the sink since the morning. "They're ice cold, but should be thawed through."

Selene handed him a cookie sheet. "Put them on here, and find a spot in the fridge for them. Who wants breakfast for dinner?"

Everyone agreed, so she pulled sausage, eggs, buttermilk and the rest of the ingredients to make biscuits.

While she mixed the dough, Aris put the chub of sausage in a frying pan and crumbled it.

Selene slid the biscuits into the oven and set the timer, and then added flour to the sausage. She whisked a dozen eggs and seasoned them, and put the griddle across two burners, dropping a dollop of bacon fat onto it. When it melted, she poured the eggs onto it.

Levi stirred it until the flour browned a little and then added milk. Once it reached the proper thickness, he turned the heat down and added a little salt and a lot of pepper.

He then mixed the scrambled eggs and added a large handful of cheese to them.

Within a few minutes, he plated the eggs, sausage gravy and the biscuits. Selene grabbed the butter from the fridge while Jed set the table.

"I'm hungry," Jed mumbled. "That smells so good."

Aris nodded as he reached for a couple of biscuits. He split them and put a large pat of butter on each side. Jed, Levi and Selene mimicked him, and then they all added a scoop of eggs and cheese on their plates. Lastly, they spread the sausage gravy over the top of the buttered biscuits.

The kitchen was silent, except for the clanking of forks on the plates as everyone devoured breakfast. Jed shoveled the last bite on his plate into his mouth, and then split and buttered another biscuit before he loaded it with gravy.

After they finished eating, Jed leaned back in his chair and let out a loud belch. "Damn, that was good."

They all worked to clean up, and then Jed turned the TV on to catch the local news. "Well, would you look at that?" he asked, pointing at the television. "I didn't see the news crew there today."

"I didn't either," Selene said.

"You guys were too busy oogling each other. I noticed their truck over by the stage," Levi said.

The news showed clips of Cody Gene and his band, kids waiting in line to visit Santa, and an extended clip of many of the booths lining the street, including theirs.

"So," Selene said once the news anchor's jingle, a bright Christmas tune, came on as the station transitioned to a commercial at the top of the hour.

Jed's head swiveled toward her when she didn't continue. "'So', what?"

She tried to hide her grin, but the corners of her mouth lifted anyway. Still, she made him wait for it.

When he pursed his lips at her, she broke out laughing. "Hmm. Hold on. It's gonna be better if I show you."

She padded down the hall to her room. They heard the printer running. A few minutes later, Selene came back down the hall with a piece of paper in her hand. She handed it to Jed. "Don't say anything when you read it, Dad."

Jed narrowed his eyes as he took the page from her. He raised his eyebrows and then narrowed his eyes at her. "Does this mean what I think it means? How did you do this?"

"You can do just about anything online nowadays, Dad."

"Uh, are you going to let the rest of us in on the secret?" Levi asked as he tapped his foot impatiently.

Selene took the paper back and stood in the middle of the living room with her arms crossed. "Hmm. Slide closer to Aris, Levi."

He narrowed his eyes and curled the corner of his lip at her. "Excuse me?"

"Just do it, or neither one of you will find out what's going on."

When Levi didn't move, Aris sighed and slid closer to Levi. "Happy now?"

Selene smiled sweetly at them. "That'll do." She took a step toward them and then stopped. "Maybe I should make you guess."

"Fuck off, Selene," Levi growled.

"You're getting coal in your stocking for cussing so much, Levi," Jed said.

"Fuck my life," Levi growled again.

Selene and Aris laughed, and even Jed finally gave in.

"Okay, okay. Damn. So impatient. At least Aris is sitting there quietly," Selene said, grinning.

"Bet he knows what it is," Levi said.

"You'd lose that bet, Levi," Aris said. He held his hand out and wiggled his fingers. "Give it."

"No." Instead, Selene held it up in front of her so they could both read it.

Their eyes tracked upward to read the title as she held the paper in front of them. *Warranty Deed.*

Silence fell thick for a heartbeat, and then Jed leaned back in his recliner with a satisfied grin. "Well, Girl, you sure made the both of them speechless. Don't think I've ever seen that happen before."

Aris finally found his voice. "Is that the place I think it is?"

"Part of it butts up against the eastern line of our property. The land crosses the street and butts up to the eastern edge of your property. It's a weird shape, but it's about three hundred acres."

Jed and Levi jumped up, whooping loud enough to rattle the picture frames on the wall. Aris's laughter joined theirs, but eventually faded into a frown.

"Wait. Are you moving here? I don't think that land has a house on it."

"I am, and it does, but it's beyond repair." Selene tucked a strand of hair behind her ear. "I'll stay here until I can build a house on it. The barns are actually in good condition. I'm going to get a bunch of horses. I might even start a breeding and training program. I don't know yet. The bakery might take up too much of my time."

They talked for about an hour, and then Jed yawned. "I'm turning in. It's going to be an early morning."

Selene and Levi agreed and headed off to their rooms. Aris grabbed the heavy quilt from the back of the couch and covered himself with it. He left the television on with the volume turned low.

Aris waited for half an hour after Levi stopped moving around in his room. *He ought to be asleep by now.* He quietly stole down the hall to Selene's room. Luckily, the bathroom was between the two bedrooms at that end of the house, and Levi's room was on the other side of it.

Selene had almost drifted off, giving up hope that Aris would sneak into her room, when she heard the quiet click of the doorknob. Her breath caught, and she lay perfectly still, the hush of the room amplifying the turning of the knob and sending anticipation through her.

She remained silent as Aris paused so his eyes could adjust to the dark.

"You awake?" he whispered.

"Yeah. You know you're gonna get caught if you stay in here."

Aris sat on the edge of her bed and peeled his socks off. He unfastened his jeans and slid them and his boxer briefs off at the same time.

Selene moaned when she saw his semi-hard cock in the dim light of the alarm clock.

"You have to be quiet," he said as he lifted his shirt over his head and threw it on the floor with his jeans. He lay next to her, pulling her against him. As his lips found hers, he pulled the blankets over both of them.

She reached between them and wrapped her hand around his cock, rubbing it up and down as she pressed the head against her clit. She moaned into his mouth as his hips moved of their own accord, putting more pressure on her sensitive nub.

Aris broke the kiss. "I can't—I have to—" He flipped her onto her back and kneeled between her legs and entered her more forcefully than he meant. He quickly covered her mouth with his to muffle her moans. Her hips rose off the bed to meet his as her fingers dug into his shoulders.

Aris broke the kiss as he arched his back, trying to reach further into her. He barely stifled his moan when Selene wrapped her legs around his waist to change the angle and buried her face in his neck. Her muscles trembled as he slid his hand under her hips to lift her as he ground into her.

When the contractions became stronger, he barely fought through them. As her muscles relaxed, he said, "I need to see it again, baby."

He slowed his movements as his hand found its way between them. His lips found hers to muffle her moans as he rubbed her sensitive nub.

She broke the kiss and whispered, "Now, Aris. Now. Fly with me."

Aris arched his back and pressed his lips together to muffle his moan as her muscles gripped him, milking him dry. He collapsed on top of her, supporting himself on his elbows so she could breathe. "Damn, baby. It gets better every time. I love you," he whispered.

"Love… you… too," Selene barely breathed out.

They lay together, holding each other until Aris heard her breathing even out. He got up and quietly dressed, and then went into the bathroom to change into his sleep shorts before he moved back to the sofa.

CHAPTER 35

Selene woke to a dark room. She leaned over to check the clock and caught a whiff of Aris's scent on the pillows. *I didn't dream it. He was here.* "Four-thirty. You'd think I'd be able to sleep in for once, but no. Of course not."

She stepped into the bathroom and turned the shower on to let the water warm up. She hated to wash Aris's scent from her, but she didn't want to walk around smelling like sex all day, either. She noticed Aris's

367

shampoo in the shower and the towel he'd draped over the end of the shower curtain rod.

Grinning, she stepped into the shower to wash and condition her hair and then lathered her body with her favorite body wash. Inhaling the lavender scent as she rinsed, she mumbled, "It feels good not to have to rush anywhere today."

When Selene finally stepped out, she dressed in a pair of soft, comfortable sweat pants and a t-shirt. That was one of the benefits of getting up so early—she could take her time, and the water would heat up before one of the guys was ready.

Aris was still sprawled under the quilt, his breathing deep and even, when Selene slipped quietly through the living room. She padded into the kitchen, the chilly tile making her toes curl. The house slept on, undisturbed—at least for now. But Selene knew the familiar rattle of the coffee pot would stir everyone soon enough.

Still, she couldn't help it. The need for her morning cup tugged at her harder than the promise of a quiet house. She reached for the peppermint sticks, vanilla, and cocoa, setting them softly on the counter. The wrapper crinkled under her fingers as she unwrapped a candy cane.

She poured cream into a small pot, the liquid glimmering in the dim kitchen light, and set it on the stove, the soft click of the knob breaking the hush.

As the coffee began to brew, the rich, bittersweet aroma curled around her—wrapping the kitchen in warmth. Steam coiled from the spout, and anticipation grew with each slow drip and pop from the machine, promising the indulgent start of a new day.

While the coffee brewed and the cream heated, she flicked the back porch light on. It was snowing heavily, but the wind was still. The flakes were thick and stuck together. It was perfect for making snowmen or having a snowball fight.

Turning the light off, she turned to give the cream a stir. Just as she mixed the ingredients for the first candy cane latte, Aris padded into the kitchen.

"That smells good. What is it?" he asked quietly.

She handed it to him and made another one for herself. "A candy cane latte. It's really good."

Aris took a hesitant sip and grinned. "It sure is." He leaned over and licked the whipped cream off her top lip and kissed her. He set his coffee on the counter and then took hers and set it next to his.

Backing her against the counter, he pressed into her as his tongue found its way between her lips.

Selene drew Aris closer, sliding her fingers into the soft hair at the nape of his neck. His breath caught against her lips, and the heat of his body sent a shiver through her core as he pressed her against the counter.

She could feel his hard cock against her stomach. Breaking the kiss, she whispered, "I want you right now, but we're gonna get caught."

"You sure are," Jed's deep voice rumbled from across the kitchen.

Selene's cheeks flamed. "Well, hell," Selene muttered without meeting Jed's eyes.

Aris, already pulling away, mouthed a silent "Fuck," as he scooped up his mug. He tried for casual, but his grip trembled just a bit. "Good morning, Jed," he managed, turning toward the door. "Wonder what it's doing out there?"

He flicked the switch, flooding the porch with pale light, revealing thick flakes swirling past the window. "Snowing pretty hard."

Selene busied herself at the stove, pretending to wipe stray drops of cream from the counter. She couldn't help the pink spreading up her neck. "Dad, you want one of these candy cane lattes?" Her voice was light, but embarrassment colored the words as she avoided his gaze.

"Yeah, Little Girl. They smell good. I'll make it."

"Might as well make one for me, too," Levi said as he sauntered into the kitchen.

370

Aris's hard-on hadn't disappeared completely, but it was less noticeable, so he turned the light off and sat at the table.

Levi narrowed his eyes at him as he sat, and then swiveled his head toward Selene, who still managed to avoid meeting Jed's gaze as she moved to her seat.

"Uh, what'd—"

"Nothing. You didn't miss a thing, Levi." Selene shook her head briefly.

Levi leaned back in his chair and pursed his lips. He turned his eyes to Jed as his father handed him the coffee. When he saw the smirk Jed was trying to hide, Levi slapped his thigh and laughed.

"Got busted, didn't y'uns." He nodded smartly as he stood and stepped over to the fridge to pull out ingredients to make breakfast.

"Shut up, Levi," Selene said, giving him a playful shove.

Jed let out a guffaw, not able to hold it in anymore. "You should have seen their faces, Levi."

"Oh, hell," Selene muttered.

"It's not too late to put coal in your stocking, Little Girl," Jed said, between laughs.

Levi set the griddle on the stove and arranged bacon strips on one end. He formed sausage patties and put them on the other.

Selene grabbed a loaf of Levi's homemade bread and sliced it thick like Texas toast, and then mixed eggs with cinnamon, nutmeg and sugar to make French toast.

Once Levi put the meat onto a cookie sheet, he slid it into the warm oven, and then laid the slices of bread on the griddle. Since it was homemade, it'd crumble too easily in the egg mixture, so he toasted it in the bacon grease first.

Selene toasted the bread on both sides, coated each slice in the egg mixture, and placed them back onto the grill.

Jed grabbed the maple syrup and butter from the fridge and then reached into the cabinet for the canister of powdered sugar, which he handed to Selene. He then set the table.

As each piece came off the griddle, she cut it diagonally and arranged it on a platter. Once the platter was full, she sprinkled the powdered sugar over the top.

Pulling the meat out of the oven, she set the two trays next to each other and snapped a photo to upload to the bakery's website, and then set the trays on the table.

"Dig in, y'all," Selene said, taking her seat.

"Have you decided where you're going to put the house, Selene?" Aris asked.

"Not yet. It'll be a bit before I start working on that. At least until the spring. I want to walk the property to find the best spot."

Aris held back the smile as he took a bite of bacon.

"What are you up to, Aris?" Levi asked when he noticed.

"Who? Me?" Aris asked, feigning innocence.

Levi tilted his head as his eyebrows lifted.

"Don't look at me like that. I ain't done a thing," Aris said with a grin.

They took their time eating as they bantered back and forth. Selene finally gathered the dishes and put them in the sink.

"I'll wash, and Aris can dry since you two cooked," Jed said.

"That works. Now that it's light out, I want to see how much snow we got," Levi said. He disappeared down the hall and then returned with sweats pulled over his legs and determination in his step. He rummaged through the junk drawer until his hand closed around the battered yellow tape measure.

A rush of ice-cold air slapped his face as he cracked open the back door, the chill biting into the warmth that lingered from breakfast. Levi stepped onto the porch, boots crunching through a thick blanket of snow. Heavy flakes fell in the morning light, creating a hush over their piece of the world.

He slogged through the white blanket of snow as wet flakes clung to his hair and shoulders. His breath plumed white as he moved away from the shelter of the house, careful to avoid measuring a windblown drift.

He plunged the tape measure into the snowpack until his fingers stung from the cold, snapping a quick picture for proof. While he was out, Levi set to work, scraping the icy buildup from the back steps with brisk, efficient strokes. The muffled sound of the shovel against packed snow echoed through the quiet yard. When the porch was clear, he circled the house, his tracks marking the pristine white, and began clearing the front steps, working up a sweat despite the biting chill.

While he was out, Selene uploaded the photo of their breakfast. "Fresh-baked bread for French toast, Texas style," she titled the photo.

Levi stomped the snow off his boots and stepped inside. "Mighty cold out there, and it doesn't look like it's gonna stop snowing any time soon. We got about eight inches so far. I'm kind of surprised it's not more."

He hung his coat on the hook by the front door and turned to Selene. "How long ago did you upload that picture to the bakery's social media?"

"About an hour ago," she said.

"Perfect." Levi pulled his phone out and selected a few photos of the landscape, showing the falling snow, and then the picture he took of the measurement. He selected "reels," and then added the song, "White Christmas," to it. He then uploaded it to the bakery's social media with the appropriate hashtags and location marker. He typed in, "A White Christmas in Evermist," and hit the 'post' button.

They gathered in the living room, the familiar scent of pine mingling with the warmth from the fireplace. Jed picked up the remote and flicked through channels until cheerful holiday music filled the space—bells chiming, strings dancing, the sound shimmering through the air like morning frost.

"Let's open the gifts," he announced, voice tinged with anticipation. He knelt beside the tree, needles brushing his sleeve, and reached beneath the twinkling lights for the neatly wrapped packages. Each gift crinkled as Jed read the tag aloud, then passed it to its recipient.

Settling by his own pile, they took turns unwrapping. Tearing paper gave way to laughter, glimmers of surprise, and the sweet, fleeting hush that fell with each reveal, the

375

holiday music quietly threading through their leisurely, grateful morning together.

When they finished, Jed and Levi gathered all the wrappings and put them in the compost bin. He saved the bows for another year.

Levi had baked pies and a Yule log the day before, so Selene and Aris prepped Cornish game hens, potatoes, a green bean casserole and the other fixings for Christmas dinner. Once the turkey was in the roaster and the other items in the fridge to cook later, they all went back into the living room.

Aris lingered as the holiday laughter faded into quiet contentment. His heart thudded beneath his sweater, each beat echoing the soft hum of country melodies drifting from the television. He reached into his pocket, fingers brushing velvet, and felt the weight of the tiny box—a promise held tight in his palm.

The twinkle of lights cast gold across Selene's face as she sat curled on the edge of the sofa, the glow painting warmth along her cheeks. For a moment, he watched her, the old ache and hope in his chest swirling together, remembering every winding turn that brought him to this room, to her.

He knelt before her, the carpet pressing into his knee, and hesitated just long enough for her gaze to find his. Music mingled in the stillness, strings and gentle lyric: God bless the broken road that led me straight to you...

Aris swallowed, voice roughened by nerves and love. "Selene," he said softly, reaching for her hand, "There were days I didn't know where I was headed, years I thought I was lost. But every detour, every wrong turn—it was a road meant to bring me right here, to you."

He pressed the box into her palm, holding it and her hand in both of his hands, the velvet warm from his touch. "You're the answer to every prayer I didn't know how to say, the crossroads I'm grateful for." His words trembled a little, "You're the reason none of it—none of the heartache—was wasted."

He opened the box. The diamond flickered in the lamplight, hope shining clear in his eyes. "Will you marry me, Selene? Will you let me walk this road beside you, wherever it leads?"

Selene stared at Aris, her breath hitching as the warm velvet brushed her palm. The soft sparkle of the ring blurred behind sudden tears, and the world seemed to shrink to Aris kneeling before her, Christmas lights swirling gold through the haze.

For a moment, she couldn't speak. The music, the gentle hush, the hopeful tremble in his voice—all wrapped around her chest, making her heart beat wild and high. She reached for his face, fingertips shaking as she traced the faint stubble along his jaw.

Her lips parted, laughter bursting through the tears. "Aris, are you serious?" Her voice wobbled, fragile and bright. "I—I can't believe—God, I love you."

She half-laughed, half-cried, clutching his hand tighter. "Yes. Yes, of course it's yes," she whispered, pulling him into a messy, breathless kiss as the holiday music built and the whole broken road behind them suddenly felt golden and right.

EPILOGUE

In the soft blush of early spring, sunlight streamed through open windows, dust motes swirling in the cool air as Selene and Levi coaxed Jed into sorting through Jeanna's things. The room held the faint scent of lavender and old paper, the quieter echoes of someone once vibrant threading through shelves and drawers.

Jed stood by the doorway, his shoulders tense—a silent wall between memory and acceptance. Grief had become familiar, but the betrayal less so. He lifted a scarf, the fabric rough between his fingers, then let it drop with a sigh.

While Jed lingered, unable to choose, Selene quietly tucked a few cherished mementos aside—a faded photograph, a bracelet Jeanna wore on Sundays, all set gently on the dresser where he might find them later. Levi chose a small trinket box, its latch crooked, remembering the cheerful way Jeanna used to hum as she cleaned the house. Selene kept a silk handkerchief, the scent of Jeanna's favorite perfume still just barely lingering.

By the time afternoon sunlight slanted gold across the floorboards, the room felt lighter. They tucked away pieces of Jeanna, now cherished in quieter hands.

The air outside was crisp, layered with the earthy scent of thawing soil and the faint sweetness of apple blossoms from the orchard behind the house. Selene paused by the tailgate, one hand absently cradling her growing belly, feeling the gentle nudge of life within. Boxes thudded softly as Levi stacked them in the truck bed, a few old jackets slipping loose and fluttering in the breeze.

Jed shuffled down the porch steps, his arms full of folded quilts, his movements slow but steady. A sparrow sang in the budding maple, and for a moment, the world seemed hushed and forgiving.

Selene's thumb traced invisible circles against the curve of her bump, heart fluttering with gratitude and uncertainty.

Levi caught her gaze, offering a crooked smile—half comfort, half a shared secret—as he brushed dust off his hands. "You good?" he asked quietly, nodding at her stomach.

She nodded, tears pricking behind her eyes. Sunlight caught on Jeanna's photograph, glinting through the tissue paper before Selene tucked it safely into her purse. Jed watched, wordless, as the last box found its place. The truck's engine rumbled to life, scattering birds and memories alike, and as Selene climbed into the cab, the old house seemed to exhale, ready for something new.

A soft early September breeze stirred ribbons and wildflowers woven into the chairs, the scent of fresh-cut grass mingling with the sweetness of baby powder and cake. Selene sat in Aris's arms under a pretty white arbor, their newborn, Aris Jedediah Beckett, tucked against her shoulder, tiny fingers curling in sleep.

Sunlight glittered on the pond, and laughter tumbled across the yard, echoing around friends and family gathered for their wedding, not far from the spot where their future home would rise.

After they spoke their vows, the reception unfolded—a swirl of toasts, gentle music under the trees, and the glow of new beginnings. Selene and Aris stole hesitant glances at each other, warmed by the sight of Jed snapping pictures and Levi tossing a cousin's child in the air.

That evening, after the guests trickled away and their child dozed in his bassinet as Levi gently rocked it, Aris traced circles over Selene's knuckles as they walked the edge of her land. "I can't wait until we start building," he said. "I love our plans to combine both properties and build a horse breeding and training operation."

Selene nodded, imagining a home on this very field—a wide porch curled around the front, the kind of kitchen that would dazzle any chef and make every holiday a feast. Tall windows would flood the house with morning light, and the library at its heart would shelter every dream, every story they'd ever hope to tell. Five bedrooms, stacked high with laughter and love, would fill with the sound of children chasing sunlight all summer long.

In the hush of twilight, their dreams stitched together—solid as the foundation soon to be poured—and as Aris slipped his arm around Selene, the future gleamed golden and certain, every hope echoing in the promise of a home built for all of them.

A NOTE FROM THE AUTHOR

Thank you for joining me in the pages of "A Twisted Infinity Christmas." This story is a tale of love, hope, and the magic that winds its way through the holiday season, even in the most unexpected ways. As I wrote this book, I found myself reflecting on the meaning of infinity—the notion that love, memory, and connection can keep looping through our lives, no matter how many twists we encounter.

"A Twisted Infinity Christmas" is a celebration of second chances and the strength found in embracing both heartache and joy. I hope that, as you read, you discover moments that make you smile, spark warmth, and maybe even rekindle a bit of holiday wonder in your own heart.

Thank you for supporting my writing and for letting me share this story with you. If it touched you, please consider leaving a review. Your words mean the world to authors and help our stories find new readers.

Wishing you comfort, connection, and love
that lasts beyond every twist of the season.

Warmest wishes,

Rhea Morrigan

ABOUT THE AUTHOR

Rhea Morrigan is a contemporary romance author whose stories blend Appalachian grit, heartfelt emotion, and the raw spirit of mountain living. From her home on the Cumberland Plateau in Tennessee, Rhea draws inspiration from misty mornings, soulful walks through the woods, and the warmth of small-town life, all brought to life in her much-loved Buck Hole Hollow Series and other steamy, deeply human romance novels.

A paralegal and content strategist by day, Rhea crafts stories at night that capture resilient heroines, flawed but redeemable heroes, and emotionally honest relationships facing real-world challenges. Whether weaving legal drama, blue-collar ingenuity, or second chances into her books, she writes with a commitment to authenticity and a deep love for the southern settings she calls home.

Rhea lives with her loyal German shepherd and her spirited umbrella cockatoo, and finds joy in crocheting, pyrography, and, most of all, sharing stories of hope, heartbreak, and the healing power of love. With every book, she invites readers into

worlds where romance is as rugged and beautiful as
the mountains themselves.

OTHER BOOKS BY RHEA MORRIGAN

Discover more heartfelt romance from Rhea Morrigan, where Appalachian grit, strong heroines, and swoon-worthy love stories come alive in every book. From the deeply emotional Buck Hole Hollow Series to stand-alone stories of redemption and second chances, Rhea crafts each book to sweep you away into small-town secrets, family bonds, legal drama, and unforgettable characters.

If you enjoyed this book, please consider leaving a review on your favorite retailer, social platform and/or Goodreads. Your reviews help authors reach new readers and keep the stories coming. Your support truly makes a difference!

(Next page for listing).

Buck Hole Hollow Series

Adley

Marley

Sarah

Shannon

Brynne

Jade

Stand-Alone Novels

A Twisted Infinity Christmas

Short Stories

Psychological Horror

The Last Drink

Paranormal Romance

Ages (Flash Fiction)

You can find all of my books on Amazon in paperback and ebook formats.

COMING SOON BY RHEA MORRIGAN

You can see what is in the works by visiting my website RheaMorrigan.com. Currently, I am working on a 12-book series (Watauga Lake).

I may add more stand-alone novels, flash fiction or short stories while working on the next series, so keep your eyes peeled!

Rhea Morrigan